PIT BULL

In a Cumbrian hamlet, young Susan Shaw depends on the support of Clem Harker during her mercenary husband's extended absences. Staying with Harker during the summer is his friend, Jack Pharaoh. When Susan's husband arrives, he soon takes exception to her neighbours, the Rankins. For their son, Paul, owns a pit bull and boasts that it could rip a man to pieces. Tensions explode as Shaw rises to Paul's taunts. After the boy's body is discovered, only Pharaoh refuses to accept the verdict of accidental death. When he decides to investigate what really happened, he is forced to confront unspeakable savagery and retribution . . .

Books by Gwen Moffat
Published by The House of Ulverscroft:

LAST CHANCE COUNTRY

GRIZZLY TRAIL

DIE LIKE A DOG

SNARE

THE STONE HAWK

THE RAPTOR ZONE

RAGE

THE CORPSE ROAD

OVER THE SEA TO DEATH

A SHORT TIME TO LIVE

MISS PINK AT THE
EDGE OF THE WORLD

DEVIANT DEATH

CUE THE BATTERED WIFE

NON-FICTION

HARD ROAD WEST

GWEN MOFFAT

♦

PIT BULL

Complete and Unabridged

ULVERSCROFT
Leicester

First published in Great Britain in 1991

First Large Print Edition
published 1997

The right of Gwen Moffat to be identified as
the author of this work has been asserted
by her in accordance with the
Copyright, Designs and Patents Act, 1988

British Library CIP Data

Moffat, Gwen
    Pit bull.—Large print ed.—
    Ulverscroft large print series: mystery
    1. Detective and mystery stories
    2. Large type books
    I. Title
    823.9′14 [F]

    ISBN 0–7089–3780–2

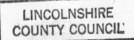

Published by
F. A. Thorpe (Publishing) Ltd.
Anstey, Leicestershire

Set by Words & Graphics Ltd.
Anstey, Leicestershire
Printed and bound in Great Britain by
T. J. International Ltd., Padstow, Cornwall

This book is printed on acid-free paper

1

HIGH summer on the northern Pennines and even the breeze was warm. On Clouds Scar the limestone pavement was dazzling and heat waves shimmered above the rock. A car drifted across the Scar and stopped at the point where the road started to dip. When the engine was switched off the birds took over, a curlew's long trill fading through the larks' song. Below the edge the Vale of Eden stretched to the Scottish border. A gleam of water marked the Solway Firth.

"The rain's cleared the air," Clem Harker said cheerfully. "Last summer visibility was never more than a few miles." His eyes moved. "There's a golden plover."

"Where?" The driver shifted in his seat and winced.

"Can't see it. You can hear it. A thin pipe on one note."

"You can pick that out in all this racket?"

"Oh yes. You would if you lived here, if you were interested. You never were."

"Hell, Clem, I was running a rescue team!"

"So was I. You put more into it. Now maybe you can find time for other things."

The two men fell silent while all around them the birds went noisily about the business of rearing young and defending territories. After a while, and not looking at his companion, Harker asked: "Do you regret it?" His face didn't change: an unremarkable face except for the eyes which now reflected his tone, curious but friendly. With his unfashionable haircut and clipped moustache he had a dated look. If he were photographed in sepia he could be a survivor of the First World War.

Jack Pharaoh was a different kettle of fish: big-boned and dark, craggy rather than fleshy — although he could have been that once — his cheeks were wasted like those of men who have to work hard to keep their weight down. The corners of his mouth drooped and he

2

didn't smile much. Now he moved as if to ease his legs and inhaled sharply. "I had no choice," he said. "And that doesn't answer your question, except at a tangent. Since I had no say about being thrown out of the Service, I had to accept the situation. Regret doesn't come into it."

"You weren't thrown out."

"As good as. Invalided out. What's that?"

"For God's sake — "

"Forget it." After a pause Pharaoh went on: "Mood swings, they're called. I'm getting used to — to my circumstances — but only gradually. The intervals between fits of depression get longer."

"You don't mean clinical depression? You're not . . . " Harker hesitated, blinking with embarrassment.

"No, I'm rational enough — now at least — to pull myself out of the pit without treatment. But there are times when this feeling strikes suddenly: what am I doing here? You know?"

"I never had it."

"You *know* what you're doing?"

"I don't ask the question."

"No, you wouldn't."

"But then I've been lucky. Of course" — smiling — "I never stuck my neck out. I never married and I didn't take risks on rescues. I don't like danger — and no one would call me a passionate man."

"No? Neither am I any longer."

"You were all of that. And there are other — pleasures besides climbing and . . . and . . . "

"Families? There may be plenty of women around but who's going to start another family at fifty? Who wants to, with the state the world's in?"

"That's trite."

They stared at each other, Harker defiant and flushed, Pharaoh angry — but then his eyes cleared. "Got you on the raw there," he said with satisfaction. "Sex has reared her head, has she, my man?"

Harker ducked the question. "You're not as uninvolved as you make out."

Pharaoh eyed him shrewdly then turned back to the view. "That could be a problem," he murmured, and nodded at the valley. "What *am* I doing here?"

"You mean *here*! I thought you were asking a much more profound question."

4

"We always said you'd make a good priest."

"Come off it, Jack. As to what you're doing here, it could be that you're looking for something: a job, a new interest, some — passion? — to replace . . . no" — as the other moved impatiently — "to fill the vacuum. And you look down there" — they regarded the rolling pastures and the woodlands spread below them — "and what you see is peace, beauty, people living contented lives in their neat little niches . . ."

"Like you. And all of it alien so far as I'm concerned."

"You're not there yet. But you come from here, Jack: way back."

"Not me. My grandfather came from the Lakes. This would be strange country to him."

"It's all the North. People don't vary much, basically. That's the point. There are plenty of folk in this valley who are bereaved and abandoned and crippled."

Pharaoh gaped. "Is that how you see me?"

"It's how you see yourself that matters."

The other inhaled deeply and his hand

went to the ignition key. As the engine fired a Range Rover passed, the woman driver clearly startled as she turned her head and saw Harker. She lifted her hand belatedly.

"Neighbour?" Pharaoh eased on to the tarmac.

"A visitor from Scotland. Esme Winter. She's an author, writes historical books."

"She does well out of it; Range Rovers cost a bomb. Or is there a husband?"

"No, no husband." Harker waved at the other vehicle. The passenger was looking back and gesturing wildly.

Pharaoh glanced sideways. "Who's the other one then, who's so eager to attract your attention?"

"The daughter."

"And what does she do in this neck of the woods? Or is she visiting too?"

"She lives in the hamlet. She's married."

"What does he do? I'm having to drag this out of you, Clem. Is there something between you and the mother or don't I ask?"

"The daughter's married to a mercenary."

"A *what*?"

"A mercenary soldier."

6

"Oh yes? He's having you on."

"I haven't met him, only Sue — his wife. He's never been here. She meets him in London mostly when he's on leave, and that's not often. They haven't been married that long, they met at some alpine lecture in Glasgow . . . " His voice dropped, "About the only thing they have in common: mountains."

"It's usually enough."

"She's very young."

"You mean gullible? She married a drifter and he kidded her he's a mercenary?"

"I believe her. Actually he has been a soldier."

Pharaoh was shaking his head. "That I can take because there can't be anything here for a youngster except farming, and that's not exactly a growth industry, but this kind of country doesn't produce mercenaries."

"Well, he's not a local but what kind of country does?"

Pharaoh negotiated a bend above a stony ravine and rolled down to the next bend. The road was empty, the Range Rover having pulled ahead. "Mercenaries are peasant types," he said, "but they're street boys rather than farm lads, and trainable; that's crucial. The trainers like a clean slate: get a man young enough, it's like a dog; you can mould him."

"Most mercenaries are former servicemen. This guy was SAS."

"So the Army's done the first part of the job: shown them the techniques, taught them to kill. A mercenary is a drifter who's come home; he fits a niche all right, but he doesn't — Jesus!"

He slammed a foot on the brake as he came out of a bend to flashing lights and a barrier descending across the road.

"I should have warned you." Harker was contrite. "I was thinking."

"There ought to be a sign! I didn't see one."

"There is. It's hidden by a flowering hawthorn. We don't trim our hedges in the dale."

"I'll know next time. How long do we have to wait?"

"Only a minute or so."

Pharaoh was leaning out of the window studying the system. "This is a Mickey Mouse set-up. Suppose there's a power cut at night; there's a streetlight but everything would fail: warning lights, even the barrier. A stranger could drive slap into the path of a train."

"The electrics must be on a different system, independent of the grid. We get a lot of power cuts in winter, in the blizzards."

"I forgot the winter. It's not all sweetness and light, is it?"

The train burst on them like a bomb, hurtling past at a speed that had Pharaoh staring in amazement. "Are they allowed to run at that speed?" he asked as the barrier rose and they crossed the line.

"Where've you been over the last decade? You talk as if you were stationed in the Falklands rather than North Wales. Trains move nowadays, Jack. Sixty's slow."

"Over an unmanned level crossing?"

Harker shrugged. "There are footpaths, rights of way, crossing main lines — but I have to admit it wouldn't be a good idea to stall your engine here."

"Now why would anyone choose to stall on a level crossing?"

"Panic." The question had been

9

facetious but Harker responded seriously. "People approach, see the lights flashing, barrier starting down, and they get confused, hit the accelerator hard, car stalls."

"That's happened?"

"Not yet."

Below the crossing there were scattered trees. They passed a farm track and the trees became lush woodland. The verges were lacy banks of cow parsley under unkempt hedges where wild roses lay like big pink snowflakes. The woods were full of song. A cuckoo called close by, disturbing as an owl in daylight. They passed the entrance to a drive on the left. "So where's your place?" Pharaoh asked. "I'm getting dehydrated in this heat."

"Turn here." A shabby signpost stood at a junction, one arm pointing to Kirkby Oswald: 7 miles, the other to Clouds.

"Why Clouds?" Pharaoh turned and braked, glimpsing the potholes.

"It means rock, a mass of rock. The edge where we stopped is the rim of Clouds Scar. It's a plateau with limestone pavements and sinkholes: a sensational place. You have to know it well to go up there in mist. Here's my van; pull in behind it. You must explore the Scar while you're here. How far can you walk?"

"Ten miles maybe. I'm all right on the flat; it's gradients that are the problem: up *and* down. And long drives." He was levering himself out of the car as he spoke, using the seat and the door for support. He had stopped behind an ancient Morris with an extending ladder on its roof rack. Ahead of the van the track continued under old beeches which would once have formed a grand avenue but now there were gaps and, a few yards ahead, the tall snag of a trunk with huge shards of yellow wood pointing upward.

"That's an eyesore," Harker said. "We have to do something about it. It came down in the February storms. I cut the rest of it up but it looks as if I'll have to get a professional in for the stump. That's going to cost."

"But that's not your job surely?"

"My job, but Fawcett land. The Fawcetts have no money to spare. I'm looking for someone to do it for free."

"So there's no one else around here

11

who spends his retirement doing unpaid work for pensioners?"

"There's not many people who can afford to these days. I own my house and I've got an adequate pension. And it's not just pensioners; it's anyone who's strapped for cash. What else do you suggest I do with my time? This is what I always wanted to do when I came out of the RAF and I'm doing it. When I get tired of being a handyman I'll do something else." He smiled as they started to unload the car. "We've all got a niche, Jack. I'm lucky, I found mine. So" — his tone lifted — "let's get this stuff in the fridge and find some beer."

Ahead of the van there was a neat gate under bushes of pink and lemon broom. A discreet board on the gate said Fox Yards. "'Yards' means earth," Harker said. "So there were foxes here once. There are still, in the woods."

Loaded with groceries and rucksacks they went up a flagged path to a white cottage under a roof of green slate. There were mauve and purple clematis on the walls, poppies and delphiniums on either side, and the hedges were clumped with more broom heavy with blossom and loud with bees. Pharaoh limped a little on the path but Harker said nothing until they were slumped in chairs in his living room and had sampled the first long draught of cold beer. Then he sighed with pleasure and said casually: "I get cramped on long drives. I need to stop and straighten out the kinks every hour, or even less as I get older. Not always convenient on motorways: to keep stopping."

Pharaoh lowered his glass. "I feel better already, but drives of over a hundred miles are hell. I was glad of your company on the last stretch. It was good of you to walk over and meet me."

"The other way round. I always wanted to cross the watershed and walk down Ewedale and you meeting me at the other end solved the problem of how to get back. Is it your back that's troubling you now or the leg?"

"Both, except that driving is much easier on the knee since I bought an automatic. But they say the lumbar vertebrae are fused. No position is comfortable for long. Well, be thankful for small mercies. Yes" — as Harker's eyebrows rose — "I could have been killed, could have landed headfirst on a rock. I was lucky I fetched up on a boggy bit of turf and not with my head; there was enough rock around, goodness knows."

Harker opened his mouth, and thought better of it. Watching him, Pharaoh divined the thought. "I don't blame the chap who was lowering me," he said. "In fact, I don't have any feeling towards him at all. Everyone makes mistakes; it was his bad luck that he had a man on the end of a rope when he made his. He must have suffered too, but he'd have been in a sight worse state if I'd been killed. All the same, I should have seen that the rope could shift and run over a sharp edge once my weight was on it. It's always the leader's responsibility."

"It was dark, and filthy weather. You'd have been concentrating on the ropes to the stretcher, not paying much attention to your own rope. That was the lowerer's job."

"Post mortems, Clem; we were always against those. Debriefing, yes, to learn from the mistakes, but not to go on and on, for ever afterwards: what might have happened if only — "

Harker's eyes strayed to the open door. The gate had clicked. There was no sound of footsteps but a shadow moved on the flags of the doorway. A girl stood there against the sunshine: vivid and slight, sparkling with energy or some strong emotion. "I wanted Mum to stop," she said eagerly. "She wouldn't because you had company . . . " She paused, glancing at Pharaoh with a twitch of a smile, but her eyes stayed on him as Harker introduced them. This was Susan Shaw. As Harker was explaining that she lived across the lane, through the woods, she interrupted impatiently.

"Clem, love, you're not going to believe this: d'you know what I found over in Tranna Mire? There's a bunch of dead ewes in the willows. That's Rankin, Clem."

"In Tranna Mire?"

"You know, beyond Juno's place — where the woodland narrows between the railway and the road. No one goes there; it's all marked private. You know the old gate and the notice saying 'Trespassers will be shot' that Rowland put up? That's the place. Fawcetts used to raise their pheasants in that wood." She turned to Pharaoh. "Our landlord's paranoid about poachers," she told him. "The point is" — she returned to Harker — "Mouse Gill rises in that marsh and flows into the river. How many people downstream of us take their water from the river?"

"I'm not sure that — "

"Or swim in it — in summer when the water's low, and warm: a forcing ground for bacteria? What did those sheep die of, Clem? It's obscene."

Pharaoh sipped his beer, enjoying the look of her. She was in her early twenties, with long legs in stone-washed jeans, and a black tank top providing the foil for her tan. She had a face like a marmoset: wide-mouthed with flaring nostrils and large intense eyes shadowed by a mass of brown curls. She wasn't beautiful but there was an attraction about her that was far from elusive. Pharaoh stared, observing the emotions in her face, her body echoing her expression. It was the body that stirred him most; this girl exuded sex as a rose gives off scent. Now she asked, wide-eyed: "What are we going to do, Clem?"

"I'm not sure. Would it be a police matter, or the RSPCA?" He looked at Pharaoh who licked his lips delicately and collected his thoughts.

"Try the police. It's a health hazard, and illegal not to bury dead sheep anyway. Who's the owner of them?"

"Have they got Rankin's mark on them?" Harker asked.

"That's odd." She wrinkled her nose. "You can't get close because of the stench but I didn't see Rankin's mark. There was a blue splodge on one. Rankin's is red. The foxes had been there, or a loose dog. It's impossible to tell how they died."

"It's not Rankin's grazing," Harker said thoughtfully. "Rowland doesn't let the woods; there's no grazing anyway, under the trees. How close are these carcasses to the road?"

"A few hundred yards. Something with big tyres, like a Land Rover, has been through the gate recently, the one under the notice about shooting trespassers."

17

The men exchanged glances. "A load of dead sheep," Harker said meaningly. "It's not the first time it's happened."

"What do you know about sheep?" It was too ingenuous to be rude.

"Rescuers go where other people don't," Harker told her, "searching for lost people, bodies, that kind of thing."

She shrugged and returned to her original concern. "What could they have died of: all at the same time? What did those others you found die of? Foot-and-mouth: could it be that?"

"They could have been killed deliberately. Perhaps someone's been sheep-stealing."

"If you're going to steal sheep you don't kill them."

"You do if the police are getting too close," Pharaoh put in.

Harker nodded. "The police were making inquiries down the dale a while back. It looks as if someone stole a bunch off the fells and then got cold feet. He wanted shot of them quick. It doesn't have to be Rankin; it could have been anyone pulling in off the road." He gave a grim smile. "It could have been someone wanting to put the finger on Rankin."

"If it was, that means everyone in the dale is under suspicion," Susan said darkly. She hadn't sat down. Now she went through the room to the kitchen. Pharaoh looked at Harker who smiled and raised an eyebrow. She returned with a bottle of beer, handed it to Harker who twisted the cap and handed it back. Their movements were smooth and economical: the behaviour of people well accustomed to each other.

"Who is Rankin?" Pharaoh asked.

She sat on the arm of Harker's chair and gave the visitor her full attention. "He's our neighbour: a yob, with a yob for a son and a slag for a wife." Harker frowned but she had her back to him. "They've got no manners," she went on, "no sense of responsibility; they're brutal and dirty and — and — what are they?" she demanded of Harker, twisting to face him.

"This is poor land, up here at the head of the dale." He was trying to take the sting out of her words. "Farmers have the devil of a time making ends meet."

She gasped, then turned fierce. "Rowland and Phoebe never lost their manners, and they're so poor they couldn't run a car, except you manage to keep it on the road — and who buys the spare parts?" It was thrown out like an accusation and Harker blinked. "This is Rowland Fawcett, our squire," she told Pharaoh, jerking her head sideways, "at the end of the lane. They run a Cortina that has to be thirty years old at least; it's all they can do to find the petrol. D'you know what this guy does?"

"Susan!" It was a warning. She hesitated. He put a hand on her arm. "That's my business, Sue." Their eyes locked and she softened. With an enchanting smile she leaned down and kissed him on the temple. "He's a dream," she told Pharaoh, rising, retrieving her beer from the floor and walking to the doorway. "What the hell are we going to do about those sheep?" she murmured, staring moodily across the lane. Pharaoh passed a hand over his mouth to hide a smile.

"I'm going to start the supper," Harker said. "No, I don't need help," as Pharaoh made to get up, "I can't do with anyone else in my kitchen. You two can get acquainted. You'll eat with us, Sue?"

"Thanks, but Mum's doing something with halibut." She sparkled at Pharaoh. "We eat like yuppies when my mother visits. You're to come to supper tomorrow, you and Clem." She moved outside, turned back and gave him her exquisite smile. "Come out and enjoy the sunshine; this is probably our last day of summer."

"You've been ill," she went on as he settled himself somewhat uncomfortably on a slatted garden seat. It was certainly lovely out here, the delphiniums and scarlet poppies catching the sun, brilliant against shadows in the hedge. She sat on a log facing him, studying his face. "You don't want to talk about it," she stated. He saw through the subterfuge immediately but it was immaterial. He smiled. "I need a cushion. D'you think you could — ?"

She rose with the grace of a cat and fetched two cushions. On the log again she picked at a dandelion, transparently casual. "So tell me about your fall," she said diffidently.

"Why should I?"

21

"I know it was . . . I'm just curious. Are you sick of talking about it?"

"I don't talk about it." He didn't add 'to strangers' because he didn't want to hurt her.

"Why not?" she asked.

"Because I think about it a lot?" He was questioning himself rather than her. His face was cool, relaxed. "It was a dirty November night on Snowdon," he said reflectively. "Two climbers had fallen: one to the foot of the cliff and he was dead, the other had stopped on a ledge about fifty feet above the bottom. He'd fractured his pelvis and others things besides but he was still alive. RAF Rescue — my team — were called out and we reached him without too much bother and put him on the stretcher. I was being lowered with him when my rope broke." She said nothing. "That's it," he added lamely.

"And you broke your back."

"I didn't, actually. Some vertebrae were chipped and my knee was shattered. I'm a bit stiff now. It slows me down." He regarded her without expression. "Not where it matters."

"It's terribly romantic, and noble. But you won't see it that way. You had to give up climbing, Clem says."

"I didn't have to, but I can't climb at the standard where I was before, so I stopped. I'm competitive."

"You can be competitive at other things."

"Name one."

He had pushed her into a corner and this girl didn't like to lose the initiative to strange men. She took the only way out she could find. "You're not married?" she asked.

"I'm not married." A pause. "What does Clem do about finding petrol for the Fawcetts' car? Does he steal it?"

She dimpled. "He puts a few gallons in the Cortina's tank when Rowland isn't looking. Clem keeps a can of petrol in his van. Was he like this in the RAF?"

Pharaoh thought about it. "For the last five years or so he was stationed in the north of Scotland and I was in Wales so I didn't see a lot of him. There wasn't much call for his kind of altruism in the RAF."

"You don't think saving lives is altruistic?"

"It's a job. We had around twenty years of mountain rescue, Clem and me; it was what we did, like other men fight fires or crew lifeboats." In the face of her steady regard he ploughed on, a trifle desperately: "You don't think about lives being at stake, that people's lives depend on your speed or skill, or on a diagnosis being correct: broken back or skull, internal bleeding and so on. You have to be technical, unemotional. You're doing what you've been trained for. In time some of us got quite expert at it but the concern was always with technique, not saving lives, with *how* it was done, not what was done. The guy you saved could be a worthless sod: a wife beater, child abuser, whatever; if he was brought down alive it was a good rescue: successful, an inspiration to the men."

She looked away. He didn't think she understood; she could be bored. "So what are you going to do now?" she asked.

"Get another beer."

"That's not what I — "

"I know what you meant. Will you help me up?"

Her jaw dropped then snapped shut. "You're not helpless. Don't you have any pride?"

"Not at my age. Ten years ago you wouldn't have needed persuading to put your arms round me."

"Oh, you poor old guy!"

For a moment he thought her eyes were wet but he lost sight of that as she took his hand and pulled him to his feet. With her arm round his waist and his across her shoulders, they entered the cottage to find Harker in a butcher's apron laying the table.

"I didn't mean you to get that well acquainted," he said tartly.

"She tried to seduce me." Pharaoh disengaged himself.

"*I* did? He's a wolf," she told Harker. "He's trouble. He needs a — Let's set Juno on him."

Harker nodded in approval. She had just saved herself from a gaffe. "That's an idea. Invite her to supper tomorrow. And Lanty," he added flatly.

"Oh, Clem! Here we go again. You'll never grow up. See you tomorrow then — if not before." She turned to go, and looked back at Pharaoh. "Preferably alone," she added.

"What was all that about?" Pharaoh asked, not looking at his friend, turning a bottle to read the label.

"She's impersonating a *femme fatale*."

"I mean Lanty. Lanty who? And what?"

"Lanty Dolphin is Juno's son. Juno's a widow. They live across the road, back in the woods. We passed their drive. It's a big Victorian house and Juno means to do bed and breakfast. We're doing it up. I mean, I'm helping. Lanty and Susan are . . . friends."

"Is that a euphemism?"

"Why should it be? In a place like this you know everyone. I don't know what the relationship is. It's not my business. They've been thrown together: working on the house." He was moving round the table fiddling with knives and forks, glancing distractedly at his watch. "He's too young for her," he muttered.

The room seemed dim now that the

girl had gone. They looked at each other and each saw a sense of loss in the other's eyes. Embarrassed, they looked away.

"We'll go up on the lime tomorrow," Harker said quickly. "We don't have to walk far if you don't feel like it; we'll take a car to the pass and it's a smooth level walk past the klints. That's what the limestone pavement's known as locally. It's great country: clean and bare, very different from the dale which is rather lush, don't you think?" He was coaxing Pharaoh into another mood. "No complications up there," he promised.

2

"**I** COULDN'T get him to say anything about his wives."

"You didn't *ask* him." It was a statement rather than a question, and Esme Winter's tone was as much resigned as shocked.

Susan was sitting at her own kitchen table eating olives. "Of course I asked him. He talked about his fall, and that had to be more traumatic than losing two wives."

"And his daughter."

"Yes, he was fond of her. But breaking his back, even though he says he just chipped it: that happened to *him*; he suffered. The other was just emotional, and Clem says he wasn't getting on well with his second wife either; he only stayed with her because of the little girl."

Esme sighed and picked up her glass of sherry.

"You think I'm hard," Susan threw at her.

28

"No, just young." At this moment she looked both young and hard, and her mother contemplated her with the calm that masks compassion. The child had yet to discover the meaning of pain.

Esme Winter didn't look like a woman who had suffered herself. In her mid-forties she had the beauty which her daughter had missed, except for the eyes. Her hair, straight and long, held a reddish tinge, and this evening she had pinned it on top of her head but in the heat of the kitchen strands had escaped to give her a Spanish air, heightened by the aquiline nose and lustrous eyes. She was dressed for the country, indeed, for this shabby cottage, in jeans and a blue cotton shirt. Tanned and without a trace of make-up, her one touch of elegance was gold earrings inlaid with silver.

"Where did you get those?" Susan asked.

"They were a present. From Roger. You don't know him."

"Is it serious?"

"No."

Susan sniffed and her eyes wandered round the kitchen where the huge

29

range, the packing-case furniture and worn armchairs made a bizarre setting for olives and avocados, for bottles of French wine and brandy on the side, and the Range Rover in the yard. Her mother said: "I've not been serious with anyone since the divorce. I'm truly fond of your father; it's just that I can't live with a man, perhaps with anyone, for ever, cheek by jowl. But ours was an amicable divorce, Sue; what Clem told you about this fellow Pharaoh's divorce, wasn't like that — "

"It wasn't in the same league as you and Daddy!" Susan was horrified. "He was married to a slag, she even took money — "

"Yes, well, service life must be disturbing for young girls. And if he put his job first — "

"And climbing. He was superb on rock. His wife didn't climb. Clem said that was the trouble, but you know Clem."

"Not all that well. However, Pharaoh's was an unpleasant divorce, but he put it behind him and he found another lady" — her voice rose — "and then you say that marriage wasn't working out either?"

"After eight years, Mum! Anyone'd be bored living with the wrong person for eight years. But he adored the little girl. That's probably what he can't adjust to: losing her."

"Both of them." The correction was firm. "For my money, when you're not getting on with your wife, losing her in a car crash would mean more guilt than usual, not to speak of the child. The violence of the shock must have been awful." She shook her head in horror, visualising it.

"He doesn't have to feel guilt. He wasn't there. He had nothing to do with it."

"There's always guilt. And then he had his own accident, and he had to leave the RAF. I'm surprised he didn't tell you to mind your own business when you — confronted him."

"I didn't push it, and he wanted to talk about the fall . . . " Which wasn't true, but Susan made no bones about skirting the truth, let alone exaggerating. "He's terribly sexy," she went on. "He has an air of deep tragedy; remember reading Pater to me when I was little: 'the head upon which all the ends of the world have come and the eyelids are a little weary'? He thinks saving lives is just a job."

"Did you remember to ask them for tomorrow?"

"Of course. That's why I went there."

"In the circumstances you might have forgotten."

"Clem said would you ask Juno too. He means to throw them together, do them both good. Clem's sweet, isn't he?"

"*Clem* suggested Juno might be good for this guy?"

Susan studied the table. Esme moved to the stove. Outside, beyond a barn on the other side of the yard, an engine was started and revved in short bursts. A dog began to bark. "Oh, Christ!" Susan leapt up and slammed the door. She whirled to the window.

"You can't close that," Esme said quickly. "It's far too hot. Maybe it will stop soon. It's been quiet since we came home."

"Because they were there. Now Paul's going out on his Honda, and his mother and father will be off to the pub so that bloody dog will keep it up until someone comes home. I told Clem about — " She stopped.

"Told him what?"

"There's a dead sheep in the wood. It's illegal not to bury sheep. It's a health hazard."

"It's the same in Scotland; the rock's too near the surface to dig a hole. Look on the bright side: the occasional carcass provides food for the foxes."

At the window the girl frowned and bit her lip. "I wonder when they'll let it out, and how. I can't see anyone in that family walking a dog. Surely they can't be going to keep it in the barn; I mean, not let it out at all?"

"They can't use an Alsatian for sheep. And it's going to fight the collies anyway."

"If it is an Alsatian."

"I thought you'd seen the animal."

"No, they haven't had it long. Paul brought it home. Tilly told me when I asked why the dogs were barking all night: said Paul had got it from one of his mates, and I assumed it was a collie at the time. She didn't tell me it wasn't. Now I reckon that bark is too deep for a collie."

"It could be any big dog, a Labrador perhaps, or a setter."

"Hell! You know" — she turned to her mother — "I wish we led normal lives: Martin and me. I mean, how often do I see him? A few times a year if I'm lucky. It's months now since he was on leave and then we met in London."

"Why wouldn't you complain about the dog yourself?"

"I did — once."

"Yes, you live too close to the Rankins." Esme was testing broccoli. She said carefully: "When Martin comes home you can talk about moving."

"I shall, definitely. I told you so. I'd move out now but then he'd come and there'd be no one here. It would be ghastly; imagine: all the way from some stinking hell-hole in the jungle or the desert — this must seem like paradise — and he gets here and there's no one in the cottage, even the furniture gone, and no one to say where I am."

"Apart from the fact that he'd quickly find out from the Fawcetts, I don't think a man of Martin's calibre is going to be much bothered — " Esme checked and slammed the lid noisily on a saucepan.

"At finding his wife missing?" Susan completed waspishly.

"At the unexpectedness of it." Esme was stiff. "There *is* the telephone, and there are letters. He might not be able to phone from Africa but he could call Clem from the airport when he lands."

"He could. He doesn't. It's just — well, he hates committing himself, he wants to feel free. You know what he's like. . . . Look, we're not going to go through all that again, are we?"

"I wouldn't dream of it. If you'll get the wine out of the fridge, I'll dish up."

★ ★ ★

"The trouble with isolated communities," Harker said, "is that if you've got an awkward neighbour there's nothing you can do about it except move. The Rankins are getting on her nerves."

"What's the problem? Apart from stealing sheep — and she didn't know about that until yesterday, if he did steal them."

Harker's pace slowed. He appeared to be studying wheel tracks in the turf. A lapwing flapped noisily above their heads, trying to lure them away from its chicks which would be hiding in a crevice.

It had been a nostalgic evening for the friends: reviving old rescues, deploring new methods, and new men. This morning, with the sun rapidly gaining strength and the upland air scented with thyme and alive with birds, Pharaoh's interest was in his surroundings; not his immediate environment but the hamlet of Clouds: in Harker's neighbours, and particularly in Susan Shaw.

"The Rankins have got a new dog," Harker said. "It barks." He stopped and frowned. Pharaoh faced him, making no comment on the triviality of a barking dog. "They're so close," Harker continued. "Originally, you see, it was all one unit: the farmhouse and buildings, going back to the year dot. Rowland maintains that the tenant paid a rate

36

of a shilling a year to Henry the Third in the thirteenth century, but the oldest part now is Sue's place which is seventeenth century. It's the original farmhouse. Rowland's father built a new house for the tenant and since then the cottage has been occupied by labourers until Rankin came. The Rankins moved here from Northumberland; pretty poor land, I imagine, because their farm was sold for forestry. They answered Rowland's advert when his last tenant retired. Murkgill isn't a prosperous farm by any means but the rent will be higher than what they were paying before. They can't afford to employ help so the cottage would be empty but for Sue, who doesn't care about the amenities. There's no bathroom. The heating is a range in the kitchen and an open fire in the parlour. In winter the bedrooms are like ice boxes." Pharaoh's eyebrow twitched. "So Sue tells me," Harker said quickly and went on: "There's only the barn between the two houses and now they've shut this new dog in the barn and the barking's driving her up the wall." Still Pharaoh said nothing. "You have to be careful," Harker continued, "they're a rough lot: the Rankins. She wasn't standing any nonsense to begin with; she caught young Paul thrashing a sheepdog and told him if he did it again she'd send for the RSPCA. It seemed to end there but she'd started a garden, growing her own vegetables. She worked hard on that plot: digging, manuring, planting, and she came home from shopping one evening and found some bullocks inside. The gate was pushed to, not latched, but the beasts couldn't get out. She had a fine old set-to with Rankin over that. The worst of it was, him and his wife were sweet as pie, she said, but they didn't trouble to hide their amusement. And Tilly Rankin told her not to annoy young Paul: *warned* her. Sue said it was a threat. She didn't protest about the dog barking, she asked about it just and Tilly didn't apologise; she said it was a new dog and left it at that. Bad neighbours, like I said."

"What's Fawcett's attitude towards them?"

"He's careful too. No doubt Rankin's got security of tenure, and the rent's worth a bit. In any case, you can't evict a family because the son thrashed a dog. As for Sue's garden: she's careless; she could have left the gate unlatched." He shook his head. "The Rankins have got the upper hand, and they're wily as foxes; we have as little to do with them as possible. Look at me, with my garden: flowers in front, vegetables at the back. I can't keep my gate padlocked, not because of the nuisance it would be to me, but because a padlock would be a signal to the Rankins that I'm afraid of their cattle. So if I put their backs up Paul could well make a hole in the hedge and push them through."

"I don't believe this. You're bothered about a boy?"

"You don't get it, Jack. I'm not afraid of him, but owning property, having a garden, all the work you've put into it: it's like having pets. You've got to be careful. Tell you something — " They were moving again but now he stopped short, his eyes earnest. "No way would I keep a dog, let alone a cat, while the Rankins are at Murkgill."

Pharaoh shook his head. "I still find it incredible. It's holding people to ransom.

Why don't you all get together and intimidate *them*, put the fear of death into them?"

"Who would get together? You haven't met anybody yet, bar Sue. The Fawcetts are old, and they're all alone up at the Hall except for Beth Potter, who looks after them, more or less, but she's not young either. She'd speak her mind all right but it's no good standing up to the Rankins; their way is to do something really nasty behind your back. As for Juno and Lanty: they're as extrovert as they come but they steer clear of the Rankins. They can do that; they live furthest away. And Lanty shoots. He's a big fellow and he virtually patrols the woods after pigeons and crows. And rabbits. We're never short of fresh meat at Clouds. Lanty's all right but you couldn't . . . " He hesitated.

"Couldn't what?"

"I was going to say you couldn't expect him to confront Rankin, but I was forgetting Lanty's taken a shine to Sue." His tone was heavy. He looked along the path and grimaced. "Come on, this was supposed to be a walk;

we're spending all our time gossiping."

"I'm interested."

"We can talk at home. For God's sake, man, let's enjoy the day. We don't get enough sun as it is; let's not waste what we do have."

They were in the sun whether walking or talking. It was surprising how irritable Clem became at mention of Lanty Dolphin. Pharaoh was amused to discover such undercurrents running below the surface of the community, but then in mountain rescue he'd had little to do with domestic life. He wasn't the kind of man to whom a wife would relate gossip, and it never occurred to him that life in married quarters, for all its discipline and rigid hierarchy, or because of that, might have had undercurrents too. He shook his head in wonder and concentrated on their immediate surroundings, amazed again to find that his friend had become so absorbed in the countryside that he seemed genuinely interested in wild flowers. Something called a bird's-eye primrose was just a pink daisy to Pharaoh but he didn't say so.

"And there's an orchid." Harker pointed to a depression.

"You're kidding. No, you're not. It's nothing like an orchid, Clem."

"Come and look."

"Well, I suppose it is." Harker had lifted a floret with delicate fingers. "Yes, same structure. I never knew orchids grew outside rain forests."

"You're pig-ignorant. Here's something more in your line." He led the way to another depression but this was funnel-shaped and at the base was a hole all but masked by anemones and ferns.

Pharaoh nodded his appreciation. "There'd be a few dead sheep in the bottom of that if it was wider." Harker was walking on to another hollow, in line with the rest but more sensational. It was as if the others had been trial shafts but here Nature had struck pay dirt. The green turf sloped to a gaping maw the sides of which were fluted columns of rock like dark marble. No ledge was visible on the columns, and no handholds.

"Oh yes?" Pharaoh was excited. "How deep is it?"

But Harker had moved again and was waiting above a maze of jagged crevasses, bridged in places by angular boulders. The ground above was not all that steep and a man might scramble down trusting that, if he did slip, a bridged boulder would arrest his plunge into the depths.

Pharaoh stood on one of these boulders and dropped a stone. He looked up at Harker. "I didn't hear it land."

"Probably fetched up on something soft. Listen."

"I can hear water dripping. I can hear that land, as if on — what? A tyre?"

"More interesting than orchids?" Harker suggested as his friend scrambled back to the lip. They looked down at the dark columns descending into the bowels of the moor. "Were you ever up here in snow?" Pharaoh asked.

"Not right here; I give the sinkholes a wide berth in winter. Even in summer I'm careful; very careful when the cloud's down."

"Have you got a rope?"

"Oh yes, I've still got all my gear, but I'm not going down that hole. Would you?"

"Perhaps not." Pharaoh sketched a grin. "Instinct got the better of me there." His tone changed. "But what a place for hikers: townies coming across this plateau on a bad night, with a weak torch and the cloud down. Snow too, perhaps."

"It's just as well this track isn't marked on the map. You don't see walkers up here. I've never seen anyone except Paul Rankin on his Honda, or his dad. They graze their sheep on the Scar."

"It seems you're seeing your first walker today then, unless that's one of the Rankins."

"Where? Why, so there is."

About half a mile away, across acres of white rock, a figure showed on the skyline.

"Big pack," Harker remarked. "He could be doing the Pennine Way, except that it doesn't cross Clouds Scar."

"He's changed direction. He's coming towards us."

Harker lifted binoculars. "Funny," he murmured, then: "I suppose not."

"What's funny?"

"He's military — well, wearing military

gear, but what's he doing on his own? He's not on the track, but then officially there isn't one. He's probably planning an exercise for the troops." He became practical. "So — how far would you like to go?"

Their path ran along the dividing line between the lime on their left and heather moor on the right. Ahead of them the ground started to rise gently to a hill with an escarpment towards the west.

"Good view from Black Blote," Harker said.

"I'm game." Pharaoh saw the question in the other's eyes. "I can always turn back," he added.

"Great. We'll have lunch on the summit."

It was brave talk; neither could forget that a year ago the summit could have been the top of the Matterhorn or the Eiger rather than a Pennine hill.

The sinkholes came to an end and, as the gap between them and the lone walker decreased, a tarn showed on the left with sheep grazing round it. The stranger must have been close to the tarn when they first saw him and now he was about to intercept their line. They observed him with interest, noting the short hair, the camouflaged trousers and khaki shirt. They, in turn, were being summed up by pale eyes in a deeply tanned face. He walked easily even under the weight of a pack, and he appeared to have the arrogance that Pharaoh and Harker associated with high Army rank, at least until he nodded to them and grinned.

"Great morning," he said cheerfully, glancing from one to the other. Like them he was of medium height but unlike them he was in splendid shape, with not an ounce of spare flesh: chunky but not muscle-bound, alert but not tense. His mouth was thin and fastidious, almost prim, the eyes clear.

"Could you be on your way to Clouds?" Harker asked.

"Yes." He showed surprise. "Are you from there?"

"I am. I'm Clem Harker. This is Jack Pharaoh; he's staying with me. You must be Martin Shaw." The man nodded. "I'm a friend of Susan's," Harker went on. "She didn't say you were coming."

46

Pharaoh, watching for Shaw's reaction, saw only polite interest.

"She doesn't know. I didn't know myself when I'd be able to get away, or if I could find space on a plane. I got a lift with a friend up the A1 and I've walked over from Ewedale. I slept under a rock." He gestured eastwards. "I was going to go straight down to the village but I saw you and I reckoned you were on the right path."

"There is a way down where you were," Harker told him. "There are some old quarries under the edge, and the line of a sledge road that goes down to a railway viaduct. Clouds is below that."

Shaw nodded and said that now he was here he'd go down by the road. They parted and the others resumed their stroll towards Black Blote Fell. They were silent for so long that when Harker did speak it sounded unnatural. "So that's Martin Shaw," he said heavily.

"Where's he come from — recently, I mean?"

"Africa. He moves around. Last time Sue heard from him was six weeks ago. He was in Mozambique."

47

"There are mercenaries in Mozambique?"

"That's where the letter came from. She didn't tell me more and I don't ask questions, not about him."

Pharaoh shot him a glance. "You reckon he's into something illegal?"

Harker shrugged. "All I know is she doesn't want to talk about him, and for a talkative girl, that's significant, wouldn't you say? What did you make of him?"

"He looks hard. Does he climb?"

"I'm sure. They met at a climbing lecture — I told you — he was in the SAS. Chaps who look powerful don't necessarily make good climbers though."

"This one had an air about him."

"Yes, he knew where he was going all right."

They lapsed into silence again and tramped on slowly, Pharaoh taking the soft turf in his stride. Behind them Martin Shaw moved lightly past the sinkholes heading for the road.

★ ★ ★

"You're going well," Harker said as, settling themselves by the summit cairn,

48

they contemplated the blue line of the Lakeland hills.

"I am." There was satisfaction in the tone but Pharaoh made no comment on those mountains which he had loved with the kind of passion most men reserve for women. "We've come all of three miles," he observed with amusement.

"We might walk along the ridge a bit and — tell you what: why don't I take the van back and you go home across the Scar and down by the old quarries: the way I was telling Shaw about?" He looked diffident. "It's a bit steep at the top."

"I'd like that. It's a pleasant walk so far but . . ."

"You need something to get your teeth into."

Two hours later he was repeating that to himself, standing at the edge of the Scar and staring down a rocky slope that looked daunting and which, a year ago, he wouldn't have thought about, but dropped down it at a run. He glanced behind him and saw Harker at a distance going towards the road. This was a reciprocal of their first sight of Martin

Shaw. The tarn was quite close, almost on the lip of the Scar; so Shaw must have been about here when they spotted him. It was odd that the man hadn't gone straight down; there was nothing wrong with *his* legs or spine, judging by the way he moved. But then Harker said Shaw had never been to Clouds so he wouldn't know that the hamlet was close, only a mile away. The cottages appeared to be hidden by the trees but the Hall showed up well: a pile of stone and slate with a stable yard at the back, while away to the left was the farm of Murkgill and its barns. One of those roofs would be his own but then Shaw wouldn't know that, Pharaoh thought, and then wondered why he should be concerned with the fellow. Dismissing him, he returned to contemplation of the descent.

The Scar was indented at this point, a bay having been gouged out of the escarpment, and in the bottom was a slanting depression that became a gully lower down. Water in the bed of the gully was catching the light and, hundreds of feet below, the railway crossed the beck by a fine arched viaduct. Beyond the viaduct were green fields, some pale where silage had been carted, and then came the woods about the hamlet. Directly below and quite close, once he could reach it, were the turfy zig-zags of the old sledge road.

He had rested for long enough; if he didn't go down now he should retreat and overtake Harker before he reached the van on the pass. He stood up and started down the slope, leading with the bad leg; that way it had less work to do. He went slowly and carefully, watching every step, trying to make sure he didn't tread on something that would move. To his delight he managed the descent without one twinge and when he had worked his way down to a level bench and looked back he felt a sense of achievement. Before euphoria could take over he turned to see what he should do now.

A sheep trod took him across the bench and down a slope that was still rocky but at an easier angle. The sledge road was close below but before he reached it he came to a chasm: one of the abandoned quarries Harker had mentioned. There was seepage under the walls and small plants growing in cracks. He scouted around, wondering what Harker would have found of interest: a rare fern perhaps. He looked at the vegetation blankly and then found himself studying the rock, which was almost black, like that which walled the sinkholes. In the mud at the foot of the chasm there was the mark of a cleated boot. He made his own imprint beside it. His mark was larger and much fresher than the other.

He started down the sledge road, passing more places where the stone had been quarried, and coming on the remains of a cabin. It was roofless but it would provide shelter from wind; proof of that was a collection of rusty cans. Rankin probably used it when he was shepherding. There was a faint but familiar smell which didn't go with the cans because it was a fresh smell and they had been here for years. He sniffed. It was just like bacon, fried bacon — which was ridiculous so far as Rankin was concerned; why would he have cooked his breakfast here this morning? How would he cook? There was no sign of fire; some kind of camping stove must have been used.

A movement caught his eye; a tail in a crack. He bent stiffly and picked up, not a tail, but a fresh piece of bacon rind. He dropped it for whatever small scavenger that had been removing it and turned to search the vicinity, but he could find nothing, not even a matchstick, to indicate that anyone had camped here. Someone had been extraordinarily meticulous about cleaning up.

★ ★ ★

"So? People have been there. What's so remarkable about it, Jack?" When Pharaoh reached Fox Yards and told his story, Harker was more amused at his friend's curiosity than at the cause of it. "There are walkers everywhere nowadays," he pointed out. "In the remotest parts of Scotland you can't get away from ramblers; they get into every corner."

"You said you never see people on Clouds Scar."

"We did today. We met Martin Shaw.

53

There you are! That's where he slept — "

"He said he spent the night in Ewedale: that's the opposite direction. And if he did sleep in the old quarries why didn't he come down that way? Why sleep there at all when his home — and his wife — are within a mile? Why, you must be able to see his roof from that point."

"He wouldn't know which one was his." Harker was pondering. "Perhaps he didn't sleep there, just cooked his breakfast, didn't know Clouds was so close . . . "

"He knew. He said he was considering going down that way and then he saw us."

"Ask him. We're eating there tonight."

"So we are. I don't think I will ask him."

"I wouldn't, either. Damn! And there's Lanty coming to supper as well." He glanced at the telephone. "I'll leave it to Esme; if she doesn't want Lanty there she'll find a way of putting them off." He took a long pull at his beer. "Handsome fellow, isn't he? Shaw, I mean. Perhaps he's got himself into trouble and what he was doing was watching from a point of vantage to see if an avenging husband had arrived in Clouds." He grinned as he envisaged it. "But I expect it's quite simple: some loner came through last night, an innocent traveller who has no connection with Clouds, and he's moved on. No one saw him arrive and no one saw him go."

"Except perhaps Shaw. He was up there ahead of us."

3

AT Murkgill Cottage Martin Shaw had been received with reservations in what was technically his own home. Susan, once she had recovered from her amazement, seemed a trifle strained, while her mother, outwardly cool, was deeply resentful. Someone else's social gaffe had put her in an awkward position, and Esme deplored bad manners.

"I have to go back tomorrow," she said, when Shaw was out of hearing, washing in the scullery.

"No, Mum!" Susan was stricken. "You came for two weeks; you can't go just because he's come home. That would be rude."

"This place is too small, sweetie." Esme used endearments only when she was tense, and Susan was well aware of it. She started to try to justify Shaw's behaviour.

"His contract ended suddenly," she

explained. "And he didn't know if there'd be an aircraft available, if they'd let him on it. . . . Mum, he's not in a nine-to-five job! It's like wartime every day for him. You don't understand." Esme shredded lettuce carefully, her face set. "He would have phoned," Susan insisted, "he knows he can phone Clem and leave a message for me. He didn't have any change when he landed." She bit her lip. "And then he was on the road," she added weakly.

"I'm not criticising him."

"Well, then. Don't go, Mum, please."

"I'm not going to make an issue of it." And she did seem to relax a little. She smiled. "What do we do about — Juno? Shall I go over to Clem's and try to reach her again?"

"I told you: there's no need to put them off. Martin will take it all in his stride. After all, what can he expect: turning up without warning? It's his own fault if he walks into a slap-up dinner party." There was a touch of bravado in the statement which her mother chose to ignore, changing the subject.

"Doesn't Clem ever lock his cottage?"

"I've never known him to. Maybe he

leaves the door open specially for me to use the phone when I have to. Otherwise there's only Juno and she's twice the distance. One doesn't want to bother the Fawcetts, and no way am I going to ask Tilly if I can use the Rankins' phone."

"The dog's been quiet today."

"Be thankful for small mercies. It'll start now" — as Harker appeared at the open door, Pharaoh behind him. "Hi, you two; come and meet my mother, Jack."

Smoothly, Susan took over the domestic preparations, sending her mother and the men out of the kitchen. Esme went without protest, appreciating that the girl needed time alone with her husband. They carried their drinks round the outside of the cottage to an overgrown plot at the back where shabby garden chairs stood in the long grass.

"Pharaoh?" remarked Esme as she sat down. "That's a Lakeland name."

"My grandfather came from Coniston; he was a foreman in the slate quarries. They moved to South Wales when the bottom fell out of slate in the twenties, and he went down the pit, after coal. My father was brought up in Swansea."

"And you?"

"I was born in Wales but I left to go in the RAF. I don't go back." There was a pause. "I have no family," he added in a neutral tone, and looked around him. "Would this be where Susan tried to grow vegetables?"

"That's right." Harker glared at the small gate, now open.

"This is good soil," Esme remarked, regarding the flourishing weeds with disapproval. "It's a pity she lost interest."

"She didn't." Harker was surprised and, too late, they realised that Susan didn't take her mother fully into her confidence. "A bullock broke in," Harker said.

She nodded and automatically her eyes went round the fence, looking for the weak spot. Pharaoh said easily: "Do you live in the country, Mrs Winter?"

"Esme, please. I live on the Clyde" — she wrinkled her nose — "in a *villa*, but my windows look straight down the firth to the Isle of Arran. The view compensates for a house that is totally without character, although I have to admit that houses built at the turn of the century are solid, 'well appointed' as estate agents say." She looked at the rear wall of the cottage and sighed. "The trouble is," she murmured, "these old families: people at the end of their line, with no business interests, no rich relatives: they're decaying along with their estates."

They had followed her without trouble. "No money for bathrooms," Pharaoh supplied.

"Not even for running repairs," Harker put in. "The Hall is lethal: rotting staircases, woodworm, loose slates, you name it. Murkgill — the farm buildings — aren't much better, and look at this place!" He was quite angry.

"She found this place on her own," Esme explained to Pharaoh. "Martin had gone — to Africa, suddenly" — her face set — "and Sue was at a loose end. Nowhere to live, I mean once she was *married*, so she decided she'd make a home in the Lake District. Quite impossible, of course; rents are astronomical there, but an agent in

Penrith told her that Rowland might have an empty cottage. She came over here and the Fawcetts were only too pleased to have the place occupied. No wonder; it's a hovel. Martin has to admit that and agree to move. No way is she going to stay here." She nodded as if confirming a point and changed the subject. "My goodness," she exclaimed on an artificial note, "he's a fit young man, don't you think?" She regarded Pharaoh candidly. "He said he'd met you."

"A good body." Pharaoh was watching Harker who looked as if he'd been shot. "He must get a lot of exercise. Surely he can't work out in Africa; not in the bush anyway."

Harker hadn't heard a word of it. "She'll — they'll never find another place as good as this," he protested.

"As *good* as this?" Esme was incredulous. "You just said — "

"It's cheap. She pays ten pounds a week rent. She'd have to pay forty for anything comparable. She doesn't mind discomfort. I can help — " He stopped. They were staring at him but when he checked, disconcerted by their combined attention, Pharaoh shifted in embarrassment and Esme smiled. "We'll have to see," she said, and Pharaoh glanced at her, alerted by her tone and puzzled. Harker merely looked miserable.

A woman came through the gateway: a big-boned woman in slacks and a shirt in bold jungle prints. She had a wide forehead, high cheekbones and black hair tied back in a scarlet bow. There was about her a suggestion of eastern Europe, of the Far East, of Russian steppes. She advanced with confidence, smiling serenely. She was accompanied by a young man who was well over six feet and boyishly good-looking, but too soft for his age which couldn't be much more than twenty.

Introductions were unnecessary but they were performed all the same, Juno Dolphin's gaze lingering on her son who seemed fascinated by Pharaoh. He resembled a large dog who had learned his basic training but lacked finesse. "We're banished from the kitchen," Juno was telling Esme. "This is so exciting: high drama for Clouds; I've never met a mercenary before. We've only just got back from Carlisle. When did he arrive?"

"This afternoon. Without warning." Esme was glacial. "Sue is overwhelmed."

"Oh, she would be."

Two pairs of maternal eyes surveyed the men. Harker blinked and looked bewildered; Lanty Dolphin, sprawled on the grass, shifted his long legs; Pharaoh regarded Juno attentively.

"With that name," she told him, switching subjects effortlessly, responding to his gaze, "you must have local roots."

"A Cumbrian grandfather. Where does Juno come from?"

"My mother was into the classics. My sister is called Minerva, which is, unfortunately, abbreviated to Minnie."

Pharaoh and the women chatted politely but Harker was preoccupied, while Lanty stared sullenly at the cottage as if trying to visualise the scene within.

The evening held its own vibrations. It had been a hot day and the wall of the cottage retained the heat. Shadows from the wood were creeping towards the garden but the atmosphere was languid, particularly so to Pharaoh after the thin air of the uplands. Doves called sleepily but the songbirds were quiet. When people stopped talking they were aware of the low sweet hum of insects in the woodland canopy.

"How quiet it is." There was a sheen on Esme's forehead. "It's amazing; we haven't heard the new dog for hours."

"Yes, where is that barking dog?" Juno asked. "We heard it all one night. When was it, Lanty?"

"I told you: it's Rankin's. No one else has a dog like that."

Juno smiled. "Unless Rowland bought a Rottweiler."

"What makes you think it's a Rottweiler?" Harker asked. "Have you seen it?"

"It's a hefty animal. You can tell by the bark. It's not a sheepdog."

"Well, folks," Susan came round the corner of the cottage, "we'll eat soon." Martin Shaw was behind her, clean and shining; short curls wet and tight to his skull, his chest and biceps straining a white T-shirt. In the golden light of evening his eyes were colourless in a face like mahogany. Lanty had stood up, his size dominating the company.

Susan licked her lips. "Can we freshen people's drinks? Martin?"

They surrendered their glasses and murmured their preferences. As Shaw turned away they watched him speculatively. On the other side of the cottage an engine started, revved and receded. Lanty remarked to no one in particular: "Someone's been in the wood." No one responded to this, as if they were all accustomed to Lanty. "I mean a hiker," he explained, "on his own, wandering around our place. We could do with a dog ourselves." He was resuming the conversation as if there had been no break.

"Lanty," observed his mother, "is becoming crime-conscious."

"You should join the police," Susan said dryly. "Work your way up to the CID."

"Why would anyone come in our woods — we're nearly a quarter of a mile from the road — unless he's casing the joint?"

The women stared at him. Pharaoh asked: "What was he like?"

"I didn't see him, I saw his track; it was a smallish boot but it was a Vibram sole, nothing fancy, more like a climbing boot actually." Lanty stared at Susan's bare feet. "Bigger than yours," he murmured.

"Why d'you ask?" Harker turned to Pharaoh who felt suddenly ridiculous: connecting tracks in the woods with the mark of a smallish Vibram sole in the quarry.

As he hesitated, Juno said: "What kind of dog could one have in sheep country — I mean, to be safe?" And Shaw was returning with the drinks so Harker forgot his question as they debated the breed of dog that might not chase sheep.

Dogs were not an innocuous subject; observing Pharaoh fish a fly out of his Scotch, Esme exclaimed angrily: "My neighbours breed Airedales. I have to keep my kitchen windows closed against the bluebottles even when I'm cooking, particularly when I'm cooking. I find it outrageous that other people should disrupt my lifestyle with impunity." She

66

gave a furious laugh. "Society's changed out of all recognition; why should I adjust to the new standards?"

"You could run," Susan said meaningly. "Move house."

"Or beat them on their own terms," put in Shaw.

After a pause Pharaoh asked: "How would you go about it?"

"Throw some rotting fish into their garden," Susan said.

"No." Shaw regarded Esme coolly. "Not retaliation but constructive action. They make your life unbearable so you get rid of them."

Lanty's jaw dropped. "Waste them?"

The pale eyes considered him. "If you like." It was said without interest. "I meant drive them out."

"How?" Susan was fascinated.

"What are they afraid of? What's valuable to them?"

"Their pets?" Esme swallowed. "Their *children*? Is that how the mercenary mind works? It sounds almost petty — and sinister at the same time: terrorising the neighbours."

"Intimidation," he corrected. "When

the other side appears to be superior you look for the weak points, that's all. It works on all levels: military campaigns, guerrilla warfare, bad neighbours."

Esme laughed but her eyes were snapping. "And then the neighbours retaliate against you. In no time you have the kind of society that you have in Corsica: blood feuds, a society run on the revenge ethic. Ethics? It's back to the Dark Ages."

He spread his hands and his eyes were candid. "It was just a scenario."

"Are you allowed to talk about your work?" Juno put in brightly. "I'm intrigued to know what you actually do."

"I've been training recruits in Mozambique."

She smiled wryly. "No jungle warfare: crocodile-infested river crossings, night patrols, all the glamour that's implied when we think of mercenaries?"

"No, ma'am; there's no glamour. No more than there is in mountain rescue." He looked at Harker. "Some people say it's squalid."

Harker stared. "What is?"

"Killing."

"The sun's going down," Esme said as a shadow touched her face. "Shall we go indoors?"

As they started to move a newcomer came round the corner and stopped at sight of the gathering: a thin woman in tight jeans and a T-shirt, with lank yellow hair. There was a hard look about her emphasised by a sharp nose and bony chin. Her eyes were small and at this moment they were anxious, perhaps frightened. These emotions were incongruous on the predatory features. The jumpy eyes found Susan.

"I was just — looking," she said with a transparent attempt at casualness then, intensely: "Have you seen the dog?"

Susan shook her head.

Harker said: "Your new dog's loose?"

Tilly Rankin turned on him. "Did you see him, Clem?"

"I haven't, Tilly. How long has he been gone?"

For a moment she looked desperate, then she hardened. "Only a short while," she snapped, but her eyes went to the shadows on the fringe of the wood.

"You'll let me know if you see him?"
She turned to go.

"Just a minute." She checked at the
sound of a strange voice. Shaw stepped
forward. "I'm Martin Shaw," he told
her. "Your neighbour." His lips thinned.
"What do we have to look for?" And
then, as she gaped at him: "What kind
of dog is it?"

"Brown," she whispered. "It's just — a
brown dog."

"What breed is it?" Esme asked.

"What business is it of yours?"

Shaw broke the shocked silence. "What
breed is it?" he repeated quietly.

Tilly tossed her head in a travesty of
nonchalance. "It's a terrier, just a brown
terrier, that's all." And she put her head
down and ran out of the garden.

Behind her the women stifled laughter
but none of the men was amused.
"Rankin," Harker said heavily, "is going
to lose some sheep."

"That's not a terrier," Lanty said.
"Not with that bark."

"Oh, I don't know" — Esme was still
smiling — "Airedales have big throats."

Susan looked at her husband. "That's

ghastly! An Airedale among the sheep. I think we ought to — "

"The Rankins aren't going to thank you — "

"There's Paul and his father, sweetie: three of them to search — "

"Leave it." Shaw cut through them like a knife through butter. "As the woman said, it's not our business. We were going to eat. Shall we go indoors?" Flustered but obedient they started to move out of the garden, Pharaoh and Harker bringing up the rear, retrieving glasses.

Pharaoh said: "It's nothing to get bothered about, surely?"

"Not for us, but definitely for the farmers unless they find it quickly. A big terrier will kill sheep just for the fun of it, lambs more likely, this time of year. The Rankins are going to have to pay heavily for that dog."

4

AT two o'clock in the morning Clouds was flooded by moonlight and quiet as the grave but not totally still. A shadow moved at the back of the Rankins' house, an eye gleamed, but there was no wind to carry scent and the old collie, asleep on a mat outside the scullery door, made no movement. An owl called upstream of the viaduct.

Windows were wide open and curtains hung motionless. Sleepers stirred as the temperature dropped in the hours before the dawn and, only half awake, people reached for discarded blankets, hunching against the chill.

The scream ripped the night apart. Shaw was awake almost as soon as it started, staring at nothing, all ears. Beside him Susan asked sleepily: "Wha's that?" and snuggled close, naked and warm. "That bloody animal," she murmured, without feeling. Shaw said nothing, listening to a bedlam of barking. Susan was suddenly wide awake.

"Martin! Martin, wake up! Hark at those dogs."

"I'm awake."

"That's not — Oh, how odd." The barking had stopped, as if a switch had been thrown, and the night was silent again. "What on earth made them do that? They stopped as if — as if they were ordered: all of them, at once. Rankin's dogs were never that obedient. It's impossible. Why don't you say something, Marty? What are you thinking?"

"Be quiet."

"*Marty!*"

"Be quiet, love. I'm listening."

They were silent for so long that she tired of it and turned away, pulling up the blanket. "It wasn't the new dog," she muttered. "It was the collies." Suddenly, quite close, a chain rattled and one dog started to bark: loud and angry. "Oh shit!" She pulled the blanket over her head.

★ ★ ★

73

"You'll have to do something about it," she said at breakfast.

Shaw considered the statement. "Would a confrontation be a good idea?"

Esme put down her cup with a clatter and stared at her daughter.

"Well, what do you propose?" Susan asked, ignoring her mother.

He said reasonably: "I'm thinking that if you're going to depend on me to sort things out, when I go you're going to be vulnerable."

"You must move." Esme couldn't contain herself. "She can't be expected to put up with this, on her own."

"She's got Harker, and Lanty Dolphin."

Susan's jaw dropped. "You mean as substitutes for you?"

"It's not their place to protect her." Esme was furious. "*You're* her husband."

"You need a husband's protection?" he asked his wife, and she bit her lip.

"I wasn't implying she's defenceless," Esme snapped. "Merely that you might pull your weight, occasionally."

"Mum, for God's sake!"

"It's all right, Sue; she's got a good point. All the same" — he regarded his mother-in-law earnestly — "the Rankins are awkward cusses from what you've told me." Esme pursed her mouth. He stared at her, through her, and she looked away. "I'll have a word with Fawcett," he promised. "He may be old but he's still their landlord; he must carry some weight. But when you come down to it, what have you got? A barking dog — and he didn't bark yesterday."

"Because he was loose," Esme said. "And God knows what the animal got up to when it was running free."

"Or when it came back." He studied their faces and they stared back: Susan distressed at the antagonism shown by her mother, Esme stony-faced.

★ ★ ★

"Phoebe says we're to go up for coffee, the three of us." Harker replaced the receiver and turned to Pharaoh and Shaw. "The Fawcetts are feudal; they have to inspect every newcomer to Clouds, so they need to see both of you."

"Good," Shaw said. "So we can bring

up the question of the dog quite naturally."

"I don't see what they can do," Pharaoh said. "What anyone can do. Would it be possible to stop a dog barking by muzzling it?"

"It has to open its mouth to bark," Harker pointed out. "But could Rowland persuade George Rankin to muzzle it?"

"Did you hear a scream?" Shaw asked.

Harker was puzzled but Pharaoh stiffened. "You heard it too?"

"What was it?"

"Someone screamed? When?" Harker's eyes went from one to the other.

"Did you think — ? What did you think?" Pharaoh asked of Shaw.

"It wasn't a rabbit."

"Where does the scream come in?" Harker pressed. "You're talking about the dogs waking us up?"

"The first thing was a scream," Pharaoh said. "That's what I heard. I was awake — I mean, it didn't wake me up; I'd been awake for some time. Had you?" Shaw nodded and Harker looked away quickly. "So there was this scream," Pharaoh resumed, "without any

76

warning, then the dogs erupted, several of them. Where does Rankin keep his dogs, Clem?"

"Shut in a stable."

"What about cats?"

"It wasn't a cat," Shaw said.

"There are cats around," Harker said slowly, trying to make sense of this business.

"Then," Pharaoh went on, "the dogs stopped barking and after a while one of them started up again. Now tell us what you heard."

"The same, but the solitary one at the end wasn't among those barking at the start."

"His old dog's loose," Harker said. "It's on its last legs: deaf as a post and crippled with rheumatism; they ought to put it down."

"I think that happened," Shaw said.

"Are you serious?" Harker was incredulous. "You think the new dog came back and killed it? My God, what kind of brute is this?"

★ ★ ★

77

"It's a bull terrier," Rowland Fawcett said equably. "She says it has to go." Nodding towards his wife.

"The boy is looking for a good home for it," Phoebe said. "More coffee, Mr Pharaoh?"

The coffee was powdered, the coffee pot, big-bellied and chipped, was Spode and probably as old as its owner. Phoebe Fawcett was a thin old lady with yellowish skin and white hair as fine as a baby's. Her eyes had the pale ring of age and her smile was vague but sweet. "They act as if they're still big landowners," Harker had warned. "It's a defence mechanism, the survivor's attitude. I go along with it."

Rowland Fawcett had met them at his front door, which was set deep inside a porch and approached by worn steps. Pharaoh, anticipating that age would have robbed the old man of some of his faculties realised, as he mounted the steps with his accustomed lurch, that shrewd eyes were on his leg.

Fawcett had been a big man once but he had shrunk; so much was obvious from the way his clothes hung on him: faded tweeds with leather at the elbows

78

and cuffs. He sported a large straggling moustache and a few grey wisps of hair on his big brown skull.

The front door opened on a dim passage that ran across the house with rooms opening off it. One of these was the drawing room, its mullioned windows open to the sun and an old Jack Russell dozing on a threadbare Turkey carpet. It was a high room and massively beamed; on the yellowing walls were portraits so old and dirty all that could be seen of the sitters were moon faces and pale hands. Upholstered furniture had worn to shades between brown and grey, but a battered cupboard was hundreds of years old, and two piecrust tables were quite exquisite. The fireplace was deep, plain and framed with sandstone blocks. Chiselled in the stone was a date: 1604.

Phoebe Fawcett had brought coffee; she was followed by a heavy woman in a green overall carrying a silver tray. It was Beth Potter. They sat and discussed the weather, the need for rain and this year's lambing season until Harker, judging his moment, asked if Fawcett knew the breed of Rankin's new dog, and Fawcett said it was a bull terrier.

"That explains it," Harker said. "We thought it was an Airedale; Tilly said it was a brown terrier. Obviously it's a big dog, with that throat on him. What are you thinking, Jack?"

"Have you seen it, sir?" asked Pharaoh.

"No. They keep it chained, except yesterday. It slipped its collar. Rankin came over, looking for it, asked me to keep our dog indoors. This bull terrier's a fighter. That's why m'wife said it's got to go. Me too. Can't have an untrained dog on a farm, particularly if it gets loose. We have to think of our neighbours."

"Tilly was terrified," Phoebe told Harker. "She came here after Rankin left, and begged me to keep all the doors closed. She said Patch" — gesturing to the Jack Russell — "wouldn't stand a chance. We can't have that, you know."

"It's a pit bull," Shaw said.

All except Pharaoh looked bewildered. "Did you see it?" he asked.

Shaw nodded. "This morning. I looked in the barn."

"What's a pit bull?" Fawcett asked

and, with the insistence of the old: "Rankin told me his dog's a bull terrier."

Shaw looked at Pharaoh who said carefully: "I'm not sure. They're mostly bull terrier but there could be something else, mastiff perhaps. It's not the breed but the strain that's important; the animals are bred for fighting: dog-fighting."

"That's illegal," Fawcett said.

"So is cock-fighting," Harker put in without expression.

"No one has fighting birds on our land."

"The spurs were inherited," Phoebe said comfortably and, turning to Pharaoh: "We have some very old spurs: they were fixed on the birds' legs and inflicted terrible wounds. Only the black sheep of the family indulged in it." She gave them her sweet smile. "There was heavy betting."

"There was dog-fighting too," Fawcett said. "And bull-baiting. So it's been revived, has it?"

Shaw said: "The dogs are imported from the States. I don't know whether dog-fighting is legal there." They hung

81

on his words. "I met a man in Cape Town," he told them. "An American. His dog was killed by a pit bull. His was a Rottweiler." They all looked at the Jack Russell.

"Why would anyone want to buy a fighting dog?" Phoebe asked.

"They'll get rid of it," Fawcett assured them. "I told Rankin it had to go." He turned to Shaw. "They tell me you're ex-Army. Who were you with?"

"SAS, sir."

"Ah, I remember the Commandos being formed, but can't say I ever came across the SAS. I served for the duration only. Mrs Fawcett ran the place herself for five years while I was away at the war."

"I had help," she told them. "There were two men in their sixties and three land gels. No tractors of course in those days; we had seven or eight carthorses, and fell ponies for riding. I loved it, even in the winter." She was looking at the sun on the carpet but not seeing it. "We were fortunate; the gels could turn their hands to anything on the farm, and I had people in the house. We called the maids farm workers too, that way we held on to 'em. They were doing more useful work here than in factories. They were a lot happier too. I miss those days."

After a while Pharaoh, to keep the ball rolling, asked Fawcett what his war had been like.

The old fellow's face lit up. "I was in North Africa. I had a good war, as they say, although I was in some unpleasant places: Africa, Italy. You'll know what I mean" — the old eyes were on Shaw — "you *choose* to go there. You like that country?"

"My contracts take me to the south, mostly: Angola, Mozambique: very humid places."

They waited for the next question. "I never served with coloured troops," Fawcett said delicately. "Met some Gurkhas on a troopship once but they're not the same, are they?"

Shaw considered that, his face giving nothing away. At length he said: "Blacks are like white soldiers, but more extreme; when they're brave they're reckless and when they're frightened they panic. Either way they're dangerous. And on the whole they don't take kindly to discipline."

"That's what I would have thought."

There was a pause. The Fawcetts clearly had no idea how to pursue this conversation, contract soldiering being as alien to them as hospitality was ingrained. What did one say to a guest who was a mercenary?

"Why do you do it?" Pharaoh asked, wondering if Shaw would cite money in this company.

But the man was unmoved. "In the SAS," he said, "you're trained for a certain kind of operation." He held Fawcett's eye. "We were the élite. And then we were disbanded. Men at their peak: so highly trained there's nothing in civilian life to match it. What would you do, sir?"

"I would never leave my land in the first place. The war was just an interlude in my life. You have no land, me boy; there's the difference."

"The old families had their adventurers," Phoebe put in gently. "A few centuries earlier and Mr Shaw would have been fighting with the East India Company, building the Empire."

"Why were you in mountain rescue?"

84

Shaw asked of Pharaoh.

"Not for the danger. I joined because it was what I was best at."

"What did I say about danger?"

Pharaoh hesitated. The atmosphere was electric. Harker said: "I got the impression that danger was part of the attraction for you. Did I get it wrong?"

"I'm not reckless."

"Like climbers," Harker observed earnestly, addressing Pharaoh. "He knows his limits. Do you climb, Martin?"

"I did some in the SAS."

"Where are you stationed now?" Fawcett asked.

"I'm between contracts, sir. I'll most likely go back to Africa."

"I suppose there's always a war somewhere."

"War or peace, it's immaterial; Third World countries like their troops to be trained by British personnel."

★ ★ ★

"You turned his questions neatly," Harker said as they made their way down the rutted track that was termed a drive.

"You were all over the place: Cape Town, Mozambique, Angola; you put up a smokescreen."

"Old soldiers don't understand mercenaries."

"He tried," Pharaoh said. "How would you explain it to us, now there's no one's feelings to hurt?"

"The same way." Shaw was surprised. "There was no alternative. You think I should have stayed in the SAS: waste all those months of training, years of experience, hanging around waiting for a terrorist-hostage situation or a plane hijack like at Entebbe? I don't wait for action; I go and find it."

Harker began to say something, and checked himself. Pharaoh glanced at his friend but before he could speak Shaw went on lightly: "We didn't accomplish much there, did we? You reckon Rankin will get rid of that dog or they're just stringing the old people along? I think I'll go and have a word with Rankin."

"Well . . . " Harker was concerned. "He can be an awkward customer."

"So?"

"He's going to be in a nasty mood

86

today. We don't know how many animals the dog killed while it was loose. Rankin won't want the police to find out. Your approaching him may send him over the edge."

"Maybe." Shaw was unconcerned. "Why didn't you tell Fawcett we think the pit bull killed the collie? The old man wouldn't have stood for that."

"He wouldn't believe it. Rowland's still living in an age when 'Down, sir!' would halt any dog in its tracks."

"He knew what fighting dogs were about," Pharaoh pointed out, adding thoughtfully: "A dog that's capable of killing a Rottweiler wouldn't hesitate to attack a human being."

They came to a gate and a path through the woods. Shaw left them there to go back to his cottage and the others continued to Fox Yards. In his garden Harker regarded his delphiniums absently. "Shaw doesn't realise what he's up against," he said.

Pharaoh laughed. "From what I've learned of the Rankins they're fairly evenly matched. What's needed here is someone who can give them a taste of their own medicine. Something's got to be done about the dog, and obviously the Fawcetts don't realise the extent of the danger. And if the animal slipped its collar once it can do it again. The Rankin woman was terrified last evening. Does her husband knock her about?"

"Tilly? Never. Oh, George is a brute all right but he's no match for Tilly. To hear her sound off sometimes you'd think she was on drugs, having a bad trip; I've heard her from here when the wind's in the east, and it's more than half a mile. She's the aggressive one; the menfolk are quieter, more — sly. They're a strange family; your typical Cumbrian farmer is bluff and outgoing — the wife too — hard to get to know but good solid folk once they accept you. The Rankins, on the other hand, are all right to your face, providing you don't upset them, but they're devious. Beth Potter says Tilly is a gypsy, although by gypsy she means the kind of travelling people who work the fairs. She may be right, but whatever they are young Paul inherited bad genes. That boy's unpleasant. His parents are getting to a state now where they're afraid of him. He's a wiry lad and could be stronger than his father. He brought the dog home, remember. For my money someone found the animal was too much to look after and was forced to get rid of it, and d'you know" — he faced Pharaoh — "it wouldn't surprise me if that lad didn't have some bright idea about staging dog-fights." He shook his head. "No, that wouldn't surprise me at all."

★ ★ ★

"What do you know about dogs?" Paul Rankin asked cheekily.

Standing at the door of the barn he was as tall as Shaw but graceless and with nondescript features except for the eyes which were inclined to drift sideways. He smiled a lot, showing big white teeth.

"We have pit bulls in Africa," Shaw said. "We use them on patrol."

"How d'you keep them quiet?" The eyes touched Shaw's and veered away.

"We train them."

"How?"

"With the whip. How else?"

"Does they fight?"

"No one can stand up to a pit bull."

"You mean — " The eyes came back, excited, and Paul held his breath. "You mean you set them at people?"

"That's what they're trained for." Shaw was patient. "A pit bull has more power than an armed man. A man will stop if the other guy's got a better weapon; those dogs stop at nothing. They go for the throat and they stay there. In fact, if you need to persuade a black to talk you can't let the dog have him first because the fellow's going to be dead by the time they've choked the brute off. You extract information *then* you give him to the dog."

Young Paul stood aside. "Come and see this 'un," he said.

★ ★ ★

"You want to watch him." George Rankin spoke with his mouth full. "He's up to something."

His wife and son stared at him across the kitchen table. It was midday: dinner time for the Rankins who were eating a

90

greyish stew with large helpings of chips. Rankin was a harder, chunkier specimen than his son and physically he appeared to have the advantage, but he made no attempt to check the lad's tone which was not merely bullying but puerile. "I could take him any time," he said.

Tilly looked nervous. "Don't be daft. He's not an ordinary soldier. He's illegal. Them mercenaries is killers."

"*You're* being daft; this in't Africa. How'd he get a gun through Customs then? He's not armed."

"They're taught to use knives," Rankin said. "And unarmed combat, like rabbit punches. You seen it." The Rankins were addicts of television violence.

Young Paul was showing his big teeth. "A dog's afraid of nowt," he said meaningly. "And they go for the throat."

"Don't you ever — " Tilly started shrilly but she was shouted down by Rankin.

"Stop yer ranting, woman! Did you put another chain on that dog?" He glared at his son, but there was as much fear as anger in his attitude.

The boy looked from one to the other, gauging how far he could go. He licked his lips. "I'm not afraid of t'dog. I can do anything I like with 'im."

"You couldn't stop him last night," Tilly said quickly, and her hand flew to her mouth.

"I wasn't there. 'Course, they *are* killers, but so what? That old dog didn't know much about it; put him out of his misery, didn't it? Shaw says they use pit bulls to put them niggers out of their misery too. You know something: I could go out there to Africa, be a mercenary, take the dog along. I'd get more money with the dog; he's worth ten men. And me, I'd put my age up; I don't look sixteen."

His parents exchanged looks, carefully noncommittal.

"Yes, well . . . " Rankin stood up from the table. "We don't want the police here. You find another chain for that dog. And fasten collar tighter."

Paul pushed back his chair and stretched his legs. "I ain't done nothing."

Rankin swallowed. "No one 'cept us knows about last night. I buried t'old dog but if your animal took a sheep as well, and *she* finds the carcass," he nodded in the direction of the barn, "she'll tell Fawcett and that Harker. They'll know what did it. We don't want no police poking about round here."

Paul glowered at the table. They watched him, waiting to see how he'd take it. "She won't talk," he said finally. "Nor won't Harker, nor Fawcett. None of 'em will." He gave them a wide grin of triumph. "I got t'dog now," he reminded them.

Tilly looked at her husband. "What made you say Shaw was up to something?"

"Someone's been hanging around. There's tracks in the woods, and that there bulldog don't bark when t'lad's home, not normally. So why'd it bark the last few nights — I mean, before last night when it were just annoyed because it'd been chained up again? It knew someone were about the other nights."

"You never said nothing," Paul sneered. "I don't believe it."

"I didn't think till this morning. I found tracks last night but I didn't think nothing to it — could be Harker or the girl — but when I were looking for a soft place to bury the old dog, I looked at those tracks again and I followed 'em. I'll tell you something funny: someone been keeping a watch on *her* cottage, and that's not all. Sometimes he saw as how he'd left a mark where it could be seen and he covered it with leaves and stuff."

"Rubbish," Paul scoffed. "Someone watching them at t'Hall more like: see if they got owt worth thieving. Why watch her? She ain't got nothing."

"You're thinking someone's after her?" Tilly was interested but not concerned. Paul stared.

"Shaw came home two days since." Rankin was thoughtful. "Someone had been in the woods at night. Now he's making up to the lad. Why?"

Paul gave a snort of derision. "Making up to me? Come off it."

"His wife and Harker can't hardly bring themselves to pass the time of day with us," his father said. "She uses Harker's phone rather'n come here. What d'you expect, after you put them bullocks

94

in her vegetable patch? That girl'd set the police on you soon as look at you only she knows what might happen. . . . What I'm saying is, that girl's trouble. She hates us. So why's her husband getting matey with you — eh?"

5

MAIL was delivered late at Clouds. "Who knows you're here?" Susan asked, handing a letter to her husband. "You only arrived two days ago. Who d'you know in Newcastle?"

"I've got friends." He was expressionless. "People know I'm on leave." He took the letter and turned away to read it in the yard. It was a short letter, no more than one side, and his attitude told her nothing. Behind her Esme had come out of the kitchen and was starting up the stairs.

"I have to write some cards before I go to town," she said. Susan murmured a response but her eyes were on Shaw. He came back, stuffing the letter in his pocket. "I need the van," he said.

"I told you when you arrived: it's got a flat."

"Then why the hell haven't you mended it?" He was suddenly vicious and she was appalled.

"I can't mend a puncture myself, Marty!" She got a grip on herself then and turned on him shrewishly: "I have to do everything myself; you're never here. I don't even have a spare wheel; that's clapped out too. I depend on Clem for repairs and he's been so busy; I hate to keep asking him. I can't pay him." Her eyes filled with angry tears. "Here I am, driving an old banger — and that's not even on the road — while you're off playing war games — you don't contribute one penny . . . " But he was walking away round the side of the cottage. She followed, glancing up at the open windows, lowering her voice: "How do you think I feel: Mum visiting in that lovely car and all I've got to drive is a load of scrap?"

He was staring at their old Datsun van, one of its rims squashing a dusty tyre. He looked at her coldly.

"Why don't you get a job?"

It silenced her momentarily. She looked away as if searching the barn and the yard for inspiration. She found it. "Who was that letter from?"

He opened his mouth, thought better of it and went to peer through the back windows of the van.

"It's like that, is it?" she asked venomously.

He turned and regarded her for a long moment. "A mate of mine: the one I flew home with, has run into trouble. He needs my help."

"Well?" She was confused. "So what?"

"I have to get to a telephone."

"Use Clem's. He doesn't mind."

"It's private."

"Oh yes, I can see that." She was fierce again. "If your mate's in trouble you wouldn't hide it from another man, there's nothing private about that, men always stick together. It's a woman, isn't it: that letter? Some woman's writing to you."

"If you say so."

She gasped and took a step back, to be brought up short by the wall of the cottage. Shaw walked away. Susan slid down the wall and lowered her head to her knees, sobbing dryly. An engine started, revved up and, as it changed note, there were shouts from the front of the cottage. The Range Rover went past but she didn't raise her head. After a few moments Esme rushed into view, cursing. She halted as she saw her daughter and stared, bewildered.

"What happened? What did he do?" She knelt and took the girl in her arms. "Darling, what's he done to you?"

Susan's sobs turned to uninhibited weeping and it was some time before she quietened enough for Esme to leave her, returning with a glass of brandy. Standing, looking down at the girl, she switched deliberately from comfort to belligerence.

"You know what that bastard did? Drove off with my 'Rover! Just like that." Susan sighed but it turned to a gasp. Esme winced. "Why would he do a thing like that?" she asked gently. "What did you quarrel about?"

"It was nothing." The girl was listless, remembering. "He wanted wheels to go and telephone. Wouldn't go to Clem's, said it was private. He bawled me out because I hadn't had the flat mended." She stopped. "That's all," she added lamely.

"Oh. He wanted to telephone. It wouldn't have anything to do with the letter that came for him, would it?"

"I suppose so. He said a mate of his was in trouble."

"And?"

"I reckon it was a woman writing to him. I said so. I think he admitted it."

"You think."

Susan shrugged. "I'm sorry about your car, Mum."

"Yes." Esme was icy. "I look forward to — Oh, my God!"

"Now what?"

"My handbag: it's on the passenger seat. I was going into Kirkby; I'd only popped upstairs to write some cards. Everything's in my bag: my wallet, my cheque book; I've got — "

"It's all right." Susan was cold in her turn. "Martin's not a thief."

★ ★ ★

As he drove down the track Shaw kept an eye on the rear-view mirror, the last thing he wanted at this moment was to be chased by a pair of hysterical women.

100

When they didn't appear he thought that Esme could be going through the woods to alert the police by telephone from Harker's place, so he turned left when he reached the road because they'd never expect him to go all the way to Ewedale in order to find a public telephone.

He had forgotten the level crossing, and the barrier was down. He swore and turned, fumbling with the unfamiliar gears, lurching into the ditch, climbing out again, gunning the engine. The handbag fell from the passenger seat, spilling its contents across the floor.

He put his foot down and the Range Rover responded with a surge of power. As he passed Murkgill's entrance he glanced right. The track was empty. Would she dare to ask Harker to block the road further down? Could Harker do it in the time? He went fast through the wood, past the Dolphins' road-end, past the Clouds junction. There were meadows before the main road and there — at right angles and completely obstructing the lane — was a trailer and a Land Rover, the trailer backed into a gateway on the left, the Land Rover in the entrance to a field on the right. The Rankins were loading sheep, a pair of collies working a bunch of ewes towards the back of the trailer. Father and son were out in the meadow, closing in as the first ewe paused at the trailer's tailboard. The Rankins ignored the Range Rover.

Shaw's hand found the horn and stayed there. The sheep scattered in all directions and George Rankin erupted, cursing ewes, dogs and driver. Paul swaggered across the grass, squeezed past the trailer and approached the driver's side of the Range Rover. The horn was silent.

"Move it," Shaw said tightly.

Paul licked his lips; he had been expecting to confront a woman. He looked beyond Shaw and saw a stylish handbag on the floor, its contents spilled, and among them a plump wallet.

"Move the trailer before I ram it," Shaw said. "It'll come apart like matchwood."

Paul grinned. "Be my guest."

Shaw glanced in the mirror and saw an empty lane; he considered the battered Land Rover. The Rankins had been here too long to have blocked the way in response to a demand from Esme.

"Pull forward into the field," he said reasonably, and Paul, feeling his power, relishing a situation where he held the whip hand over a hard man, aware of his father approaching, said in a ridiculous travesty of a doting mother: "Ask nicely, then."

The driver's door slammed open, making contact but not doing much damage. Paul staggered and just managed to retain his balance until Shaw's fist connected with his jaw. His head snapped on his spine and he fell, the back of his skull making a nasty crack on the tarmac.

Shaw turned in a quick crouch as Rankin came past the front of the Range Rover, his stick raised like a cudgel. He stopped dead as Shaw's hand went to his ankle. Rankin had seen too many movies not to know what that meant. He lowered the stick and took a couple of steps backwards, staring.

Shaw went to the Land Rover, put it in gear and eased it forward, dragging the tailboard over the tarmac, the flanking wings swinging. Wood splintered. He came back to find Paul leaning on the door of the Range Rover, looking sick. His father was closing the gate into the meadow — and Lanty Dolphin was standing on the grass verge, a shotgun over his arm, observing the scene with fascination.

Shaw took Paul by the shoulders, whirled him like a rag doll and sent him staggering across the verge. His feet tangled in the ditch and he fell headlong, his body in nettles, his face in the thorn hedge.

Rankin shrank back against the gate and Lanty stepped quickly into the hedge, eyeing the Range Rover with apprehension, but he need not have worried. Shaw drew away smoothly, his indicator started to flash and he halted at the Stop sign where he turned right on the main road down the dale. Behind him three pairs of eyes followed the Range Rover's roof until it disappeared behind high hedges.

★ ★ ★

Shaw wasn't gone for long. When he returned the Land Rover and trailer had disappeared but the sheep were still in the meadow. He passed the Clouds junction and the Dolphins' road-end and turned on Murkgill's track, driving well now that he'd got the hang of the gears, enjoying the feel of the smooth vehicle.

The yard was empty but the door of his cottage was open. He parked neatly and walked indoors. Esme was sitting at the kitchen table with a face like stone. Susan was at the stove, her back towards him. He crossed the room, put his hands lightly on her arms and kissed the nape of her neck. She tried to turn but his hands tightened, holding her.

"It isn't a woman," he said softly. "There isn't any other woman."

She went rigid. At the table Esme glared at the scene.

"How about some beer?" he asked. "It's hot out there." He released his wife and went to the scullery where they kept the refrigerator. Susan threw an agonised look at her mother, smiled tremulously and blundered across the room and up the stairs. A door slammed. Shaw came back with three bottles.

"Shall I open yours?" he asked. "You'd like a glass?"

Esme said grimly: "You and I are going to have a talk." He paused, attentive. "How about starting with an apology?" she asked.

He nodded. "I'm sorry about the car."

"Why didn't you ask?"

"You wouldn't have let me have it."

"Have you touched it?" His eyes widened. "Scraped it," she hissed. "You know what I mean."

"No, it's untouched." He smiled.

"What's funny?"

"I did threaten to ram the Rankins' trailer. They were blocking the road."

"You — " She rushed outside, glanced at her car, then went to the passenger's door. Wrenching it open, she snatched her handbag from the seat. She hesitated and glanced at the cottage. Apparently she was unobserved, but she turned her back before taking out her wallet.

She returned slowly to the kitchen, carrying the bag and wallet separately. Shaw was sitting at the table facing her, one hand on a bottle.

"Give me the money," she said tightly.

"What money?" He was looking at the wallet.

"Two hundred pounds, near enough."

"You shouldn't carry that much cash on you. It was in the wallet?"

Her voice rose. "I've taken all I'm going to take from you; now I'm sending for the police. But I'll have my money first." Behind her Susan was standing in the doorway, her face white with shock. Shaw flicked a glance at her. He was quite composed. "I had a run-in with the Rankins," he said. "The bag had fallen on the floor and everything spilled out of it. I got out of your 'Rover to go and pull the Rankins' outfit off the road. I left George and Paul by your car — oh yes, Lanty Dolphin too; he was there."

"I don't believe this!" Esme's shoulders dropped and she turned, saw Susan, said abstractedly: "This has nothing to do with you, sweetie," and turned back. "You're telling me one of the Rankins or Lanty took two hundred pounds from this wallet? You're telling me *that*? Turn out your pockets!"

"Mum! That's crazy!"

Shaw was trying to hide amusement

and Esme, beside herself with anger and frustration, took a step forward. Susan darted to her husband, wildly feeling the outside of his pockets. He stood up, making it easy for her, lifting his arms.

"Look, Mum: nothing! Where's he going to hide that much money? It was the Rankins — Paul's capable of anything. He'll go and get it back for you, won't you, Marty? Look, love, Mum's upset; you took her lovely new car without asking — and she'd left her bag in it — two hundred quid, Marty! It's a fortune!"

Esme had a grip on herself now. "No time like the present," she said coldly. "Shall we go and confront the Rankins right away?"

"Would that be a good idea?"

"Of course it would, Marty; you have to. The bag was in your charge; you're responsible."

He looked at the girl bleakly and she swallowed. He glanced at the window. "Where's the dog?"

"Oh no." Esme was incredulous. "Are you suggesting you're afraid to go over there because they might have the dog in the house? Right, I'll go myself."

Shaw grimaced and followed her outside, trailed by Susan.

★ ★ ★

"He didn't take no money," Tilly shouted from her back porch.

"He were knocked out by 'im!" She gestured furiously at Shaw. George and Paul were nowhere to be seen although the truck and trailer were in the yard. "He attacked our lad; he's mad, that son-in-law of yourn, *and* he threatened Rankin with a knife." Esme and Susan turned wide eyes on Shaw who stood in the yard, his eyes ranging over windows and doors. "I'm going to law about this," Tilly cried. "My boy's got a cracked skull and he's all bruised and cut and shocked."

"No Rankin was ever shocked," Susan said coldly.

"Where's the money?" Shaw asked. "Give Mrs Winter her two hundred pounds and we'll call it quits."

"You dare — ! You bugger!" Tilly came out of the porch and he held up his arm as he would stop a horse. "Stay there," he said, and smiled. "Don't forget the knife."

At that Esme turned and stalked out of the yard. After a moment Susan followed her. Shaw faced Tilly.

"When I go away again," he said distinctly and in a pleasant conversational tone as if formally taking his leave of her, "you're going to have to watch your step. That goes for all of you. I've got friends. Nasty accidents can happen on farms, fatal accidents. Do I make myself quite clear?"

6

A T Grammery Bank, the Dolphin place, Harker and Juno were stripping wallpaper in one of the bedrooms at the back. In the garden Lanty was scything nettles, watched by Pharaoh from a wooden bench.

"Jack's worn out," Juno murmured, glancing out of the window. "He was on his feet too long, painting that bathroom."

"He needs to keep busy," Harker said absently and then, with unaccustomed heat: "What the hell's going to happen when he goes?"

"Jack?"

"Shaw. And why should he thump Paul? It must have been for something more than cheek."

Lanty had come straight home and the three of them stopped work to listen to his account of the confrontation in the lane. After Shaw drove away George Rankin had explained that what he called the attack on his son had been prompted merely by Shaw's finding the trailer blocking the road. The man had gone mad, said Rankin, he would have stabbed both of them to death had Lanty not been a witness — or it could be Shaw was frightened of the shotgun.

"Do you believe he carries a knife?" Juno asked now. "I mean strapped to his leg? Or is that just George being paranoid?"

She was peeling a long strip from the wall but his silence prompted her to turn, to find him regarding her with something approaching shock. She turned back to the wall. "*Is* he violent?" she wondered, picking at a bulge of plaster.

"Not . . . to my knowledge." He paused. "Not in his own home."

"Good." It was emphatic. She scraped away diligently. Harker moved to stand beside her and look down into the garden. "Lanty wears his heart on his sleeve," she said lightly. He turned and met her eyes. "Being older you're discreet," she went on. "All the same it would be as well to keep a low profile for a while, until he goes away."

"What *are* you talking about?" The words didn't go with the jumpy eyes.

"You're both in the same boat: you and Lanty. It's obvious, at least to an older woman. A son's behaviour is transparent anyway: to his mother, and quite natural; they're both without partners — well, she was without a partner."

"Is Lanty still — " Harker stopped. "None of my business," he muttered.

"A moot point." The sound of her scraper was loud in the empty room. From below a woman called: "Anyone home?"

"That sounds like Esme Winter," she said. "Maybe we'll learn more now. Is that ghoulish?" She glanced at him. "Or just prudent: to know what's going on so we don't put our foot in it?" She lifted her voice: "I'm coming, Esme." She laid a hand on his arm. "It's the wrong moment to get on your white charger," she said quietly. "I'll bet that man doesn't fight clean, Clem, and I'm rather fond of you. Not to speak of Lanty. Let's keep the peace while Martin's with us, shall we?"

He shrugged. "You don't have to

worry about me. She doesn't know I'm here, not when Lanty's around."

"Well, that's something." But there was resignation rather than relief in her tone. "That leaves me only one man to look after."

Esme was pacing the tiles at the foot of the stairs. Beyond the open door the Range Rover gleamed in the sunshine. Esme was flushed with temper. "Have you got a room?" She spat it out.

"Come along to the kitchen." Juno smiled serenely. "Have some coffee, or a drink. Would you like a drink?"

"Anything." Esme allowed herself to be ushered across the hall and along a passage. "I have never, ever been treated like this in my whole life!" They entered a cluttered kitchen and Juno pulled out a chair. Esme remained standing. "And by my own son-in-law! He had the temerity, the insolence — "

Juno glanced towards the window as a figure passed.

"Let him come" — Esme interrupted herself wildly — "I'm sounding off like a fishwife; this is what he's done to me. We need a man here — Lanty's too young; where's Clem? His van's outside." Lanty opened the back door and stopped dead, regarding Esme with apprehension. "Give Clem a shout," she ordered. "Tell him he's wanted. And there's Jack Pharaoh," she added, seeing him through the window. "What a nice solid fellow he is." She strode to the door which Lanty had left open. "Jack! Please. We need you."

She was in no mood for restraint or argument, and perhaps Juno thought that there would be comfort in numbers. She poured coffee as they gathered round the table, all anticipating some enthralling item of gossip, so it was something of an anticlimax when Esme, having had a little time in which to collect herself, told it from the beginning but omitting, in her indignation, the arrival of the letter. It wasn't until she reached the part where she had discovered that two hundred pounds was missing from her wallet that they sat up and took notice.

"He says either the Rankins stole it or you," she flung at Lanty.

"I didn't go near the Range Rover!"

"He's not accusing you directly." She

was dismissive. "That's his way of wriggling out of it. He stole it, I'm certain of that. He wasn't carrying it, that's for sure; Sue patted his pockets. That means he hid it somewhere on the road."

There was silence, the more marked because Esme had been talking so loudly and fast that no one could ask a question. She continued flatly, her voice starting to crack: "So we went to Rankin's, and Tilly blew her top, put all the blame on Martin, of course. Said he hit Paul, threatened them both with a knife. What did happen, Lanty?"

Lanty was happy to tell it again. "I was coming up the lane and here's George's truck and trailer blocking the way, but I could see what happened through the gap between 'em. Shaw moved as fast as a rat; he thumped Paul, then George rushed at him and he went for his ankle. I didn't see a knife but it was that action, you know: either for a knife or a gun. George thought so too; he backed off immediately."

"Were the Rankins in my Range Rover?"

"No, not in it. Paul was hanging on the door but unless he was shamming, he wasn't in any state to reach in and pinch a wallet."

"He'd have to open it and take the notes out." She shook her head. "I never thought it was them. It had to be him." She appealed to Juno. "You see it's impossible for me to stay there — and yet I can't leave Clouds; Sue is devastated. He has to go now. I'll stay till he leaves and then she's going to need a shoulder to cry on. If you can't have me, Juno, I'll go to a hotel in Kirkby."

"There's no need for that. We can make room if you don't mind a frightful muddle — "

"What does Sue think?" Harker cut in roughly. "I mean" — as people turned to him — "does she agree with you, or is she standing by him?"

"Clem." Juno's tone was heavy with warning. He ignored her, waiting for Esme's response.

"She's loyal. That's her problem right now: division of loyalties." She returned his stare. "She's a sensitive child but perhaps a little immature, and she's never run into anything like this before. I was always against — " She checked, looked round the table and her eyes came to rest on Pharaoh who, conscious of his position as a guest in the community, had been keeping quiet. "What do you think, Jack?"

"I'm wondering what made it so important that he had to take your car right then."

"He'd had a letter, and that meant he had to get to a telephone right away, and he wouldn't go to Clem's place because it was a private matter, and their van's off the road."

"Must have been a hell of an important letter," Lanty growled. Pharaoh said nothing.

Harker turned to Esme. "Since Shaw arrived has he said anything about where he was immediately before he reached Clouds?"

"Immediately before?" She was bewildered.

"The night before," Pharaoh clarified, and Juno looked at him sharply. Lanty was frowning.

"He slept out on the moor." Esme

waved a hand. "Why is that important?"

Harker glanced at Pharaoh. "I was wondering if the letter could relate to something that happened before he turned up here. Obviously someone has his home address. Or had it been forwarded?"

"No. I saw the envelope before he took it. There was one address, one postmark: Newcastle."

Juno was smiling. "You're not suggesting there was something sinister about the letter, Clem?"

"Of course not." But it lacked conviction.

"Sue reckoned it was from a woman." Esme sounded spiteful. "At first he admitted it. They quarrelled and that's when he went off in my car. When he came back he went out of his way to deny that there was a woman involved; he told her that in front of me. Maybe," she added nastily, "he was told to deny it, by the person he telephoned."

"Did he hit her?" Lanty asked, and Harker's eyes widened.

"To my knowledge he's never been

violent." Esme's face was taut. "I mean, not to women."

"What's he doing now?" Pharaoh asked.

"For my money, he'll keep out of the way. We left him talking to Tilly — yes, I remember! He mentioned the knife himself. What happened was he demanded the money, my two hundred pounds, from Tilly: told her that if she gave it back we would call it quits. Those were his words. Tilly lost control. I thought she was going to scratch his eyes out. She sprang out of the porch — and he just put his arm up, palm out, and said: 'Remember the knife'. I was so disgusted I came away, and Sue with me. I'm prepared to write off the money now. All I want to do is to get her away from here. She can come and live with me until she's sorted herself out, but no way am I going to go home and leave her in this place." She thought better of that, seeing them stiffen. "You're all good friends of hers, I know, and I'm very grateful that she's had you to turn to" — her eyes rested momentarily on Harker — "but you can't go and live in the cottage with her, and when he's gone — well, she shouldn't be there on her own."

Harker stood up. "I have to go to town," he announced. "I'm going to take that flat to the tyre people — "

"Oh, I should have done that, Clem — " Esme stopped in confusion, guessing he might have an ulterior motive.

"I'll take the two wheels," he told her firmly. "She must have a serviceable spare."

"The child has no money. I'll give you — oh damn!" She remembered that she had no money either. "Would a cheque do? He didn't take my cheque book, nor my credit cards."

"You can pay me when I get back."

"You can save me a journey," Juno told Pharaoh, and he realised that she wanted him to accompany Harker. "If you'd get me some chicken breasts," she went on, "some French bread, and we'll have a bottle of burgundy — a poor man's *coq au vin*, Esme; how's that? You're a sweet man, Clem, always running errands for people; I don't know what we'd do without you. You'll remember that, Jack,

121

or do you need a list?"

As they drove down Grammery's drive Pharaoh said: "It's just as well I'm with you; Juno saw that immediately. If Shaw can thump a boy because a trailer's blocking his road, what's he going to do to you if you utter one wrong word to his wife? He might use the knife next time."

"You've been watching too much telly."

"Perhaps the heat's bothering him," Pharaoh mused.

"After Africa? You're not thinking straight."

It was hot. The drive wound through hardwoods and conifers with cool shadows in the depths but after standing in the sun the van was like an oven, even with the windows open. Pharaoh stared through the windscreen. The heat wave was affecting everyone. He was tense himself as they approached Murkgill where, at the gable end of the big barn, the way divided: left to the cottage, right to the Rankins' house.

As Harker turned his van in the yard they could hear the dog barking above the sound of the engine. Susan appeared in the cottage porch, her eyes huge and a little wild.

"I'm taking your wheels to Kirkby," Harker told her, his tone so neutral that it sounded cold. He glanced at the kitchen window. "Your mother's buying you two new tyres."

"How sweet of you. And Mum." She looked past him to Pharaoh who watched her — and the shadowed doorway — without expression.

"I have to go to town myself," she said. "I'll come with you."

Harker shifted involuntarily. "Should you?" He put a world of meaning into it.

"I have to." She looked towards the barn. "I can't stand that row." Feeling flooded her face. "I can't take it any longer, Clem."

"Of course you can't! Come on: let's get those wheels in the van."

"Is Martin coming with us?" Pharaoh asked politely.

"He's sloped off somewhere." Now she looked like a sulky child. "He has to get rid of the bad taste; it's not nice to have your own family accuse you of being a thief."

"Your mother is buying the tyres, Sue," Harker reminded her.

"It's not good enough. She ought to apologise . . . "

But he was getting out of the van with a busy air and walking to the corner. "You got a jack and a wheelbrace?" he called back.

In a few minutes they had the wheel off the old Datsun and were on their way, Susan sitting in front, Pharaoh on a crate in the rear watching her profile as she turned to Harker. She was pale and her jaw was clenched until she spoke. As they emerged from Murkgill's track and turned right she asked, as if surprised that she hadn't done so before: "Is Mum staying with Juno? Great, she said she'd go there." Then, sulkily, "I suppose she told you what happened, what's supposed to have happened?"

"Yes." Harker sounded tight-lipped. Pharaoh could see only the back of his head.

"You don't believe he took that money,

do you?" She was pleading, and Harker unbent a little.

"I only know what I've been told — "

"But you've met him!" It was almost a wail, and then she changed tack. "Two hundred pounds: why, he earns more than that in a week!" Harker stared at the windscreen and Pharaoh hoped he was sparing some concentration for the road. "The Rankins are capable of anything," she persisted. "He says Paul was hanging on to the door when he came back from pulling the trailer out of the way. And there was George: they had heaps of time to reach in, either of them, take the money out of the wallet and throw it back. It's just the kind of thing they would do; they'd know it was Mum's handbag. Paul would love it: get two hundred quid and drop Marty in the shit at the same time."

"That's how it must have been," Pharaoh put in quietly, and she turned to him, her eyes shining with gratitude. She looked at Harker in triumph. "You see! And Jack's just a visitor; he takes the objective view. You don't like Marty, Clem; you're prejudiced. You think he ought to have a proper job. Well, I've got news for you: he's going to take a commission in the Liberian army. There!" she threw it down like a gauntlet but then, aware of her own childishness, added carelessly: "The pay is one thousand pounds a month, tax free."

"Good." Harker didn't look at her. "When's he leaving?"

"We're having a holiday first. We're going to tour the Continent."

"In what?"

"What?"

"That's right. Your mother's buying you a couple of new tyres but for the Continent you're going to need a new car. The Datsun'd fall apart before you reached the ferry."

"We shall hire a car, of course."

In the back Pharaoh sat like a cat, watching and listening. They passed old stone houses and magnificent barns but he saw none of them; he was thinking about love and infatuation and lust, and trying to be objective.

"When are you going?" Harker asked.

"He has to go to London first, to sign the contract. They've been trying to persuade him for ages, the recruiting people. Marty's good with native troops." She interpreted Harker's silence as contradiction. "They're a sight easier to deal with than young Paul," she added heatedly. "That boy's out of control. He doesn't have any discipline in the home; why, even Tilly and George are afraid of him now he's as big as his father. But of course" — she caught herself up — "Marty knows how to deal with Paul Rankin. He didn't lose his temper, you know; he just dropped him with one punch."

"And the knife?" Harker murmured.

"What knife?" It was too innocent.

"Forget it." He sighed and changed the subject. "Are you going to stay with your mother in Scotland or look for somewhere on your own?"

"When?"

"When he goes abroad again, of course."

"Oh, I'm not leaving Clouds."

"Are you sure? Your mother thinks you're leaving. And you can't stand that dog."

"The dog's going to be got rid of.

And my mother knows nothing about it. Marty's going to buy the cottage and then we'll modernise it. There's a job for you, Clem. Mum will lend us the deposit money."

A lay-by showed ahead. Harker slowed, pulled in and stopped the van. He turned to her. The two of them might have been alone for all the notice they paid to Pharaoh. "Look, love," he began earnestly, "do you have any idea how your mother feels about this business? About losing the money, his part in it? About everything, in fact?"

"She'll do it for me."

"She'll do a lot for you; she'd lend you money to buy a place of your own, I'm sure; what she won't do is provide money so that you can stay with him — "

"It's not your business! You can't bear for me — "

Pharaoh coughed loudly and she turned in astonishment. She had indeed forgotten him. "If you're going to make the tyre depot before they close . . . " he said meaningly.

Harker drew a deep breath and reached for the ignition. "You're right," he said grimly. "None of my business. I apologise. However" — it was too light, contrived — "if you're going to stay at Clouds, that's all to the good. Personally I'd rather you stayed."

"Don't let Marty hear you say that." It was a spark of her old flirtatious manner and, as far as Pharaoh was concerned, it confirmed her inability to understand the situation. As her mother said: she was more than a little immature.

★ ★ ★

"He's won her over," Harker said. "Odd, isn't it, how susceptible women are to charm and a hard young body?"

They were sitting on a low wall outside the tyre depot waiting for a mechanic to put the new tyres on the rims. Susan had gone to do the shopping.

"I don't find it odd," Pharaoh said. "Kids love glamour. Remember the way the village girls used to mob the team at the Saturday night discos?"

"Susan isn't a village girl — and she could do a lot better for herself than that lout. I mean it" — as Pharaoh raised his eyebrows. "Stealing from his own mother-in-law! When you said it could have been the Rankins that was just you trying to cool it; you don't really believe that. Why'd he do it, Jack?"

"It didn't have to be him. If he came into town or stopped on the way to use a telephone, with the windows open and the bag on the seat, anyone could have reached in and picked up the wallet. He's not necessarily a thief, just irresponsible."

"Maybe he stole it so that it would look bad for the Rankins." Harker hadn't been listening.

"Do you think he's serious about the Liberia job?"

"I suppose so. Is there a war in Liberia? But he said he trained troops in peacetime too; a bit dull for him: training men when he's more accustomed to shooting them, but if he wants to keep Sue then he's got to work. And no doubt he'll have the opportunity to waste a few dissident tribesmen occasionally. He'd consider that a bonus."

Pharaoh gave him a sharp look but all he said was, "Tribesmen in Liberia are probably armed with Soviet rocket launchers by now. Or American."

"That might even things up." Harker's eyes gleamed, then shifted. "Here's Sue. And she's loaded. Where did she get the money to — " He stopped, horrified at the implication of his own words. Susan approached with loaded bags in her arms.

"I had to put this on Juno's account," she told them, unaware of any undercurrent. "Mum will pay for my share. I doubled everything because I thought we'd eat together tonight, sort of celebration. Marty loves *coq au vin*. Don't look so fierce, Clem; Juno knows Marty *and* she knows the Rankins. We all do. We know who's responsible."

"That's not the point, Sue. Your mother's at Grammery; you can't take Martin over there to dinner, not tonight anyway. At least give the air a chance to clear."

"What do you say, Jack?"

Pharaoh suppressed a sigh; people were always picking on him for an ally. He decided that if it let Harker off the hook then he would adopt an avuncular attitude. "Why don't you celebrate with Martin tonight?" he urged. "In a day or two things should have sorted themselves out." Or we might be rid of Shaw, he thought, looking into the wide eyes and suddenly aware of the shape of her lips, parted as she watched his face. "Be patient," he said and, looking past her, saw that Harker was regarding him with suspicion.

They loaded the new tyres and the shopping and drove back to Clouds. The mood was a little lighter on the return, Harker pointing out features of interest: the crag where he'd surprised a vixen playing with cubs, the copse that housed a badger's sett, the ghyll where a peregrine nested. The men worked hard to achieve a normal atmosphere but the girl was subdued. Any social graces she possessed related to her emotions and now that she was preoccupied with Shaw, other men were superfluous.

At Clouds they went first to Grammery and waited in the van while she went indoors with the shopping. Harker drummed on the steering wheel and stared at a sequoia across the lawn.

"Good job it leans away from the house," he remarked. "We have awful gales here." Pharaoh was silent. Harker turned. "You can't be comfortable on that crate."

"I'll live. I could do with a drink though. I'm sure it's getting hotter."

"It's stuffy. We could be in for a storm."

Juno came out of the house, urging them to come inside for a beer. She was followed by Susan who said her mother was bathing and then announced in a flurry that she must go straight home and cook her dinner.

They drove to the cottage and the dog started barking as they entered the yard. Shaw was nowhere to be seen and didn't appear. Susan went indoors and came out again to watch Harker and Pharaoh replacing the wheel on the Datsun. All urgency was forgotten and she looked as if she had nothing else to do. When they had tightened the last nut and stowed the tools and turned to her she wouldn't meet their eyes but pretended to find an interest in the skyline above the quarries.

"We could be in for a storm," Harker repeated.

A chain rattled in the barn. The dog had stopped barking. Susan glanced across the yard, seemed about to say something, thought better of it and sighed heavily. She stepped back. "I'll see you around." It was pathetic, forlorn. She turned and went into the cottage. She had forgotten to thank them. Harker took a step after her. Pharaoh said quietly: "He'll be back any time," and walked deliberately to the van. Harker hesitated, then followed and climbed behind the wheel.

"If this was mountain country," he said as they drove down the track, "he could have gone climbing — solo — and fallen. Nowhere to fall here." He sounded disappointed.

★ ★ ★

There was no storm on the Pennines that night, only a mutter of thunder over the Lakeland hills. At Clouds the houses were bowered in their dark and leafy woods and the air was heavy, almost stagnant. No owls called and the dogs were silent. People sweated under cotton sheets. Sometime in the small hours Pharaoh went downstairs for a drink and was startled out of his wits, crossing the living room, when a voice spoke from the gloom.

"You can't sleep either?" Harker must be standing by the open window. He peered in that direction but could see no shape against the darkness. The trees in the lane blocked out the stars.

"You might have put a light on," he grumbled. "What are you doing, standing there? Or are you sitting? Where's the switch?"

"No, don't show a light!" It was quick and urgent.

"What's up, Clem?"

"Nothing. I'm just listening."

Pharaoh felt his way round the table until he could sense the proximity of the other man. "Listening for what?"

"I came down for a drink. There was something in the garden."

"Probably an animal."

"Probably. Whatever it was, it's gone now." His tone changed. "Let's climb tomorrow — today, rather. Go across to the Lakes and do a route in Langdale."

Pharaoh gave a bark of amusement. "You'd need a block and tackle for me — "

"Now look, Jack — "

"Seriously, I haven't got any equipment."

"All we need is a rope. I've got that."

"It's too hot, Clem. Take Lanty Dolphin. Now there's an idea: that lad could follow anything you could lead."

"You reckon? I'm not all that confident — but, yes, I could take him. You don't mind?"

"Not in the least. I'm happy here."

It had been a ritual response, he thought, sitting on his bed, drinking water, but it held an element of truth; he was quite amenable to his host going off to the Lakes for the day. In any event his own reaction was irrelevant beside this curiously tactless suggestion — or was he being neurotic: interpreting a friendly gesture as a thoughtless jibe? He was over-reacting, he told himself sternly; what was remarkable was Harker's impulsive decision to leave Clouds for the day.

He was not an impulsive man. Was he so bewitched by Susan that he literally couldn't bear to be close to her when Shaw was around?

He stretched himself carefully on the mattress — lying down was something he had to do in stages — and pulled up the sheet. Lying in this narrow bed, in a room that was monastic in its masculinity (but heavy with the scent of roses), he visualised Harker's room, ostensibly similar, with nothing more than a hairbrush and a handful of change on the chest of drawers, and dust, but housing a different climate of mind. Not climate — he relinquished the term regretfully — but preoccupation. Because whereas he, Pharaoh, was fascinated by his friend's motivation, that friend seemed preoccupied by sex.

Such were Pharaoh's thoughts in the cooling hours before the dawn as he regarded the ceiling — which he could now make out as a pale square — and reflected that the current situation would never have arisen if only Harker and Susan had behaved like normal people and had an affair while Shaw was in

Africa. By now it would be over and they would be just good friends. Mesmerised by the ceiling, against which he found that he could discern the faintly darker shape of the lampshade, he felt himself drifting pleasantly, aware that, floating with the current, he touched something: a snag, a thought, but not concerned enough to feel round the edges of whatever it was: a rock, driftwood, a sleeping monster. . . . In the woods a vixen called. Distantly, shut in the stable, Rankin's collies responded. There was no sound from the pit bull.

7

AT ten o'clock in the morning, another brilliant morning and already hot, Pharaoh was leafing through a book on the northern Pennines, trying to convince himself that being relaxed at Clouds was preferable to being tense on vertical rock, when a shadow darkened the flagstones.

"'Morning," Shaw said. "Harker around?"

"He's gone climbing."

Shaw regarded him without expression, and the fact that he was waiting for some kind of explanation annoyed Pharaoh. He raised an eyebrow. "Can I help?"

Shaw seemed to come to a decision. "Yes." His lips stretched and then he smiled properly. He's a good-looking bastard, thought Pharaoh grudgingly, and aloud: "Sit down and have a drink."

"It's too early."

"Not for coffee." He pulled himself to his feet, resentful that this man should witness his clumsiness. He made coffee and brought the mugs to the living room.

"I have to go to London," Shaw said. "I was going to ask Harker to keep an eye on Susan. You can tell him when he comes back."

"I'll do that. Keep an eye on her?"

"I don't like the Rankins. You'll have heard about yesterday — thanks for running her into Kirkby by the way, and getting those tyres — I wouldn't put it past the lad to try and get his own back when I'm not here."

"You can't be thinking Paul would be physically violent? Personally? No, you mean damage to property."

"Not really." Shaw seemed unconcerned. "The cottage is Fawcett's property, and the lad wouldn't be likely to damage that. And I'm taking the van" — he grinned tightly — "so he can't slash the new tyres. As for Susan: she can take care of herself well enough; she's a right bitch when she's roused." He stopped and looked out of the window, missing Pharaoh's frown.

"So what could the lad do? You had

140

something specific in mind? Oh — not the dog!"

"The dog?" Shaw blinked. "You mean the pit bull. No, it's chained; it can't do any harm. What it is: Susan hates being on her own, and she won't listen to me. I tell her the situation hasn't changed; she's been alone in the past for months at a time, now she's bothered because I'm going away for one night."

"Why doesn't she go to Juno's?"

"I don't want her to do that. Esme's got it in for me. She'd like to break us up, Sue and me. The money being stolen is an excuse; she knows it wasn't me but she's using it as a handle. I'm not just a drifter now; I'm a thief too. Susan's climbing the wall, poor kid. She finds her mother a bit overwhelming."

Pharaoh said, for something to say: "Why don't you take her to London?"

"She doesn't want to come." He put down his mug and stood up. "I was going to ask Harker to spend the day with her, both of you, I mean; go for a walk, anything to keep her company, stop her brooding." Keep her away from her mother, he might have added. He regarded Pharaoh hopefully. "You can do that, can't you? I'll send her across."

"I'll do what I can." Pharaoh was noncommittal. What did this guy want? He said coldly: "But if Susan is afraid of being left alone, the night is the worst time." Their eyes locked. "I know what I'm talking about," he said deliberately, "I've been there. She could go and sleep at the Hall."

Shaw nodded. "Get Harker to suggest it. She'll take his advice. She respects him, he's a father figure." Pharaoh couldn't hide his surprise. "I mean it," Shaw persisted. "After all, what other man is there for her to respect in this neck of the woods? Only old Fawcett and he's too old. Harker's just the right age; she could be his daughter. So I'll leave it with you." He took a step towards the door, then paused. "I'm not bothered about young Dolphin," he said, and was gone before Pharaoh could think of a response.

As he washed the mugs and reflected that Harker had chosen a singular moment to absent himself, it occurred to Pharaoh that he'd missed an opportunity to ask Shaw if he'd been camping in the quarries before his arrival at Clouds, and then he thought that there hadn't been an opportunity, and it was better not to ask anyway. If it had been Shaw, the only motive he could have for spying on the community was to keep a watch on someone, and who was that more likely to be than his own wife? "I'll send her over," he'd said. He sounded like a pimp, and yet presumably you knew where you were with pimps; Pharaoh certainly didn't know where he was with this fellow. He felt a surge of revulsion; suddenly Clouds seemed less pleasing and the last thing he wanted was to be at Fox Yards if Susan arrived.

When he'd washed up, he took Harker's binoculars from the back of the door and set out for the fresh air of the uplands. Immediately he started to climb he felt good again and he went well: not exactly striding, but walking without strain up a path with easy zig-zags that brought him out on another limestone pavement, on the opposite side of the pass from Clouds Scar. From the edge of the plateau he had a comprehensive view of this country that he was coming to know and even to like for its small scale, its gentle understatement. Below him the minor road emerged from the woods to cross the railway line and rise in sweeping curves to the pass where they'd left the van the day they walked to Black Blote Fell. The path showed as a pale line between the limestone and the black peat hags. The sinkholes were invisible, sunk in the bottom of their grassy funnels. To the left he could see the roof and upper windows of the Hall but the woods obscured Harker's cottage,and only one corner of Juno's tall house was visible, this side of the sequoia that towered above the hardwoods.

The buildings of Murkgill, the house and Susan's cottage, were obvious, the shabby whitewash of the cottage deceptively bright in the heat haze. Visibility was decreasing with every day. Clouds was less than two miles distant as the raven flew but the Pennines were so faint as to be sensed rather than seen: the other side of a space that was opaque but brilliant, like pearls.

Pharaoh felt a surge of passion, surprising because these were only little hills. And yet they were uplands. Below him there was heat and humidity but here, where zephyrs strayed along the rim of the plateau, body and mind fused, his skin was absorbent and he basked like a lizard in a radiance that was more than air and sun. He had no problems, he even forgot that Harker was at this moment climbing on mountains which would have been visible but for the haze. The last thing he remembered as he stretched out on the turf was that the night had been restless.

★ ★ ★

The sound was an enchantment. It grew louder, more insistent, monopolising a world which had been peopled with remembered faces, speech patterns, touch ("You have a good jaw," his wife said, tracing it) and now the wild music swelled: too loud, too much. . . . Before he opened his eyes he knew it was only larks and their song faded as he sat up blinking. His cap fell off, and as he reached for it he saw Susan sitting on a rock, her chin on her hands, observing him as she might an interesting animal.

There was a daisy chain encircling his Breton cap. He smiled. "How long have you been watching over me?"

"Well, watching. I don't know. There's no time up here."

She was wearing skimpy shorts and Nike trainers, the clumpy shoes emphasising the length of her tanned legs. Her red shirt was threadbare and torn, tied under her breasts in a knot. No brassière showed through the ripped shoulder and no white flesh. She must sunbathe nude. She returned his appraisal with interest. "I've been here twenty minutes," she admitted.

"By accident or design?"

"You're vain, Mr Pharaoh."

"Not in this context. Your husband said he would send you over to Clem's."

"He said what? *Send me over?* What in hell — " There was no doubt that her anger was genuine. "He called at Fox Yards before he left? So what did you have to say to that — you and Clem?"

"What could I say? It was directed at Clem but he's climbing with Lanty today so I said I'd pass on the message when he came home."

"It was his idea of a joke. He didn't mean it. So — Clem and Lanty are climbing together?"

"Is that surprising?"

"I would expect him to take — I mean, you two — Why didn't you go?" she bit her lip in confusion. "I'm sorry."

"That's all right. I could have gone; I'm just not up to the hard stuff. So Martin's away to London?"

"Yes, he's gone to join up." She spoke absently, forgetting that he knew already, her attention caught by something on the other side of the pass. He followed the direction of her gaze and after a moment he saw a shape moving fast along the path towards Black Blote Fell.

"Is that someone on a horse?" He reached for the glasses.

"Nobody rides at Clouds — at least, no one's got a horse. That'll be the Rankins shepherding, but it's too small for a Land Rover. It must be Paul on the Honda."

He was focusing. "He rounds up sheep on a bike?"

"A farm bike, an ATV. You must have seen him on it: that little three-wheeler thing. ATVs go anywhere; that's what it means: All Terrain Vehicle."

"It's Paul all right, and he's going like the clappers."

"Surely you wouldn't expect a boy of sixteen to go slowly on a farm bike?"

"Hardly. I bet his mother goes up the wall. He's not what you might call stable. Is the bike?"

"How do you mean?"

"Doesn't it tip easily on rough ground?"

"I hope so. That could solve a lot of problems — as long as it was fatal. I'm thirsty; aren't you thirsty? I wish we had some beer — but the beer's only two miles away, well, three by the path. Come on, I'll race you — Oh, I'm sorry!" She had leapt to her feet and now she stood, poised for flight but stricken, her hand over her mouth.

He laughed. "You go on. I'd like to see you running — cantering rather; you're built like a racehorse. If you stay you'll be pandering to an old man."

"I'd what?"

"Leaning over backwards to be kind."

148

"Oh hell!" She passed a tongue over her lips, eyeing him. "I'm going to Fox Yards, not to my place." She glanced across the pass but Paul had disappeared. "I haven't got any beer. You'd better hurry or I'll have drunk all Clem's by the time you get there; all the same, I bet you won't be more than a few minutes behind me."

The gallantry was sweet: making up for her thoughtlessness. He had a terrible time descending, trying to watch the ground and her progress at the same time. He saw her reach the road and start down the middle of it at a speed that amazed him. Idly he looked beyond her and pulled up, appalled. A train was crossing the viaduct. He clutched the binoculars but he didn't raise them. He could see the red disc at the crossing that showed the barrier was down, so she'd know the train was coming. The lights would be flashing anyway; she'd stop.

She reached the line and crossed it, her speed scarcely checked at the barriers. A whistle sounded, she waved and went racing down the road and into the woods. Pharaoh let out the breath that he hadn't known he was holding. His heart was thudding like a pile driver. Didn't she realise the danger — or didn't she care?

When he opened the gate at Fox Yards she was sitting on the log drinking beer.

"You were quick." He'd made a bet with himself that she'd say just that. He went to the refrigerator and came back with a bottle and cushions to pad the slatted seat. He settled himself, drank greedily and lowered the bottle. They both spoke at once.

"Why did Clem — "

"You might have some — " He deferred to her with a gesture.

"Why did Clem pick Lanty to climb with? He could have asked me."

"He didn't know Martin was leaving. Tell me: don't you have any consideration for people's feelings?" She gaped at him. "The driver of the train?" he prompted.

"What train?"

He slumped on the seat. It wasn't worth the trouble. He took a long pull at his beer.

"Oh!" she cried. "*That* train. You were watching. Did you expect to see me splattered all up the — " She stopped, appalled; she'd done it again. "We need glasses," she muttered, and dashed into the cottage.

It was a while before she came back and when she did he said quietly: "We can't go on like this or you'll be examining everything before you speak to see if it's passable. My wife and daughter died in a car crash. My first wife left me because we couldn't get on together. It happens to thousands of people all the time. You can't avoid mentioning death and divorce and bereavement — I forgot: legs and spines too — so don't try. And no, I didn't think the train would hit you because I could see the barriers were down and I thought you'd wait before you crossed. You were over the line before I realised what was happening. It's afterwards that the onlooker starts to shake. That driver would have had a bad moment."

"Rubbish. There are thousands of footpaths crossing main lines. Drivers must see pedestrians on the track all the time. A woman was killed . . . " She faltered and finished limply, " . . . this summer."

"And two children with her. There was no barrier on that crossing. Here there is."

"So, what do you want me to do: write to British Rail and apologise?"

It was an impasse and they both knew it. She was amused: he found her teasing disconcerting. "I'm dehydrated," he muttered, and got up, realising that he too was using the cottage as a sanctuary when embarrassed. Alcohol was fuddling his brain; he should prepare some kind of meal. He surveyed the neatly stacked packets in the top of the fridge.

"Let's have fish fingers." She was at his elbow. "They don't need thawing."

"You move like a cat."

"I took my shoes off. Leave the supper; we'll eat when Clem comes home." She reached past him, her breasts brushing his bare arm, and took two bottles from the inside of the door. "Close it." She was peremptory. "You're wasting electricity."

He followed her outside. She handed him the bottles and he twisted the caps off with his hands. "Marty can do that," she said.

They could have been alone in this lush garden in the woods. There was no human sound: no suggestion of a distant engine or voices, not even a murmur of aircraft; only the drone of insects which gave the afternoon an air of animation as if the woods, and even the earth, were breathing; it was a world drunk with sunshine and heat and the sappy scent of green things.

"The second drink is always the best," she said dreamily, "when everything comes into focus and before you go over the edge."

That pulled him up. She was right, and the third drink could make him lose his sense of proportion. Deliberately he adjusted to her mood, but only up to a point: the point where he retained control. And then he wondered why it should be important not to lose control. The garden was a place of enchantment. Control seemed a waste of magic.

"This is what townies visualise when they dream of living in the country," he said. "Even the dog is quiet."

"They never bark." She'd misheard him. "Not the collies."

"They did last night: barking at the foxes."

"I didn't hear them." She lay back in the long grass and stared at the sky. "All the colour's been washed out by the heat."

"The pit bull was quiet."

"Don't let's talk about that."

"Yesterday you said you couldn't stand it any longer."

"That was yesterday." She sat up, annoyed. "And I was mad! That business with the money — for Heaven's sake, Jack: yesterday was the pits."

"You had a hard time, but you've got resilience; you come bouncing back like a ball. I suppose you feel safe with Martin around." He raised an eyebrow. "I hope that doesn't sound macho."

She frowned and looked thoughtful, then she giggled. "Well, no one would dare approach me when he's home, that's for sure — no person, that is. There's the dog, but if it's going to settle down and stop barking then we don't have that problem. Feel safe with Martin," she repeated, savouring it, and shrugged. "I don't feel unsafe without him."

"I suppose not, otherwise you'd have gone to London with him."

"It wasn't worth it; he's not going to be there more than an hour, only as long as it takes to sign on and be briefed and get his advance payment. He didn't want me hanging around outside the office, not knowing how long he might be. I'd hate to be an embarrassment to him."

It was Pharaoh's turn to be thoughtful. After a while he said, "Why would he suggest that we keep an eye on you? You're not worried about the Rankins or their dog; what are we supposed to be protecting you from?"

"Oh, that's easy — but he wouldn't tell you; he'd pretend he was bothered about the Rankins coming to rape me or something. No, Marty's frantic that Mum will persuade me to leave him. It would break him into little pieces. She won't, of course, but he's not thinking straight. He thinks Mum's got it in for him, not just since that stupid business yesterday; she never did like him. It's put me on the spot," she added with a grimace. "Clem was right; she won't lend me the money to buy the cottage, to put down a deposit, but we can go on renting. We talked it over last night, Marty and me. All the same" — she brightened — "I shall have loads of money if we haven't got a mortgage to pay; I can have a new stove and a telephone and colour television, and I can whitewash the outside and paint the woodwork. Clem can put up a solid fence to keep the cattle out and I'll have a garden again and grow my own vegetables."

"You'll be on your own."

"No I won't. There's Clem and — all the others. There'll be the telly in the winter evenings."

"Your mother isn't going to like it."

"She'll come round. She knows it's not logical that Marty should have stolen the money. And she'll think a lot better of him once we start banking a thousand a month — in a joint account. Marty promised me that. Come to think of it, it won't be long before we save enough to put down a deposit on the cottage ourselves."

"You'll have to go easy on the

improvements then: appliances, fencing the garden."

"Clem would do it for nothing. I'd just need to buy the posts and wire: peanuts."

"Is that fair on Clem?"

"He'd do anything for me."

"Should he?"

"Why not? He's got no one else."

"Aren't you rather exploiting the situation?"

"I am a bit." The capitulation surprised him, but then her natural vitality was intensified; another beer and she would fold like a kitten. "Marty says Clem sees himself as a father substitute," she went on, "and I have to be gentle with him because he never had any children." Her eyes were candid. "I like older men. Is that why I do? Because I need a father figure?"

He wasn't sure how much of this was sincere, how much alcohol-induced. "Lanty Dolphin is your age group," he said.

Her cheeks darkened under her tan. "What's he got to do with it?" He said nothing. "All right," she muttered, "but it's over — for what it was worth. It was just straight animal attraction, nothing more. We were thrown together; it was chemical. Are you shocked?"

"Not at all."

"You're not surprised?" Belligerence was spiked by resentment.

"Was Martin?"

"Surprised?" She looked lost. "He was shocked, of course — and deeply hurt, but he admits it's his own fault for leaving me here on my own, and he forgave me. Now you *are* shocked. I'm not a feminist; I believe in marriage, otherwise I wouldn't have married. Lanty was an aberration. Don't gape at me; I'm telling the truth. Were you celibate when you were married?"

His lips twitched. He must tell Clem to buy her a dictionary. "Was it Martin who said Lanty was an aberration?"

"As it happens — yes. He was very understanding and I feel terrible about it." There were tears in her eyes.

"And you assured him it was all over."

"He told you that!"

"I guessed. But if this affair was the

result of your being lonely, why don't you move into a village?"

She sighed. "Actually I would; I'd like to go to Scotland and be near Mum when he's in Africa or wherever. . . . That sounds disloyal, it *is* disloyal, but I don't see much of him; I mean: six months at a time without meeting; it's a huge void in your life, Jack, when you're still young. But he wants me to stay here, and he's my husband. He's fallen in love with Clouds; he needs its peace and security after the horrors he sees in his work."

"It must be a strain for him. I thought, when he went off yesterday, that's just what I'd do in the circumstances." There was no response. "I'd go up on the moors," he added absently.

"That's what he did." She was somnolent, half asleep. She lay back in the grass again and closed her eyes.

"He came home late. Clem said someone passed down the lane in the night."

"Not Marty. He was home for supper. I told him about Lanty." A slow blush spread to her neck.

"Was he abusive?"

"The opposite." She sat up and met his eye. "You mean does he knock me about, don't you? He would never touch me, not in that way. Mum says he's violent but I think that's because she wants to think he is. That sounds nasty; maybe she's taken a shine to him." She laughed angrily, then sobered with one of her swift changes of mood. "He's not worried about Lanty. I think men find adultery stimulating, don't you?"

"Husbands?"

"Yes, that's what I meant."

He lifted his glass and his hand shook. When he had drunk he tried to meet her gaze calmly, like another surrogate father.

"I did follow you this morning," she murmured, so softly that, straining to hear, he heard also the sound of an approaching vehicle.

"You're both drunk," Harker said, coming into the garden, studying the vacant faces turned towards him. "We had a great day. How was yours?"

160

8

THE forecast was for storms and by eleven o'clock next morning the air was heavy and humid. Animals were nervous and people were on edge, particularly Pharaoh who limped downstairs with a hangover and a stiff knee to find a note from Harker saying he had gone over to Grammery Bank. His rope and slings were still on the back of a chair where he'd left them when he came home last night, and Pharaoh regarded them sourly; that was all he needed to put the lid on a bad morning.

★ ★ ★

Paul Rankin was always a late riser so it wasn't until eleven that he approached the barn with a bowl of hound meal for his dog. The Rankins were mean with their animals and since the pit bull had been brought to Murkgill it had tasted no meat other than table scraps;

161

consequently it was always hungry. The chain rattled as Paul approached the barn but the dog didn't bark. It had been thrashed several times to teach it who was boss and now it showed no overt hostility to the boy, only an intense interest in his movements.

The barn's cross-axis was a cart-way — the original threshing floor — so there were doors at each end. Paul entered by that nearest his house, gave the dog its food, and went to peer through a crack in the door that gave on to the yard and Susan's cottage. This was a practice that stemmed less from prurience than from the need to keep an eye on Shaw, who had struck the last blow in what Paul viewed as a vendetta. Some form of retaliation was now in order but this demanded finesse. Paul had never come up against anyone who carried a knife as a weapon and once his shock had worn off he had started to scheme how it might be possible to get the better of an armed man, but so far without result.

The door and all the windows of the cottage were open but neither Shaw nor Susan was visible and the van wasn't in

162

its usual place at the gable end. He knew about the new tyre of course, and the idea had occurred to him to slash it, but he'd dismissed the thought; he would be the obvious suspect. On the other hand he might well cut the tyre when Shaw went away again. He frowned. This was humiliating. Over recent months he'd started to feel his own power; he'd had everyone at Clouds walking round him carefully, but now he was like a kid again, cut down to size. It was Shaw who had the power, but only because he had the knife — and that was ridiculous: knives were cheap. But knife *fighting*: that was something else. He swung between humiliation and contempt, the lust to hurt and the dread of pain.

Behind him the dog snuffled grossly as it shoved its bowl across the floor. Paul's eyes narrowed. The dog redressed the balance. The difficulty lay in finding how it could be used. A blowfly landed on his cheek and he jerked his head in disgust. He hated flies; they fed on shit and then came in the kitchen and walked on food. He was always shouting at his mother about the flies . . . and now she had the cheek to say that the barn was full of bluebottles because he kept the dog there.

He was about to turn away from the crack in the door when Susan came out of the cottage with a teapot. She emptied it on the cobbles and went back indoors. So it was Shaw who had taken the van, and the girl was alone in the cottage. That could be turned to his advantage.

He opened the door that faced the cottage and, without looking that way, made a show of inspecting an iron ring set in the wall of the barn. In the old days, while a wagon was waiting its turn to off-load in the threshing bay, the horses would have been tethered to that ring. He went back inside, unclipped the chain and tried to haul the dog out to the yard but the pit bull was young and unused to being led. It strained back and when he got behind in order to boot it, the animal retreated to its corner and Paul slipped on its dung. Cursing, he yanked on the chain and the dog snarled. It had wicked jaws and Paul was suddenly quiet. He went to unbuckle his big studded belt but thought better of it and reached for the riding crop that he kept beyond the length of the chain. He should have picked that up before he came within the dog's range, he reminded himself; he wouldn't make that mistake again. The dog, which never took its eyes off him, saw the movement and now, when Paul got behind, it edged away from him to the length of the chain and so, driven but still held, it was worked into the yard where it stood, straddle-legged, as Paul fastened the chain to the ring with a snap-link. The boy walked back to the door, feeling sure that he was being observed from the cottage.

When the barn door was closed the dog watched it suspiciously, knowing the boy was on the other side. Paul didn't think that Susan would draw the same conclusion. Through the crack he watched and waited to see what would happen.

The pit bull, seen head-on, looked more like a bulldog than a bull terrier; it was a very broad dog with a massive chest and bowed front legs that appeared to be too light for its weight. Its colour was between cinnamon and ginger and its nose was pink. With its queer little pointed ears like those of a pug it was extraordinarily ugly but then its merit didn't lie in its appearance, except as it related to its fighting ability.

When Susan came out of the cottage again the dog whirled with amazing agility and it was snarling before it focused on her. Its claws scraped the cobbles and it started a rush towards her only to be brought up short by the chain. The heavy head was twisted so violently that Paul winced. It would never try that move again; next time it would surely break its neck. When the dog recovered its breath it started to bark furiously. Paul grinned. He hadn't paid Shaw back but he'd put the fear of death into the guy's wife. At the first rush she had fled inside and slammed the door.

He went through the barn and started towards his house. Suddenly the barking changed tone, became frenetic. He stopped, petrified. Had it — ? Could it — ? But there was no sound of worrying: the dog was still chained. He'd had a bad moment there but once it was past he recalled the picture in his mind, and relished it: the picture of a crazed animal attacking a defenceless girl. He glanced at his house to see if his mother was watching but there was no sign of her. A movement to the right caught his eye. Susan was running to his back door. He slipped away to the left and vanished down an overgrown track into the woods.

* * *

Tilly confronted Susan stonily. This wasn't a moment for histrionics; the girl was angry enough for two. "The lad got a bad fright yesterday," she was saying. "I reckon he's got a concussion. His head's paining him."

"So's mine," snapped Susan. "It's the dog I'm talking about. Listen to it! This is me and the dog; nothing to do with your son and my husband."

"The boy's scared he'll do it again." Tilly looked past the girl. "We're all scared, we live in fear. A knife's an offensive weapon."

"He's put that dog outside deliberately! It sprang at me when I left my place; only the chain stopped it. If it ever got loose again . . . Is it going to keep up that row all day?"

"It'll settle." The tone was treacly. "He's got to put it out in the yard. We can't have it spending its whole life in the barn: no sunshine, no fresh air; it's not right, is it? Cruel, that would be. He's a nice dog, don't you think, now you seen 'im? A good guard dog; you won't be getting no visitors now, nights, when you're on your own." Again her eyes sought for something beyond the girl.

"I'd rather have visitors than that dog."

"I'm sure you would, darling."

The saccharine tone and the words ripped through her anger and Susan, gaping, realised what was implied. "You filthy old slag," she gasped, but, unlike her husband or any of the Rankins, it didn't occur to her to utter a threat. She ran back to her cottage — sending the dog into a fresh paroxysm of rage — and, seeing this, terrified of the noise, of the awful power held by such a flimsy chain, she dashed past the cottage and took the woodland path that led to Fox Yards.

As she pounded through the trees the sound of barking faded, or faded enough that she could take some comfort from knowing that the animal was still chained. She slowed to a walk, realising that she was drenched with sweat and that her head felt peculiar, as if she were drunk or about to faint. The wood was silent and not a leaf stirred. The air was stifling. From the north, towards the border country, came a rumble of thunder.

Harker's van wasn't outside although Pharaoh's car was there. The front door was closed but, as usual, not locked. She went in the house and called. There was no answer. She glanced round the living room wondering if they were both at Grammery Bank or if they had gone climbing. No, the rope was there where Clem had left it last night. If she went across to Grammery her mother would insist on going to the cottage and seeing the dog for herself, and then all hell would break loose, and she couldn't handle that. Her mother would be adamant about the dog, would insist that she leave Murkgill, and leave now. No way would she do that. She wished Martin were home. The heat was ghastly; one could scarcely breathe. In a panic she ran out of the cottage and up the lane to the Hall.

The Fawcetts were kind and comforting, the epitome of good manners, but they didn't seem to be on the same wavelength as Susan, at least where it mattered.

"It's not a very big dog then," Phoebe commented, pouring coffee at the kitchen table.

"You don't need a big dog to give you a nasty bite," Rowland chided. "Jack Russells have sharp little teeth." He handed Susan brandy in a lemonade tumbler. "Drink that, m'dear; you're quite pale. Shouldn't rush about in this heat. We're going to have a storm."

"I was terrified out of my life! Nasty bite? That dog would tear your throat out."

He nodded in sympathy. "Gave you a fright. I can see that."

"You weren't brought up with dogs," Phoebe stated, but commiserating, not condemning.

Susan drank some brandy, then coffee. They watched her benignly and she thought: To hell with their age, they've got to face facts for their own good, perhaps for all our good. She said: "You remember how worried the Rankins were when the dog got out a few days ago?"

"Oh yes." Rowland's face hardened. Here was something he felt strongly about. "A loose dog among the sheep: that could be disastrous. The Rankins were lucky they got it back before it did any damage. I assume it didn't; no one's said anything. It could have been shot, you know."

"There's a load of dead sheep in Tranna Mire. I found them just before the dog got out."

"On our land?" It was rhetorical. Everyone knew Clouds' boundaries. "How long have they been there?"

"Some time. They stink."

He sighed. "There's nothing much we can do about it except report it to the police." He looked at his wife. "If she found them before the dog got loose, if they were stinking, it couldn't have been this new dog."

171

"It's not Rankin," Beth Potter said. "Not on our land."

She was standing in the doorway, a pile of washing in her meaty arms: a big, solid, red-faced countrywoman in a flowered apron. She put the washing on the table and stood back. "He'd not foul his own doorstep," she told Rowland. "Murkgill's a nice little farm, what's left of it. He don't want to lose it. Wouldn't hurt to have the police poking around though," she added darkly. "Might do that boy a power of good."

Phoebe said: "Dead sheep in one place: that's not a dog's work. It's sheep-stealing."

"Of course it's not a dog!" Rowland glared. "I'll get on to the police."

"They'll see the dog when they come." Susan was delighted. "Then it will have to go."

"It's not illegal if it's chained," Rowland told her.

"But suppose the chain breaks, or it slips its collar again? Do you have to wait for it to kill someone, a child for instance? It came for me so fast that when the chain jerked it back I thought its neck must be broken, but it was on its feet in a second. Next time the chain could break. I hate to think how many sheep that brute could kill in a night."

"I think you should go down and see this dog," Phoebe told her husband.

"Take your shotgun," urged Beth, but no one protested when Susan stood up to accompany him. A shotgun was adequate protection against anything.

The dog was not immediately aware of them as they approached. It was facing in the other direction, barking with its legs splayed: head thrown back, eyes slitted, not looking at anything, just barking for something to do. She hated its boredom as much as its aggression.

"Noisy brute," Rowland said, walking up for a closer look, intrigued. The dog turned and started to rush, remembered the chain, scraped to a halt and broke into its dreadful tirade. It was as if the animal would burst with rage. At last Rowland was convinced. Without taking his eyes off the dog he groped in his pocket for cartridges and loaded both barrels. He raised the gun. Susan put her hand over her mouth. The dog was suddenly quiet, backing with peculiar delicacy to the barn door. When its rump touched the planks it half turned, sat down and lowered its head, twitching ineffectually as it tried to make itself smaller.

Rowland had halted. "It's accustomed to being beaten," he observed, and studied it critically. "There's a queer mix of breeds in it, but it's a powerful brute; it'd play the devil in a flock of sheep. We'll have to do something about this. I must go and find Rankin. Tell you what, m'dear, when you go out, you be sure to take a big stick and show it to him. He understands that. You see how he is with the gun."

"It's obscene. He must have been all right as a puppy. Cruelty's made him like this."

"I'm not so sure about that. Probably people who breed these dogs breed for fighting in the same way that farmers breed collies for shepherding. It's genes, isn't it? And this fellow was born vicious to my mind. Now you go indoors . . . "

She went in and shut the door. After a few minutes the dog started to bark with that steady nerve-wracking rhythm that made her head ache. She wandered round the house, moving objects and picking them up, putting them down, standing well back from the bedroom window and watching the dog, detesting it, feeling the tension increase until finally, to her horror, she found herself identifying with its boredom. She looked round wildly, remembered the drop of brandy left in the bottom of the bottle; she'd poured it last night when she came home from Fox Yards but had left it untasted and found it this morning: a glass containing two fingers of brandy on the kitchen table. She'd poured it back in the bottle.

She went downstairs, picked up the bottle — and it was empty. She stood and thought about this, visualising the shot glass on the table when she got up this morning, herself pouring it back, carefully so as not to spill a drop, pleased that there was one shot left for emergencies. Now it was gone. Someone had been in the cottage while she was at Tilly's back door or at Fox Yards or the Hall.

Her shoulder bag was on the window

sill. There had been three pounds in her purse, no notes in the wallet. Before she looked she guessed what she would find, but she was wrong. There was one pound left.

She closed the front door and locked it, then unlocked it to reach inside for a stick, observing with grim satisfaction that as soon as the dog saw she had a weapon, it fell silent. But it snarled. She assumed that this meant it had been thrashed only by men but, given the chance, it was ready to have a go at a woman.

* * *

"He's a sociopath, sweetie; he's dangerous." Esme was angry. She was sitting on Grammery's lawn with Susan. The business with the dog (although she thought it exaggerated) had intensified her conviction that the girl should leave Murkgill. Unbothered that yesterday she had been accusing her son-in-law of theft, she had merely transferred the accusation, and her rancour, realigning her sights on Paul and his family. "Rowland Fawcett's a broken reed," she went on. "It's not that he's intimidated; it's just that he has no idea how to deal with rough types that have got out of hand. Rowland couldn't be rude to save his life, and Tilly will be servile; she'll agree with everything he says, and laugh at him behind his back."

"She's disgusting," Susan said. "She's a slut."

Grammery was cheerful and bustling: a world away from the menace at Murkgill. From the house came the strains of country and western punctuated by the rhythmic slash of Lanty's scythe as he cut bracken on a bank below the lawn. He was stripped to the waist and his skin gleamed as if oiled. Now and again he glanced up the bank to where the women's heads showed through a fringe of foxgloves. They ignored him. He cut great swaths in the sweltering heat, dreaming of the months ahead when Shaw would be gone again to a far country where with any luck a sniper would put a bullet in his back.

"Come back with me at least for a while," Esme coaxed. "Martin has to see now that you can't stay here on your own. Even if Rowland could force the Rankins to get rid of the dog, if that boy is entering the house when you're out, he'll be coming next when you're *in*; at night, for instance. He's a big strong fellow, sweetie; you wouldn't stand a chance."

"Oh, Mum!" But she'd had the same thought herself before today, and been appalled, not at the prospect of being raped by Paul but that she should have considered it a possibility. He was only a kid. "That's paranoid," she said weakly.

"Not at all. That boy's crazy. He's unpredictable — "

"Telephone!" Juno shouted from the kitchen. "For you, Susan."

"It'll be Marty." She sprang up and ran towards the house. Esme sighed and looked round and her eyes fell on Lanty. She frowned thoughtfully, her lips compressed.

It was Rowland on the telephone. "I guessed you'd gone over to your mother," he said. "Well, I had a word with Tilly and she was very cooperative. She agrees that the dog has to go. She'll try to find a home for it but I don't see how she can, not in sheep country, and you can't keep a noisy animal in a town. I'm afraid it will have to be put down. Actually, I think Tilly's relieved; she said she's been worried about the sheep. I didn't mention Tranna Mire. I'll need to see those dead ewes myself and then I'll get on to the police. I have to see Rankin too . . . " He trailed off; one didn't discuss such matters with a person who wasn't family. Sheep-stealing was intimate.

Susan said weakly, "Thank you for — for everything, Rowland. I was a nervous wreck. The barking was bad enough but — well, you know . . . "

"No question, m'dear; you should have said something before; it's not right for that brute to threaten you every time you go out of your own door. And what good is a dog like that?" His voice rose. "It's not a pet, there's nothing it can be used for except fighting."

"Do you think that could have been the idea?"

"Never. Never on my property. I made that quite plain to Tilly. It hadn't occurred to her. She was shocked."

"I'm sure she was. What did George say?"

"I didn't see George. He was shepherding."

"And Paul? He must be upset."

"I didn't see him either."

"So when is the dog going to — to be removed?"

"Tilly should be making calls right now, trying to find someone to give it a home, although that goes against the grain with me: shifting responsibility. However, I'm sure they won't find anyone who's willing to take it. So it'll have to be taken to the vet. Meanwhile it's going back in the barn just as soon as young Paul comes home. I made that quite clear. No one can handle the dog except the boy. That makes you think, doesn't it? What would have happened if George or Tilly had come face to face with it that night it escaped?" He laughed grimly. "Apparently Paul caught it then."

★ ★ ★

Over the midday meal Tilly told her menfolk about Rowland's ultimatum and how she had stalled him. Paul listened avidly but his father was amused. "All the same," Rankin said, after he'd thought about it, "that dog'll have to go. It's eating its head off, and what good is it?"

"I told you," Paul was on the defensive. "You agreed there was money in it. If this guy in Carlisle can get enough folk interested . . . "

"It's too risky. The old man's suspicious already. He's only got to mention the dog to one of his mates in the police and we wouldn't stand a chance of taking it anywhere. They'd stop and search 'Rover every time we went on road."

"Then buy Shaw's van. I been on at you — "

"That van's clapped out. 'Sides, police would know it had changed hands, wouldn't they? You leave dog-fighting to folk as can afford to pay fines. You want to make a bit on the side, you get yourself a bird or two. You know where you can pick up some spurs."

Tilly giggled but Paul refused to

respond. Cock-fighting was nothing compared with the drama of a dog-fight. He retreated into a sullen silence which deepened when his father told him not to go off again, they'd be muck-spreading this afternoon. After dinner he slouched outside to look at his dog. The noise it was making indicated that someone was in the yard. He went through the barn and put his eye to the crack just as Shaw started hammering on his own front door with his fist. "Are you in there?" he shouted. "Sue!" He stepped to the kitchen window, shading the glass, then moved back to glance up at the bedrooms. No one showed in the cottage but the dog was going mad. Paul was beside himself with glee but he sobered when Shaw turned and stared at the dog. The look in the man's eyes made Paul's belly contract, and momentarily he knew an emotion that was foreign to him: he felt sorry for the dog, so helpless in its shackles. The moment passed as Shaw started towards the van but then, instead of taking it, he broke into a jog and disappeared.

Paul lifted the latch of the door and

the dog whirled, its fangs bared wickedly. He went back for the crop and emerged, presenting the weapon. The pit bull backed to the length of its chain and the yard was deathly quiet.

He walked across the cobbles and peered round the corner of the cottage. Shaw was nearly at the end of the track, evidently on his way to Grammery. He went to look in the van to try to discover why the guy had left on foot.

In the back there was a small rucksack and a brand-new spare tyre on a rim. The tyres on the road wheels were inflated so it wasn't a puncture that had stopped him. Trusting the dog to give warning of anyone's approach he opened the door on the passenger side and peered around. It could be that the petrol tank was nearly empty but the guy had taken the keys so he couldn't tell. He looked thoughtfully at the dashboard, his eye lingering on the mileometer which his father swore had been turned back because it read 33,330, or had done last week when the van was sitting here with a flat tyre and he'd tried to persuade his father to buy it, partly because of that: the low mileage.

It wasn't much more now: 33,505. Paul had a good memory for figures but he had difficulty with subtraction. However, it looked as if Shaw had done less than two hundred miles; he wondered where the man had been, and stored the new figure against a time when it might come in useful. He was a magpie for odd snippets of information. You never could tell.

The dog started to bark furiously. His father was at the door of the barn, shouting. Paul left the Datsun, showed the crop and walked over. The dog fell silent.

"I said put dog in barn," Rankin said. "Jesus, but that's a vicious brute!"

"It's what he's supposed to be." Paul unclipped the chain. "I'm coming in." He enjoyed seeing his father dodge back as he made to advance but then he found that the damn dog wouldn't move. "Heh!" he called. "Come back 'ere!"

"What's up?"

"I can't move the bugger. You come and pull on chain, I'll boot it from behind."

"It's your dog. You move it."

184

Paul was livid. He swung the crop and tried to get behind the animal but it retreated in front of him, out into the middle of the yard. He hauled on the chain. The brute dug in its legs and strained back, immovable as a rock. Now he couldn't pull it back far enough to clip the chain to the ringbolt. "Dad!" he shouted. "Bring me some hound meal. I can't budge it."

Dog and boy stood and stared at each other until Rankin shouted: "Bowl's here, inside door."

"Bring it 'ere, man! How can I reach it? I can't leave go the chain. I can't reach ringbolt even."

He heard his father walk through the barn. "I'll leave it here."

"You daft ol' git! You got to bring it in reach." His father appeared in the doorway, holding a bowl. "Bring it 'ere!" Paul gestured violently with the crop. "He'll never come past me; you're safe. Where you going?"

Rankin had put the bowl down and disappeared. In a moment he was back with a pitchfork. He came out hesitantly, watching the dog. Paul took the bowl and rattled it. The pit bull relaxed its stance and Rankin retreated, presenting the tines of the fork.

Whether the dog was afraid of the barn or the boy, its hunger was greater than its fear and it came almost eagerly, forgetting to be suspicious, its eyes on the bowl. Inside the barn Paul put the food on a shelf, clipped the chain to another ring and followed his father outside.

"You didn't give him the food," Rankin said.

"Of course not. Teach him a lesson. That's how you train 'em, that and beating. I'll beat him tonight."

★ ★ ★

They were spreading muck in the field called Killing Close below the viaduct. It was hard work, the heat increasing through the afternoon as great cumulus clouds piled up above the Pennines, and the air felt solid, reeking of high-protein excrement. They finished at four o'clock and Tilly made them wash at the yard tap before coming in for their tea. The front and back doors were open and the kitchen was full of flies. Paul swore at her.

"Storm's not my fault," she told him. "Storms always bring flies."

Before she could start on him about dogs bringing flies too he said quickly: "I'll come with you if you're going to town tonight."

"We're not," George said. "And you have to see about getting rid of that dog."

"That's why I need to go to Kirkby. I'll have to hitch so I won't be back till late." He eyed his father. "I'm doing a man's job, I should have wheels. You could buy that Datsun and keep it for me till next year." It was said without feeling; he might be able to wear them down.

"You could do that," Tilly told Rankin, surprising both father and son. It was she who had been adamant that he must wait for a car until he was seventeen. It wasn't so much his being under age that worried her but the enormous expense involved if he should have an accident when driving without a licence or insurance. Now here she was suggesting that they

187

buy the Datsun for him. "Shaw's off again shortly," she explained, "and he's going to be sending home a thousand pound a month. They won't have no use for that old van; she'll be buying one of them fancy Range Rovers like her mother, you'll see."

Rankin spooned sugar into his tea. "Someone's having you on, woman."

"No. Beth Potter were here for the eggs and the girl told them when she were up at the Hall this morning. Shaw went to London yesterday and signed on with them Africans."

"That's what *he* says." Paul was full of contempt.

"It's what they earn. The old man says those black generals is so rich that all they got to do with their spare millions is spend it on keeping themselves in power. They'll pay fortunes for English officers to train their armies."

"He didn't go to London for a start," Paul said, and stopped, thinking. He got up, found an envelope and pen, wrote two sets of figures and put the envelope in front of his mother. "What's that sum from that?" he asked.

The answer was 175. "That's as far as he went," Paul said, and walked out. Tilly started to clear the table. Rankin was engrossed in the paper. Paul was the curious one in the family.

He paused outside the back door. The dog was raging again — which was odd because he'd shut it in the barn and yet it sounded as if it was trying to reach someone. In the barn? He ran to the nearer door and jerked it open to be greeted by a flood of light. The other door was open too and the dog was intent on something in the yard beyond, or in the cottage. Paul picked up the crop as Shaw came out of his front door carrying a stick. The pit bull was suddenly quiet, retreating to the wall where it could watch both of them.

They met at the far doorway. Shaw said, slightly out of breath: "They tell me you're the only one that can handle it."

"That's right."

"Let's see you do it."

Paul didn't hesitate. He walked back, unclipped the snap-link and, presenting the crop as a lion tamer presents a chair, he drove the dog into the yard and fastened the chain to the ring on the wall. Shaw had stood aside as dog and boy went past him: alert but showing no sign of fear.

"Now take it back," he said.

Paul realised that he'd trapped himself. He stalled. "He stays here a while, he needs exercise."

Shaw didn't push it but said pleasantly: "You were in my house this morning."

Paul took a few steps so that he was within the dog's reach. He raised the crop a fraction. Shaw was expressionless but the pale eyes missed nothing. "And stole two pounds," he went on. "And there's the two hundred you lifted from Mrs Winter . . . "

Paul started to speak, then checked himself. Shaw was saying: "And a load of dead sheep in Tranna Mire which you rustled and had to get rid of quick because the police were getting close: working up the dale towards you."

Paul's lip lifted. Shaw smiled. "I compiled a dossier on you," he said. "Burglary, theft from cars, sheep-stealing. I'm going away shortly and I'll leave copies of it with different people. If you so much as say one word out of line to my wife, or lay a finger on my van, that dossier goes straight to the police."

"You got no proof." It was automatic.

"Dead sheep on this land."

"Them was dumped by someone else."

"That." Shaw nodded towards the dog.

"Sheep were dumped long afore I bought 'im, long afore he got loose."

"Prove it." Then Shaw changed tack. "I know where there's dog-fighting in the North. I know a few places the police don't. They'll be glad of any information, like who owns a dog. You'll have the CID poking around here, uncovering all those little scams you'd like to keep hidden, you and your dad."

"So that's it!" The bastard had been going round the north country over the last two days finding out where the dog-fighting was, just so he could put a spoke in his wheels. Paul grinned nastily. "Thousand pound a month!" he jeered. "Signing on for an officer in London to train niggers! You weren't nowhere near London!"

Shaw's eyes glittered and the muscles

tightened in his bare arms. Paul took a step towards the dog which, at the full length of its chain, unable to go further, stiffened and licked its lips.

"Do you know something I don't?" Shaw asked.

"I know — " He decided not to mention mileage, not right now. Don't waste it, he thought; we may have him on the hop already. "I know what I know," he said, and saw the tight muscles relax. Shaw smiled. "That's a bit girlish," he said.

Paul's face was stony but he was gloating. "Sheep-stealing!" He was venomous. "Two pound, two hundred pound! What's that beside what you're into, eh? What's the police going to say to *that*?"

Shaw's smile had faded. He looked at the dog, then back at the boy. "What I'm doing is legal, mostly. If there is anything illegal it's winked at — like killing in the bush. It's not murder when it's war."

"And when it's not war?"

"What do you know about it? You're just a kid."

"Well, now, you got your dossier on

me; I got one on you, see, but you'll have to sweat it out, won't you? You don't know what I got but" — and now he couldn't contain himself, shaking his head in amusement, screwing up his eyes — "we both know, don't we, that even if I'd stole them sheep, and shot 'em, and stole the old girl's two hundred quid, that's nowt to what you're into, is it?" Pushing it, greatly daring but inspired, he held the other's eye. "You're in a right mess," he concluded, shaking his head in mock commiseration.

He went back into the barn and closed the door. He'd left the dog but he wasn't going to try and get it in with Shaw watching. And so what? It would bark all evening — with luck — and what could Shaw do about it? He wondered what the guy was up to; probably, being a sort of soldier, he was stealing from the stores: big things like cars and guns, even rockets to sell to terrorists. As he prepared for his evening in town, he thought back over the confrontation. Yes, there was definitely something there, but the nature of it wasn't important; what was important was that he *knew*, that he was making Shaw sweat. When he left for town he walked past the cottage whistling, dancing and kicking stones, demonstrating who held the whip hand now. The dog watched him go.

9

THE wind rose in the evening, a hot wind that tore leaves from the trees and scattered young cattle as if a wild beast was after them. And yet with all this swirling confusion people still felt that there wasn't enough air to breathe, not good air.

"It's monstrous," Susan stormed. "I'd like to sit in the garden — well, not sit but stamp around; I feel restless, I don't want to stay indoors. And if I put my nose outside it'll start to bark. Can't you do something?"

Shaw was standing away from the window watching the dog. It was backed up against the wall from where it stared at a world of tossing trees and blowing dust with something that could be interpreted as apprehension. "It's stupid," he said. "All it's got going for it is a pair of jaws. It wouldn't survive for a moment in the wild."

"So what are you doing? Analysing it,

for God's sake! When you came over to Grammery this afternoon you were furious; you said then that you'd shoot it yourself if you had a pistol. Now you're assessing its IQ."

"Coming home to that welcome was the last straw. That bloody van had been breaking down all the way back — "

"And you reckon Paul put something in the petrol — *and* he's coming into this house and drinking our booze and stealing: *your* house! And I'm your wife and that's his damn dog, and I'm afraid to go outside my own front door because it might break its chain. Well, what *are* you going to do about it? Because there's nothing I can do. I give up." She was sitting at the table and she put her head on her arms and sobbed angrily.

Shaw came and put his hands on her shoulders. "Don't get so upset. It's quiet now. It'll be gone tomorrow."

She raised her head, her cheeks wet. "You think Rowland will force them to get rid of it?"

"I think Rowland will shoot it."

"You do?" she searched his face. "You mean it." Her eyes lit up. "I need a drink. Hell, we've got no booze. I'd love a drink."

"We've got no transport." He moved towards the door. "I'm going to have another go at cleaning that carburettor — "

"Oh no, Marty, *please*. It'll start barking, and it'll keep it up all the time you're out there."

"I must get the car running for you, love. Look, why don't you go over to Grammery? When the storm breaks that brute's going to be barking all night — "

"Christ! I can't bear it — "

"Go on then; Juno will have lashings of drink. And there's company. Me, I'm going to work on the van."

He walked outside and the pit bull gave tongue, forgetting the wind. After a few minutes Susan followed, carrying a bulging plastic bag. Shaw had raised the Datsun's bonnet. She said tightly, grimacing at the background noise: "I'm going to stay down there tonight. I just can't take any more of it, Marty. Why don't you come with me?"

He straightened his back. "After what I said to young Paul I should stay here."

He grinned. "We don't want a brick through a window."

"You think he'd do that?"

He shrugged. "He's the type. You get along before the rain starts. Have a good evening." He bent over the engine and Susan ran down the track towards the road and Grammery.

★ ★ ★

By eight o'clock there was a deep gloom in the dale, against which barns and houses stood out naked in the lightning flashes. The storm was about ten miles away when the first drops began to fall: big heavy spots that raised little spurts of dust. The rain increased as the thunder approached. Rolling crashes reverberated round the fells and now, beneath the clamour, the deluge could be heard sweeping wet roofs and wet woods, swelling streams that were starting to run on every slope. A tree came down between Grammery and the railway but no one heard it; everyone was indoors. Only the pit bull was pressed against the wall of the barn, cringing at the thunder claps, its ginger coat shining in the rain.

The storm hung about for much of the night, grumbling in the west, returning loudly, rolling round the Vale of Eden as if trapped there. It wasn't until the small hours that the thunder finally receded, and the lightning lessened, faded and flickered out. The rain stopped but there was no cessation of movement nor of sound in this watery world. Gutters overflowed and downpipes spurted, the becks ran fast and turbid and the river roared down the dale.

When the first light showed above the eastern fells it revealed woods still bowed under their sodden foliage, but as the light intensified and the dawn wind wandered down the slopes, shaking the leaves, the trees stood up like gods, and when the sun started to climb and its rays came slanting westwards a multitude of rainbows shimmered on every branch and blade of grass. Long swaths of mist lay along escarpments, there were waterfalls in every gully, torrents that had been mud-brown at first light now shone with amber fire and there were jewels in the spray.

Cattle began to steam. Birds came out to sit in the tops of trees and on power lines, warming their backs, all bursting with song. The light was gold and the shadows black, and in the black shadow of the barn lay the chain, fastened at one end to the ringbolt, at the other to a buckled collar.

It lay on the cobbles at the head of a miniature drift of mud. George Rankin stared at it, horrified, and thought of fines and compensation (whole flocks of sheep?) but he had the wit to note that the dog had escaped during the storm, because it was still raining when that mud collected — but that made it worse because it must have been gone for many hours.

He unclipped the chain and, frantically trying to gather it up without its jangling, he retreated to the barn and closed the door. He looked through the crack. There was no sign of life at the Shaws' cottage. He threw the chain in a corner and rushed back to the house where Tilly was frying sausages at the stove.

He slammed the door back on its hinges. "Dog's gone," he gasped.

"Oh, my God! Where's Paul?"

"He didn't come home last night. His door were open this morning. You musta seen."

"I saw his door were open. I didn't look inside. Perhaps he come home and found the dog gone and he went out again, looking for it."

"He'd 'a told us. What difference does it make anyway? Dog's missing. What is us going to do?"

"Could you catch 'im with a net?"

"Don't be daft, woman. You get on that phone, try and find where the lad is. You know his friends — " He stopped, wide-eyed. "Don't you say owt about the dog. You say as how you're worried because lad didn't come home all night — and in that storm. Say floods is out and trees down across road. Say you gotta find the lad, put your mind at rest."

"What are you going to do?"

He'd gone into the larder; he came back with his shotgun. "I'm taking 'Rover and see if I can find dog on road. It'll have gone down the dale; that's where its home were, in Kirkby. If you do find lad and speak to him, tell him to go and see his mate what give it him."

* * *

The storm had done no serious structural damage but wind and rain had found the vulnerable spots and weakened them further. Slates had shifted at the Hall and a cracked window pane had disintegrated. Water had poured into the Fawcetts' bedroom and they'd had to get up and move the bed in the night. Harker, informed by telephone, told Rowland he'd get on the roof after breakfast and see what he could do about the leaks. He sighed because his garden was in a terrible state, the taller plants battered to the ground. "I can stake those," Pharaoh said helpfully. "I'll come up to the Hall when I'm finished."

"The garden can wait. I need you in the loft. That old roof's a bugger, and there's a bad weather forecast. We have to plug those leaks before the next rain. The old people can't sleep in a wet bed."

Susan came home after breakfast to

find clothes drying on the washing line and Shaw mopping out the kitchen. In heavy rain a spring surfaced in one corner and continued to run for several hours after the rain stopped. "We've still got all our slates," she said. "I looked. Juno lost three, and Mum and Lanty have gone out to try to find replacements. They're those green Honister slates so it's difficult." He didn't seem interested. "Did you get some breakfast?" she asked brightly, glancing out of the window. "Isn't it lovely when it's quiet? How was it during the night?"

He blinked, thinking. "I don't remember, so it must have been quiet. It was probably frightened of the storm."

"There's actually something that frightens that dog? Oh yes, it didn't like the wind, did it?" She looked at the barn. "So Paul put it inside when he came home," she mused.

"Or this morning. He'll bring it outside in a minute to annoy us."

"I think I'll go up to the Hall then, see if the old people need any help after the storm. I could sort of prod Rowland into turning the screw on the Rankins — like taking the dog to the vet."

"I heard the Land Rover go past early on."

"You don't think they've taken it to be put down? It didn't make a sound when I came in."

"That would be great, wouldn't it?"

★ ★ ★

A couple of miles down the dale Esme and Lanty were measuring slates on a partially ruined shed. They were on a slight slope from which long stretches of the road were visible. Lanty, bored with the job, was watching the traffic which, at that moment, amounted to one extremely slow Land Rover.

"Lanty, you're miles away," exclaimed Esme. "This one will do; now we want two more. What *are* you watching?"

"That guy there keeps stopping and starting. He's not driving sheep; he must be looking for something."

"Lanty! You have to get these slates on the roof this morning if possible. It'll be raining by tonight. The forecast was dire. We promised Juno."

"Yes. That's Rankin's Land Rover. He's lost some sheep. I expect a tree came down on a fence. It makes a change; I reckon Rankin's more used to finding sheep: other people's."

"Look, there's another slate just the right size. I think it would be a good idea to find the owner of this hovel and you can put in an offer for all the undamaged slates . . . "

★ ★ ★

Beth Potter was draping blankets over the clothes rack in the Hall's kitchen. "We could use another pair of hands, I'm sure," she told Susan. "If you'd just help me get these spread out. . . . They sleep that soundly, them two, they didn't know rain were pouring in till it had soaked through blankets and woke 'em up."

"What are they doing now?"

"Mr Fawcett's going round woods and such seeing what the damage is. Clem and his friend is doing the roof. Mrs Fawcett is trying to find a dry mattress."

"Beth! They need an electric blanket.

All the bedding in this house must be damp."

"We don't have no electric blankets. Come on, we'll go upstairs and give her a hand with them mattresses."

★ ★ ★

Precariously perched on the roof, Harker shouted: "How's that?"

"You've covered this hole," Pharaoh responded from inside the loft. "Now what about this?" He poked a stick through a chink where daylight showed.

"Got it. I'll have to shift — what sort of state are those laths in?"

Clouds was bustling as people laboured to batten down the hatches before the next storm, the residents well aware that although this was June, the rest of the so-called summer could be wet, giving them little respite before the autumn gales. Only Tilly, in her solid modern house, was unconcerned about more rain; what bothered her was of far greater consequence. She couldn't find Paul.

Rankin had gone long ago, leaving her to telephone people in Kirkby.

Unbalanced by the urgency, by the twinges that signalled the start of one of her headaches, she couldn't remember the surname of any of Paul's former schoolmates, and in her confusion she couldn't think of a method by which she might find out. The difficulty lay in trying to discover Paul's whereabouts without betraying the reason for the urgency. The doctor would know the surnames of sixteen-year-old lads, so would the dentist, but these represented Authority, and Authority's representatives pooled information. To speak to the receptionist in a surgery would be as stupid as phoning the police station. "What's the problem?" would be the automatic response, and no one would ever believe that Tilly Rankin was bothered about her son being out all night, however stormy. She was starting to panic. When Paul came home at ten o'clock her head was paining her so much that, dosed with aspirin and still hurting, she didn't notice his expression until he cut through the start of her tirade.

"Where's my dog?" His tone stopped her in full flight. "Did Dad try to move 'im?" He showed his teeth in a mirthless grin. "How's Dad now?"

"No one moved 'im," Tilly whispered. "He got loose again."

"Well, but — " He was nonplussed. "Chain's gone too. Did that old git try to move 'im inside and he got away? Did he go for Dad then, attack him like?"

"Listen, son! Your dad went out early and dog were gone then. Chain and collar left lying. Dog got loose in the night; he must have been frightened of storm, see. He's been loose for hours. Your dad's out searching."

"I saw him; I mean, the old man. I were on bus. He didn't see me. I wondered what he were up to. Why'd he go down dale? Did someone see dog?"

"Your dad said it'd run home: to its last home."

"I'll ring Jase — "

"No!"

"Why not?"

"Well, ring him but don't say nowt about dog. If it's there, he'll tell you. Folk mustn't know dog's loose because it'll be — it might kill a sheep if it gets hungry enough."

He stared at her, remembering that it

208

hadn't been fed for twenty-four hours
— and it hadn't eaten meat for days.
"Jesus!" His eyes danced. "One sheep?
You must be joking."

They heard the Land Rover enter the
yard. When he came into the kitchen
Rankin stared at his son grimly. "Now
you go out and try to find 'un," he said.
"It's all your fault. I told you to tighten
that collar after he slipped it last time."

"If it'd been any tighter he'd 'a choked
to death. He didn't slip no collar."

"Don't be daft. It's still buckled."

"I don't believe you. Show me."

Out in the barn Paul turned the
studded collar in his hands. "You sure
you didn't buckle it yourself?" Rankin
glared at him. "OK, OK. And chain
were still clipped to ring? Were there
any blood?"

"Blood?"

"Aye, blood. Like he" — Paul gestured
viciously towards the cottage — "shot it."
Rankin's face was blank. "Or used his
knife?" Paul persisted.

"He could never get that close. Nay,
lad; dog slipped his collar same as last
time and you got to find 'un quick afore

209

he does any damage."

Paul looked at the collar. He was thinking that if Shaw had killed the dog and taken the body away, the collar would have been left undone to show that the animal had not escaped by accident: a signal to show a man was responsible; that was what he would have done himself. But maybe Shaw wanted it to look like an accident. . . . He had to have used a firearm; no way would anyone risk coming in close to attack that dog with a knife.

"He used a pistol," he said.

His father's look was calculating. He would like to believe that the dog was dead but it was too good to be true, and it was too easy for a dog to slip its collar, particularly one that thrashed about like the pit bull.

"You gotta start looking," he said stubbornly.

Paul turned and walked through the barn, letting himself out of the far door. Rankin followed and waited as the lad crossed the yard to Shaw's cottage and knocked on the door. After a moment he depressed the thumb latch but the door was locked. The Datsun was at the gable end.

"You call that lad you got the dog from," Rankin said when Paul came back.

"What'll I tell 'im?"

"Anything. You don't have no trouble telling lies other times."

They stared at each other, cold with dislike that was, in the father's case, laced with fear: not fear of his son but of what the dog might be doing at this moment.

Paul telephoned Jason Birkett, the dog's previous owner. Jason had gone to Penrith, his mother said. She sounded cool but not distressed in any way. Paul suggested he might come in to Kirkby tomorrow, bring the dog; they'd take it — She didn't let him finish. "Don't you bring that brute within a mile of this house!" she shouted. "I got my nieces coming tomorrow; you bring that beast through my front gate and I'm calling the police! I never want to see the bugger again in my life!"

"Yeah, OK — I'll get — " He stared at the receiver. She had hung up. "Dog's not there," he told his parents.

"Right," Rankin exclaimed. "Come on; I know one place he might be."

Paul said nothing as, carrying the collar and chain, he followed his father out to the Land Rover. Rankin drove to the main road, turned left and started south. Paul stared at the road, his jaw set, his eyes savage. Less than two miles from Clouds Rankin stopped at a gate. Taking his gun and followed by Paul, he walked along an overgrown track to the boggy patch they called Tranna Mire. There among scattered thorns they came on Rowland Fawcett, his Jack Russell some distance away, and at his feet a mess of wet fleeces from which rose a nauseating smell and a buzzing of swarms of blowflies. Rowland regarded them bleakly. "Who's responsible for this?" he asked.

"Someone who wants you to think I was." Rankin sounded equable but his eyes were shifty. Paul peered at the carcasses, a hand over his nose and mouth, his eyes slitted with revulsion. Rowland moved upwind, lifting his face as if to cleanse it. The others followed.

"When were they put here?" he asked.

"I couldn't say." Rankin looked back at the ghastly mass. "I got no sheep in here so I never come. Lanty Dolphin might know. He shoots rabbits in the wood. Like us now: the wife wants a rabbit stew."

Rowland eyed them: two people after rabbits with one gun between them. Rankin shifted his feet and looked away.

"These gotta be buried." Paul's voice was curiously soft, startling his father. "Illegal to leave 'em lying," the boy said. "But who'll you get to do it? Dirty job. Best get a JCB."

Rowland glared at the carcasses. They knew exactly what he was thinking: how was he going to get them buried? Paul contemplated the Jack Russell. The pit bull would *eat* it. He wondered how many cats and small dogs it had killed and he lapsed into a brown study as he pondered the mystery. If Shaw hadn't killed it, how had it escaped? What was it doing? Where was it now?

Paul was unnerved and he gave in to his father's panic: searching all afternoon, up and down the dale, looking, not for the dog, but at the sheep. The behaviour of sheep would tell them if there was a loose dog about, but flocks and cattle were grazing unconcerned. Rankin thought of traps and stopped by the woods and copses to listen for barking or the sound of a heavy body thrashing in the undergrowth. They found nothing. Meanwhile the sun was overdrawn by a milky veil that was thickening by the minute. Cloud was low on the fells and dropping lower. By five o'clock it was raining again and the cloud was down almost to the level of the railway line.

They were back in Murkgill's kitchen when a woman telephoned to say that a pit bull was among her sheep and had already killed two ewes. Tilly had answered the phone and now her eyes widened and she turned pale, but she spoke almost calmly.

"That's bad. Why did you ring us?"

"Because you got a pit bull."

"Yes, but it's chained up."

"Oh. Are you quite sure?"

"I just fed it. It's chained and locked in barn."

At the table Rankin looked as if he

was going to be sick. Paul stared at his plate.

"I'm sorry," Tilly said, adding carelessly, "You'll shoot it, of course."

"Oh, we'll shoot it." The woman hung up without saying goodbye.

"Get down there quick," Tilly hissed, as if afraid of being overheard. "It's killed two ewes at Weeping Klints. It's still there. Take your gun" — to Rankin — "and you shoot that bugger dead."

10

SINCE there was only one extending ladder in Clouds the owner was much in demand after the storm, and once they had done what they could on the roof of the Hall, Harker and Pharaoh lost no time in getting to Grammery Bank to replace Juno's slates. By six o'clock the second roof had been patched up and everyone collected in the kitchen for a well-earned drink. Lanty and Susan had come in drenched after cutting up an ash tree which had been blown down in the night.

"And there's a sycamore down over towards Tranna Mire," Juno told them. "Someone should cut that up for the old people."

"Maybe we can get around to that tomorrow," Harker said. "Is that it: just two trees down?"

"Rowland only mentioned one on his property. He called when you were on the roof. He was terribly upset, poor dear; he'd been to look at those dead sheep. He says they belong to someone in Bowderdale, miles away."

"They'll have been stolen," Lanty said. "But why kill them?"

"I don't think they were killed," Harker said. "My guess is that they died lambing, or from some other cause, but naturally — more or less; they might have been worried by a dog, I forgot that possibility. What used to happen until recently was that dead animals were taken to the knacker to be processed for pet food. Farmers got a few pounds for each carcass, but now, since mad cow disease, the bottom's dropped out of the market and knackers are out of business. I expect the owner took some dead beasts to a knacker and was told to take them away, or pay to have them buried or incinerated, whatever they do to get rid of these unwanted carcasses. So he dumped them; it's as simple as that."

"I reckon George stole them," Susan said stubbornly. "The Rankins are capable of anything. Marty's putting a new fence round our garden. He says I have to keep the gate padlocked. I daren't tell him that Paul will probably take a crowbar to the padlock and drive some bullocks in to trample my vegetables."

"Rowland can't bury those sheep," Harker said. "I suppose we'd better do it."

"Paul had the cheek to tell Rowland to get a JCB," Juno said. "Rowland thought it curious that when he found the sheep this afternoon, that the Rankins should come along while he was there, at Tranna Mire. He thought they must be looking for some sheep themselves: live ones that had got out during the storm, but Rankin had a shotgun with him."

"After rabbits," Harker said. "The Rankins have certainly been very active today; Saturday afternoons they usually take off. They're not great ones for weekend work, George and Paul, but the Land Rover's been in and out all day, and now Paul's gone up to the Scar. I heard the Honda."

"The cloud's down," Pharaoh pointed out. "He can't shepherd in mist."

"He's gone over to Ewedale," Susan

said. "He does that: goes drinking with his mates."

"That's monstrous!" Esme had entered the kitchen and caught the last part. "That boy's only sixteen! You mean, he drives home in the dark after he's been drinking? The police ought to pick him up."

"There aren't any police on that road at night," Lanty told her. "Nobody at all. Ewedale folk drink in their own dale, and people on this side go to Kirkby. There's no reason for anyone to go over the top; that's why Paul goes that way, he knows he's safe. The Honda shouldn't be on the road at all — it's a farm bike — and he's got no licence, no insurance, nothing, besides being under age. He's breaking a whole heap of regulations, but he's never been caught yet."

"Then someone should report him!" Esme was furious. "*I* would do it." She threw it down like a challenge.

"It would have to be done anony-mously," Susan pointed out. "And I hate to think of the consequences if he found out who'd done it. The police would guess, if they didn't know — and how far can you trust a local noddy not to talk?"

"What you need in this place," Esme hissed, "is an anonymous letter writer."

"Maybe tonight will see some poetic justice," Susan said, "without any of us being involved: like him coming back drunk in the fog with his lights failing, and he meets a black sheep on a bend above a very deep gully." She grinned at them. "Pity about the sheep."

"It *is* getting thick." Harker was looking out of the window. "Raining heavily too. I must get home and stake my delphiniums."

"You're staying," Juno said firmly. "After spending all day on rooftops you're not going home to cook your own supper. You're eating with us."

"The garden will be ruined — "

"You can stake the delphiniums after supper. I insist, Clem."

Susan said too brightly: "But I have to go. Marty's been working hard all day too." Her eyes flickered to her mother but Esme was at the window watching the rain.

"One for the road." Lanty popped

a can of beer and slid it across the table to Susan. Pharaoh, relaxing after the urgency, the cramped conditions in the lofts, thought he saw a change in the relationship between the youngsters. Lanty appeared dominant and demanding but Susan was uneasy, trying to avoid meeting his eyes.

The kitchen grew fuggy even though the windows were wide open. Among the older people conviviality bloomed; after cooperating during the day they had a sense of achievement. Harker and Juno were flushed and talkative, Esme joined in, seeming to have forgotten Paul, while Pharaoh, his muscles slackening under the influence of alcohol, stretched his legs, beamed at the women, finding them all beautiful, and decided that country living was absolutely delightful.

They ate late and only when Juno insisted on it, saying that the beef would be dried out if it stayed any longer in the oven. Susan had gone home long ago but Harker and Pharaoh remained, and went home in the last of the daylight. Harker sighed as he surveyed his wrecked garden: he'd tackle it first thing in the morning.

The rain eased during the night. When Pharaoh came downstairs the cloud had lifted a few hundred feet and there was only a light drizzle falling. The coffee pot was on the stove, and the door open to the garden where Harker was hard at work tidying up. He said that if Pharaoh went over to Murkgill for eggs they would breakfast when he returned.

Pharaoh put on a cagoule and walked through the wood to the farm. The path emerged from the trees close to the Shaws' cottage where the new fenceposts were in position but not yet strung with wire. He crossed the yard and walked past the end of the barn before it occurred to him that the pit bull was very quiet; Susan could have been right when she suggested yesterday that the Rankins had taken it to be destroyed. Not before time, he thought grimly; a dog like that was as dangerous as a tiger in sheep country.

He passed the front of Murkgill and continued round to the back as Harker had directed. The Land Rover was in the yard and the back door was closed. He knocked, waited, and knocked again, more loudly.

The door opened suddenly and Tilly faced him. For a moment neither of them spoke, Tilly seemingly astonished, Pharaoh taken aback by her expression. He saw eagerness, hostility, fear, all in succession, and then a desperate attempt to cover up. Whoever she had been expecting it certainly wasn't himself; he wondered who she had thought would be on the doorstep.

"I've come for some eggs," he said.

She gaped, made a curious little bobbing movement and turned back to the kitchen. Pharaoh took a step after her and nodded to Rankin who was seated at the table, immobile, staring blankly at him.

"Good morning," Pharaoh remarked pleasantly and then, because the man didn't respond: "Dog gone, has it?"

"No!" Rankin gasped.

"No, he's not gone." Tilly was at an inner doorway, an egg in each hand. "He's just quiet. He's settled now."

Pharaoh looked from one to the other.

Suddenly Tilly was galvanised into action. "You get and see to that sick cow now, George Rankin," she shrilled. "You finished your breakfast. Get out of the way, do!"

Rankin stood up and tramped outside, avoiding Pharaoh's eye as he passed. Tilly retreated into what was evidently the pantry. Pharaoh looked at the table: two places set with plates, mugs, knives and forks. The plates were clean; on the stove was a frying pan with sausages and bacon spluttering in it.

"Paul having a lie-in?" he asked as she came out with two egg boxes.

"He's a late riser." Her eyes wandered. "That'll be one pound twenty."

"He got back all right then." Pharaoh produced the correct change and took the boxes before she dropped them. "It was a wild night," he said, a little desperately, and she stared at him as if he were a snake and she a rabbit: limp and submissive, drained of spirit. Since she made no move to take the money he put it on the table. He turned to go. "Is there anything else?" he asked although, of course, he had approached her with

224

the request for eggs. She shook her head dumbly, picked up a plate and carried it to the sink. She turned and came back for the other, moving like a robot.

Pharaoh stepped outside. The Land Rover was still in the yard but there was no sign of Rankin or Paul, and no sound from the pit bull. Without thinking he wandered round the south side of the barn which brought him to the gable end of the cottage where the Datsun stood, its bonnet raised. Martin Shaw was examining the engine gloomily.

"'Morning." Pharaoh changed course and came to stand beside him. "Problems?" he asked genially.

"Bloody thing keeps stalling. I've cleaned the carburettor but it's still not running right."

"Hi, Jack." Susan came out of the cottage. "Do you have any ideas — apart from scrapping it, I mean? Do you have to drain the tank if it's sugar?"

"Sugar?"

"Marty reckons Paul's put sugar in the petrol tank, or water."

"It's his style." Shaw glowered at the carburettor. "I suppose it's possible the tank's corroded. It's an old car."

"It was Paul," Susan said firmly. "You've been for eggs, Jack. Where's the pit bull? Have they taken it to the vet?"

"They've still got it. I thought it had gone too because it didn't make a sound when I came across. This is the barn where they keep it?"

"Yes, there's the ring it's tied to when Paul puts it outside." She pointed. "It's inside now, of course — if it's here. But we haven't seen it for ages, nor heard it, come to that. It was quiet all day yesterday, Marty says. I was over at Grammery a lot. You say they've still got it? But that's not right; they told Rowland they'd have it destroyed yesterday."

"They both say it's still here. Tilly says it's 'settled'." Pharaoh grinned. "Perhaps they've tranquillised it. But the Rankins aren't tranquil," he added seriously. "They're acting very strangely."

"How, strange?" Susan asked. Shaw rubbed at the battery terminals with cotton waste.

"Difficult to say." Pharaoh stared

absently at Shaw's hands. "Frightened, definitely, but they would be, with Rowland delivering an ultimatum about the dog, particularly if they haven't got rid of it. That could account for their attitude; they're worried that I'll tell the Fawcetts it's still here. So why did they tell me it was? Odd. And there are those dead sheep," he mused. "Perhaps the Rankins are involved somehow despite Clem's theory. They seem to be floundering."

"Floundering?" Shaw straightened his back, looking puzzled. Pharaoh made an effort to assess the Rankins' behaviour in retrospect. "She got him out of the way," he said.

"Paul?" asked Susan.

"No, Paul wasn't there: having a lie-in, Tilly said. It was George she pushed out of the kitchen. She said he'd finished his breakfast so he could get out of the way. In fact, they hadn't had breakfast; she was cooking it. Then she started taking clean plates to the sink. It was weird."

"And Paul's still in bed and the dog's quiet. What's going on, Marty?"

Shaw blinked, suddenly addressed.

"Old man shot the dog?" he ventured. "And they haven't dared tell the lad?" His eyes shone.

"My God," breathed Susan. "It could be that. Go and look in the barn. If it's not there, if the chain is there, you'll know."

"It could be even simpler," Pharaoh said. "They — George and Tilly — could have had the dog destroyed, humanely, and now they're waiting for Paul to wake up and find out."

"Go and see if it's in the barn," she urged. "Take a stick."

With Shaw leading the way they crossed the cobbles to the barn door. There was no sound from inside, not even a rattle from the chain. The men opened the big double doors and entered confidently, sure now that the pit bull was gone.

"Where was it kept?" Pharaoh looked across the threshing floor and sniffed in disgust. "It was certainly kept here. What a stench!"

"Over there." Susan pointed to heaps of excrement.

"It's enough to make you feel sorry for

the animal," Shaw exclaimed, "living in that filth."

"There's no chain," Pharaoh said, advancing. "There's a ringbolt though; it must have been fastened to that. Where is he now?" They looked round vaguely as if the barn might hold a clue. And then they heard it: unmistakable, the rattle of a chain. They froze, and Shaw raised the stick.

The other door opened and George Rankin stood there, wide-eyed, his mouth slack, staring at them. In his hands were a collar and a looped chain.

Shaw recovered his voice first. "Where is it?" he asked.

Rankin swallowed and croaked. He tried again. "What you doing in my barn?" It was so weak it was scarcely a question.

"Where's the pit bull?" Susan asked.

"In . . . " His eyes were frantic. " . . . in cow house."

"Loose?" asked Shaw.

"Nay. He's tied up secure."

"Without a collar," Shaw said quietly.

Rankin looked at it as if he wondered how he came to be carrying it. "He were in cow house. He'm in 'Rover now." Alarmingly he started to shout: "You'm trespassing! You'm on private property. I'll take you to court, all lot of you — "

Shaw raised his arm, seeming to forget that he had the stick in his hand. Rankin cringed. "Show us the dog," Shaw ordered.

"Well, I . . . " He turned in time to see Tilly emerge from the front door and move towards them. "He'm gone to Kirkby," he threw at them. "The lad took 'im; he's gone — rabbiting — with his mates."

"What's the trouble?" Tilly asked, coming up, looking from her husband to the others. "You gotta problem?"

Her eyes slitted at Shaw who observed curiously: "Paul's trained him to ride on the back of the Honda, like a sheepdog?"

Rankin stared. Tilly said quickly: "I didn't see 'im go but he were training dog, of course. Sunday, isn't it; the lad has Sunday off." Her voice rose as she found the clichés she needed. "And what business is it of yours, may I ask? What you doing, standing there in our barn?

You" — she glared at Pharaoh — "you just used eggs as an excuse to come and spy on us. We ain't got nothing to hide . . . " In the face of their fascinated gaze she trailed off, jerking her head as she looked from one to the other, from them to Rankin, and beyond: to the cavern of the barn. She snatched the collar and chain from her husband, advanced on the others, who moved to let her pass, and threw the chain on the threshing floor. "There," she said. "That's to tie 'im up with. Paul took the other collar with 'im."

Shaw grinned. "He's been gone a long time."

Tilly grasped Rankin's sleeve and tried to pull him away. He looked at her but he didn't budge. "We got things to do," she urged, tugging at the sleeve. At length he moved and shambled after her.

"Do you want the barn closed?" Shaw called.

Tilly turned and screamed at him: "A lot you care: treating other folks' place same as it were your own! I don't care: leave it open, leave all gates open, pull down walls, set place afire, see if I care;

we be turned out anyway — "

They saw Rankin push her. It wasn't a blow but a hard shove, and then he had her by the arms and was hustling her round the corner of the house.

"Oh, wow," breathed Susan. "She's flipped. And has she got it in for us! What did she mean by being turned out? Could Rowland have told them to go because they haven't got rid of the dog? And where *is* the dog? It isn't on the farm, is it? I reckon it's been destroyed; I mean, you've got a collar and chain but no dog; it stands to reason."

* * *

"No way," said Harker. "No way is he going to be able to train a pit bull to ride on the back of a Honda. Even if it was possible he hasn't had the time. They've got rid of it or — Oh, my God!"

"What?" Pharaoh finished his scrambled eggs and waited, but Harker was slow to reply, working something out. "When did it stop barking?" he asked at last.

"You'd have to ask the Shaws. What are you suggesting?"

232

"Well . . . " He was uneasy. "It happened before; I was wondering if it had broken loose again. There was all that activity at Murkgill yesterday, and Paul going over to Ewedale; they could have been covering all the roads — I've just realised that. And Paul isn't there now."

"Tilly said he was in bed. No, I said that; she said he was a late riser."

"Someone must get the truth out of them. If that dog's loose they must be forced to admit it, and people can go out and shoot it. The brute could have done untold harm already; why, it could kill a child! I'm going to call Rowland — No! Let's go up to the Hall; we can calm 'em down if they get excited; it's easier talking face to face."

★ ★ ★

"I can't believe it," Rowland said. "Surely if a dog like that was loose, even for a few hours, the whole dale would know. They would if it was killing sheep."

They had found the Fawcetts and Beth Potter in the kitchen at the Hall.

Rowland had told them that he had had no communication with the Rankins since yesterday afternoon when he encountered them at Tranna Mire. "Funny thing," he said now, "but I had the impression that something was wrong: two of them after rabbits and only one gun. They were looking for the dog, of course. But how can it be running loose and no one know about it?"

"It could be," Beth put in. "Rankins don't feed their dogs right. When their collies get loose, first place they come is to our dustbins for a good feed. If that pit thing went loose because it were hungry, it'd kill the first sheep it come across and then it would eat itself silly and maybe lie up by the carcass or even run up on moors, afraid like. Killer dogs is always frightened of people."

"I hope so," Harker said. "I mean, I hope it's frightened of people — if it's loose. I hate to think — " He stopped.

"What would happen if it comes across a child?" Phoebe supplied. "You must go and see Rankin," she told Rowland. "Clem and Jack will go with you."

* * *

"The dog?" Tilly repeated, facing them at her back door, addressing Rowland. "The *dog*? He's not here."

"Where is he?" Rowland asked, for the second time.

She opened her mouth but no sound came.

"He slipped his collar." Rowland was implacable.

"I — don't know. You'll need to speak — " She looked around, evidently decided that she could cope better than Rankin and said firmly: "He slipped his collar last week."

"*And* this time?" Pharaoh suggested. "The collar was buckled." He meant when he'd seen it earlier today but as he said it he realised that the Rankins could have found it buckled a long time ago. Rowland guessed the thought.

"When did it get loose, Mrs Rankin?" he asked.

Tilly gave up. "Rankin said as how it musta gone in storm," she whispered.

"Friday night!" Rowland was horrified. He stared at his companions. "It's been

235

loose for over a day! Why haven't we heard anything then?" He turned on Tilly. "Or have you?" He was angry now, not sparing her. "Have people been calling you and you kept it quiet? No," he murmured, turning aside, "they'd have called us too."

Behind him Pharaoh asked: "Who called, Mrs Rankin?"

"Weeping Klints," she muttered. "It were down there in her sheep but when we got there it were gone."

"That's the only call you had?" She nodded dumbly.

"How many sheep did it kill at Weeping Klints?" Rowland snapped.

"Two, I think she said."

"You think!"

"Where's George?" Harker asked.

But Tilly was on the point of collapse. Retreating into the kitchen she slumped in a chair at the cluttered table and put her head in her hands. Rowland looked helplessly at Pharaoh. Harker signalled them to stay outside and went in and closed the door.

Rowland and Pharaoh stood in the yard speculating, and realising the futility of it. After a few minutes Harker emerged. "No good," he told them. "She doesn't know where they are, neither George nor Paul, only that they're searching, which is what they were doing yesterday, of course. So . . . " He looked meaningly at Rowland; it was his land, his tenant — and the Hall's relationship with the neighbouring families was centuries old.

"We must report it to the police," Rowland said, acknowledging his responsibility. "And then we'll get a party together: find the animal and shoot it. There's no way that brute can be taken alive even if anyone wanted to."

"Paul could," Harker said. "But he's had his chances. Tell me who you want to get in touch with and we can make some of the calls for you."

"I'll tell Shaw," Pharaoh said.

"Never mind him." A strategy formulated, Rowland was incisive. "The chap we want is Lanty Dolphin, he's a marksman. Give him a ring, tell him to come up to the Hall. Do you shoot, Jack?"

"I can handle a shotgun."

"Then you come with Clem. I can

lend you a couple of guns. Mind you get Lanty."

Despite the circumstances Pharaoh was surprised that the old man preferred to lend him a shotgun rather than Shaw who was the acknowledged expert with firearms. Could it be that to Rowland Shaw was an unknown quantity? But he was that to all of them. Leaving Harker to return to Fox Yards, Pharaoh went to the Shaws' cottage to tell them the news. "And to warn you," he said. "It's loose, so be careful if you leave the place on foot."

"I wish I had a firearm," Shaw said.

"It's miles away by now," Susan assured them. "That dog's been abused all its life so it would get as far away from people as it could once it was loose. It certainly wouldn't hang around here. Imagine how it must hate Paul!"

"Ye-es." Shaw looked at her absently, then turned back to Pharaoh. "What do you want me to do?"

"Rowland didn't say. It's guns he needs for the shooting party so I suppose you just carry on as usual."

"As usual!" Susan was scornful. "With

a killer in the dale — or on the tops," she added, remembering her own theory.

Pharaoh went back to Fox Yards where, between calls to rally the farmers, Harker told him that Juno's line was engaged and asked him to drive to Grammery and bring Lanty Dolphin back.

At Grammery Pharaoh found Esme and Juno gossiping over coffee. "Lanty's out shooting," Juno told him, and smiled. "Which is where you'll always find him if he's not here. Was it something special?"

They received the news with predictable horror, not because a dog was loose in the dale — country people are accustomed to tourists' dogs running wild — but because of the kind of dog; this one was no tourist's pet.

"Susan reckons it's miles away," Pharaoh said. "But to be on the safe side it's better not to go out on foot until it's been shot. Lanty's not in any danger," he added quickly, "he's armed. That's why he's wanted to join the . . . posse, I suppose you'd call it."

"It's incredible," raged Esme. "That devil Paul should be shot himself. He knew how dangerous the dog was; he terrorised Sue with it — it was an extension of his ego. What were his parents about to let him keep it?"

"I don't think his parents have any control over him," Juno said reasonably. "They're the kind of family who depend on physical restraint and once Paul outgrew his father, he became the dominant member of the family."

"I thought they were afraid of Tilly."

"They're frightened of her temper. George is probably afraid of her but not Paul. He'll always get his own back somehow. He's sly."

"Could he have turned the dog loose himself?" Pharaoh wondered.

"Why?" Esme demanded.

"Rather than have it put down?" Juno suggested. "Giving the dog a chance, without realising the consequences? But that would be insane. You don't mean it, Jack — Ah, here's Lanty," as his rangy figure passed the window. "I'll make some sandwiches for you. I'm sure Clem will forget about food."

Lanty came in, nodding affably to Pharaoh, holding up two rabbits. "Youngsters," he told his mother, "but

full-grown. They'll be tender as babies."
Esme winced.

"Lanty's careless about his use of words," Juno said as he retreated.

"I did mean it," Pharaoh said. "I don't think Paul considers consequences."

"So you've come round to my way of thinking," Esme said. She bit her lip, then went on defiantly: "All right, I was wrong to accuse Martin of stealing my two hundred pounds; it had to be that young ruffian, with hindsight — " Pharaoh went to speak, and checked, but she had seen. "It was Paul who went into Sue's cottage and took the cash from her purse," she told him firmly, "and now you all agree he's a psychopath — well, he is, isn't he: if he's unable to visualise the consequences of his actions? There's no way Sue can go on living in that cottage with that — that madman next door." She shook her head vehemently, "You have to help me persuade her, and him, both of them. Imagine Sue on her own for months at a time! You have to face it: he's not just a thief, a potential rapist — " Behind her back Lanty reappeared, having disposed of the rabbits. He stood his shotgun in a corner, not taking his astonished eyes off Esme. She addressed him: "He's a psychopath, Lanty! A boy who deliberately frees a dog that's so vicious it could kill a man! That is, is . . . " She stuttered, unable to find a word bad enough.

"What on earth are you talking about?" Lanty asked. "The pit bull's out again? I haven't seen it."

"Tell him, Jack," Juno said quickly, before Esme could get her second wind.

Pharaoh told him the gist of it, and said that he was wanted at the Hall, and to bring his gun. Lanty sat down, absently pouring coffee into a used mug, regarding Pharaoh blankly at first, and then with a dawning anger. "I'll kill Paul," he said, without inflection, when Pharaoh stopped talking and they waited for his reaction — which wasn't what they'd expected. Actually, thought Pharaoh, he didn't know what he'd expected of Lanty: this gangling young fellow who seemed to have no interests other than shooting and a natural desire for the only young girl in the community. He didn't even know what Lanty *did*, when he was employed.

In fact, he knew virtually nothing about Lanty, who was saying conversationally, without apparent feeling: "You see what this means: he's a juvenile. If the dog kills someone, he can't be charged with manslaughter because he's not an adult. George will get into trouble, of course; he'll probably be fined heavily if the dog tears someone's throat out; Paul won't even go to court. Legally he's still a child. And he's worse than the dog. He's the one who should be put down."

Esme laughed harshly. Juno regarded her son with astonishment. Pharaoh said weakly: "Well, when they find him, no doubt there'll be some straight talking."

"Oh." Lanty looked pleased. "He's missing too, is he?"

"No. I mean, he's out searching — which we should be doing too. Shall we make a move?"

"Perhaps he'll get in someone's sights when they go to shoot the dog." Lanty grinned boyishly.

11

THE search was hampered by the thick mist. The drizzle had stopped by the afternoon but the cloud had dropped again to the level of the railway and, above that, visibility would be no more than a few yards. A police car made a run up the dale on the alert for any sheep that were behaving unnaturally, but the outlook was restricted, cut off by that solid cloud ceiling.

There was no panic. No warning had been broadcast as yet and, generally speaking, the dalespeople were phlegmatic, annoyed that somewhere someone was losing sheep — had to be, they said, with a big dog at large, but no one thought it necessary to keep children indoors. There was a feeling abroad that this was something of the order of an Alsatian or a big terrier and that, like any other sheep-killer, it would run when it realised it was being hunted, would escape over the tops to another dale, kill someone else's animals. Only the police (who had received a directive on pit bulls) and the inhabitants of Clouds had any idea of the true danger.

The searchers gathered at Weeping Klints, four miles north of Clouds, since this was the last place that the dog had been seen, so far as they knew. The woman who farmed at the Klints was a widow living alone in the farmhouse, the heavy work and the shepherding being done by her married son who lived a mile further down the dale. When his mother telephoned him yesterday afternoon, he had gone out but seen nothing untoward below the intake wall, and he wasn't concerned about the animals on the moor because no one could have seen a dog among them. The cloud was down as far as the intake, the in-bye land.

The widow: plump, genial, grimly amused, told Rowland she wasn't surprised to know that the Rankins' dog was loose; the caller had said it was a pit bull and it wouldn't be the first time that Tilly Rankin had skirted the truth, let alone told a deliberate lie. "And it had to be

George Rankin came down immediately after," she told them. "I was watching, and a Land Rover came over the brae there" — from her kitchen window she had a good view of the road to Clouds — "and this 'Rover stopped. I had the field glasses on 'em, but no one got out, although they were there awhiles, and then they come on down, slowly. After a time they drove back. They realised, same as us, that no dog had been among our sheep because they were quiet. If I'd 'a looked at sheep before I phoned Tilly Rankin I'd'a known we had nowt to worry about."

"Whose land was the dog on then?" asked Rowland. "One of your neighbours?"

"We never found out. No one's lost any sheep that we know of. If you ask me the fellow saw lambs chasing a fox, playful like."

"But Tilly said the dog killed two sheep."

"You know what townsfolk is like, Mr Fawcett: they see a couple of old ewes stuck on their backs, legs in t'air, and townies think they're dead — or if they're moving, then they been savaged.

Time you get there, ewes have righted theirselves."

They didn't go all the way with that; for one thing they couldn't conceive of anyone mistaking a pit bull for a fox, but since Weeping Klints was the place where something had happened, and they had to start somewhere, they started there.

Yesterday the Rankins had covered the dale from the road. This afternoon the patrol car was on the road while groups of men set out on foot from the widow's farm: two groups to each side of the dale, some going downstream, the others south towards Clouds. They had no dogs with them; no one was going to risk having his collie shot by an excited neighbour.

Pharaoh and Harker were with two elderly farmers whom they allowed to draw ahead. They were walking on a green track which ran down the side of the dale towards Kirkby Oswald. Above them was the railway, and beyond, scree slopes now showing below the cloud which seemed to be lifting. On their left were pastures: a brilliant green after the rain and set off by their white stone walls, then came the road and the river marked by a broken belt of hardwoods.

"Remind you of anything?" Pharaoh asked.

"Oh yes. Looking for a lost walker and you don't even know where to start."

"And when you do start you feel you're in the wrong place."

They walked on in silence, preoccupied with memories, watching their feet instead of looking to either side as they should be doing. Ahead of them the farmers grumbled softly to each other.

Pharaoh asked suddenly: "Where's Paul?"

"How would I know?" Harker shot a glance at his friend. "He's with George, isn't he? Tilly said they were out looking for the dog so they'll be together."

"I didn't see the Honda."

"Well, that's it; he's on the Honda, his father's in the Land Rover."

"Yes, separate. His father was in for breakfast but Paul was out; the Honda wasn't in the yard."

"You mean it wasn't visible. He takes care of it; he'd have put it under cover so it wouldn't get wet."

"It wasn't in the barn. And where was Paul?"

"In bed, Jack, it's a dog missing, not a boy. And we should be keeping our eyes skinned — although I'm willing to bet that dog isn't down here in the bottom of the dale. If it has been here, then it's killed and moved on." He glanced up at the foot of the escarpment, the rocks just showing. "Probably gone over into the next dale. We'll have to go to Ewedale, you know; that's where Paul went."

Pharaoh looked up the slope, not idly but intently, frowning. "What are you thinking now?" Harker asked.

"Did he come back?"

Harker snorted. "You've got Paul on the brain. Of course he came back — well, I suppose he could have stayed the night with his mates. And then" — he went on slowly — "he wouldn't know that it's public knowledge now: that his dog's missing." He quickened his pace. "Come on; it's not important anyway."

They walked for two miles, until the green track curved left to meet the road. The police car came along with space for two passengers, and took the farmers back to Weeping Klints. After a while Esme arrived in the Range Rover and gave Harker and Pharaoh a lift. No one had any news; the afternoon had been so much wasted time. At the widow's farm people hung around drinking tea until they had all collected again and Rowland said they would go over to Ewedale. There were murmurs of dissent at this; Ewedale was the responsibility of Ewedale folk, and there were cows to be milked on this side. The police arrived and told them that the people in Ewedale knew all about it and were on the alert. They also said that there would be an item on the television news this evening. At this season there were so many tourists about, not to speak of hikers, that it was only a matter of time before someone spotted the dog; it had to eat. There was a low growl at this but no one spoke up; no one could think of anything more that they could do.

The men from Clouds went home: Pharaoh and Harker together, Lanty with Rowland as he had been this afternoon. "What does Lanty do?" Pharaoh asked idly as they followed Rowland's Cortina up the dale.

"He's between jobs. You mean what did he train for? He was in medical school for a year but he went off to South America on some vacation trip and he didn't come back. He did eventually of course, but after that he lost interest in medicine and he just drifted. He's tried a number of things, for a few months at a time: farming, Outward Bound instructor, garage mechanic. Now he's helping his mother get the house fit for bed and breakfast next summer. Presumably he gets some pocket money. I know Juno's got no money to spare but so long as he works he comes cheaper than professional decorators, which she couldn't afford anyway. He's an only child," he added. 'And spoiled' hung in the air.

"I wondered," Pharaoh said lamely.

"No harm in him."

Pharaoh studied his friend's profile. "Are you as objective as you appear?"

"About Lanty?"

"That for a start."

Harker shrugged and made great play

of turning left at the Ewedale junction and braking for the sluggish Cortina.

At the Hall's road-end Rowland went on to drop Lanty, and Harker turned again, weaving between the potholes to pull up at Fox Yards with a sigh of relief. "Nice to be home," he murmured as he opened the gate, his eyes going immediately to the delphiniums which, staked and tied, looked pretty sodden. "Bit of a wasted day, that," he muttered, frowning at a broken hollyhock. "Never mind; no one's in a hurry."

"We haven't found the bloody dog."

"We need a drink."

They drank, they ate TV dinners and they speculated until Pharaoh said: "This is ridiculous; we're discussing it as if there's a walker with a broken leg lying out there waiting for rescue — " He stopped.

"Instead of just a dog." Harker nodded, agreeing with the unspoken thought. "But there's this creepy feeling that there could be someone lying out there injured all the same. That's why we can't leave the subject alone. I'm going to go and see the old people; if we're worried, they could be frantic."

They walked to the Hall. The clouds had gone and the sky was clear. Beyond and above the Hall the old sledge road was obvious in the evening light. "We can make a start on the moors tomorrow," Pharaoh said.

They found the Fawcetts sitting over coffee and brandy in the drawing room. Far from being frantic their initial concern was for the comfort of their guests. When they were offered brandy Pharaoh caught Harker's almost imperceptible nod and accepted, guessing who had provided the extremely expensive Martell. Only when they were settled did Rowland remark equably: "I've sent for Rankin; we're expecting him any moment."

"Where's he been all day?" Pharaoh asked.

"Searching, according to Tilly, but as to where, she couldn't say. He was out when I telephoned but she'll send him over as soon as he comes home." Hence the brandy, thought Pharaoh: Dutch courage; he's more bothered than he appears.

"He can't keep avoiding you," Phoebe told the guests.

Pharaoh considered this. "You mean he's been avoiding us all day: the people searching in the dale? But he would, wouldn't he? Feeling's running pretty high against him; more against him than the boy, in fact. People hold the parents responsible; they should never have allowed him to keep that kind of dog. George wouldn't be able to face other farmers. He sloped off."

"He should have put in an appearance," Rowland said stubbornly.

"You're quiet, Clem," Phoebe remarked. "What are you thinking?"

Harker started; he had been miles away. "I can't think why we haven't found any dead sheep," he said.

"We'll find them tomorrow." Rowland grimaced. "On the moor. Ah, Beth — " as she appeared in the doorway. "Is that Rankin? Bring him in."

He hadn't come alone; Tilly was with him. They came into the drawing room, sat uncomfortably in armchairs, accepted brandy, and looked everywhere but at the company. Tilly was making small nervous movements of her hands, but Rankin was slow and careful, even as he raised his glass, as if he were in the presence of something that would pounce if startled by a sudden movement.

"There appears to be no news?" Phoebe's voice rose slightly but the Rankins remained silent.

"Where is Paul?" Rowland asked, but all the couple could do was stare at him.

Pharaoh and Harker exchanged glances. "Where did you go today, George?" Harker asked firmly.

"Ewedale." It was unexpectedly soft.

"*Where?*" Rowland hadn't caught it.

Rankin said nothing. "Ewedale," repeated Harker, and turned back to Rankin. "Paul was with you?"

The man stared at his glass, lifted it and drank the brandy at a gulp. Tilly regarded Harker as if he were a ghost. "Where's Paul?" she whispered.

"Eh? What's that?" Rowland cupped his ear. Phoebe moved impatiently, hushing him. For a long moment there was silence. Tilly had her hand clapped to her mouth, Rankin turned his glass in his hands, somewhere in the room the Jack Russell whimpered in its sleep. Tilly's eyes slewed wildly, searching for the source of the sound as if she'd forgotten that the Fawcetts had a dog.

Pharaoh asked gently: "When did you see Paul last?"

There was no answer. Tilly's eyelids drooped. Suddenly she looked tired and stupid.

"Was he home last night?" Harker asked.

"No," Rankin said.

"But he was home yesterday." Rankin nodded. "So he didn't come back from Ewedale, is that it?"

"*You* said he went to Ewedale!" Tilly came to life and flung it at him like an accusation. "It were you said it. We never saw him go, we were down to Kirkby, down dale, looking to see if dog were gone past Weeping Klints. You said this morning as Paul were over to Ewedale."

"I told you that," Rowland said. "It was news to you. I should have known that he hadn't been home all night; he would have told you where he'd been."

"He didn't always," Rankin said.

Phoebe frowned and glanced at Harker. Tilly saw the look. "What have you done with my boy?" she screamed. Harker's jaw dropped.

"This won't do," Rowland chided.

"Now, now, Tilly." Phoebe spoke as if to a child. "That's quite enough. You've had a hard day. Beth!" She must have been listening in the passage because she appeared as if she'd been waiting for the summons. "Make a pot of tea, Beth."

Tilly collapsed in her chair, squeezing into the back of it. She looked terrified. Rankin ignored her. Rowland got up and poured more brandy. Harker and Pharaoh declined.

"Paul must be in Ewedale," Harker said pleasantly.

"He's not back." Tilly's voice was flat. The light had gone out of her eyes as if she had given way to terror and gone beyond, into shock. "Last time," she went on in that dull tone, "he come back next morning."

"Last time?" Harker repeated.

"The night before. He were in Kirkby

with one of his mates . . . the night of the storm . . . he stayed in Kirkby. He wouldn't take the Honda to town, he's under age, so he had to stay there because of the storm. He come home next morning and he were so mad because dog were gone. It went during t'storm . . . Paul were in Kirkby — "

"Tilly." Phoebe was quiet but compelling and the woman stopped as if she'd been switched off. "Who did he stay with, Tilly? The night of the storm?"

"He didn't say."

"But he took the Honda last night," Harker reminded the others quietly. "And he went to Ewedale, or towards Ewedale." He looked out of the window at the tops of the dark trees. The sunshine had left the dale. "No," he said. "He's done a bunk."

"No to what?" Rowland demanded. "What's on your mind?"

"Nothing. Was he drinking in Ewedale last night, George?"

"No."

"You went in all the pubs?"

"Aye."

"So he went on down Ewedale.

Probably abandoned the Honda, or sold it. He's scared of repercussions over the dog. He'll be back as soon as the dog's found, and things are settled. He's just frightened of the consequences. He's only a boy, after all."

"He didn't have no money," Rankin said.

Harker opened his mouth, and closed it again.

★ ★ ★

Walking down the drive, Pharaoh laughed. "You nearly reminded him that Paul has Esme's two hundred quid. The state Tilly was in she'd have been at your throat."

"I let myself in for it. I was the last person to see Paul — well, to hear him, and now she's got it in for me just because of that. I'm a scapegoat."

"All the same . . . "

"Yes. A gully, d'you think: took a bend too fast on the way home?"

"He wasn't drinking in Ewedale."

"George won't have called at the farms. The lad's probably got friends his parents don't know about anyway. He could still be with one of them, or a group. All the same — " They stopped and turned and stared at the escarpment above the roofs of the Hall.

"We'll go and look in the gullies tomorrow," Pharaoh said. "It won't take more than an hour and then we can start searching for the dog on the tops. We might even find a trace of it down the other side: kill two birds with one stone."

"Funny," mused Harker. "We've got two missing now."

★ ★ ★

There was an item about the dog on the evening news. The police had told Rowland that they would let him know if there were any developments, but no one reported that they had seen a dog chasing sheep although there were quite a few calls relating to loose dogs — a number of them opportunist and none that concerned a cinnamon pit bull, according to Rowland who telephoned Fox Yards next morning. He said he'd talked to Rankin who sounded as if he'd been stunned. By now Paul had been absent for two days. Harker said that he and Pharaoh would go down Ewedale, come back and have a look at the Scar. "If he went after the sheep," he said, "there'll be fresh tracks."

"How can you be sure they're his?" Rowland asked.

"We can't, but it's the only three-wheeler around."

"Oh, I thought you were talking about the dog."

"There's the dog too, of course."

"Be sure and take the guns. I'll be coming up meself. I'll go by way of the quarries; we'll meet on top."

After breakfast they took Pharaoh's car and drove up the moor road to the pass. It was a glorious fresh morning, sunny with a light breeze and high fair-weather clouds. They crossed the pass and the road began to descend, gently at first between long slopes faintly hazed with green. There were numerous bridges but no houses, only the odd ruin, relic of some ancient shieling.

They didn't stop at the higher bridges; if the Honda had left the road here its wreck would be obvious, would have

261

been reported already. These were one-arched bridges over becks so small that they would have been dry but for the rain, and none ran between steep banks. But as the dale narrowed and deepened and the road traversed a steep slope, scattered with hawthorns and holly, the becks came plunging down dark rocks in waterfalls, and bridges spanned deep gorges. They stopped and peered into these black holes but all they found was one rotting sheep carcass and a rusted stove. There was silty mud about the carcass but no tracks. When the road started to run between walls they turned back; if a Honda could breach a wall someone would have investigated if only to plug the gap to keep the sheep inside. A cattle grid marked the end of the open moor and at that point they started back to the pass.

It was ten o'clock in the morning but there were few tourists about and no one had stopped on top. They parked, put on their boots, took the shotguns and started along the green path to Black Blote Fell. Immediately they were surrounded by birds, the larger ones frantic, the larks as unconcerned as ever.

"Midsummer," Pharaoh said. "Smell the thyme; you could get drunk on that. And listen to those birds."

Harker suppressed a smile. "Watch where you put your feet in case there's a chick pretending to be a stone. I fell flat on my face once to avoid a ptarmigan chick."

"Ptarmigan here?"

"Above Glen Shiel."

"There's someone on the pavement. Aren't we about where we met Shaw?"

"It was further along. That must be Rowland. Don't people look sinister carrying guns in a place like this?"

The man was silhouetted on the far side of the limestone pavement, moving towards them. "It is Rowland," Harker said. "I'd know his walk anywhere. He's not excited so he hasn't found any sign in the quarries or about the tarn, although the dog doesn't have to drink in the obvious places; there's plenty of surface water after the rain."

"Can this be the Honda?" Pharaoh had stopped and was studying the ground where the path had been muddy and had dried. Etched in the surface was the tread of a tyre.

"It's the Honda all right but how fresh is that track?"

"It's been made since the heavy rain, Clem."

"He's — he was going to Black Blote Fell?" They looked along the track to the distant slope with the pimple on top that was the summit cairn. "Did he come back?" Harker asked.

Pharaoh didn't answer immediately. After a while, as they walked on and Rowland approached steadily, he murmured: "But I haven't seen any tracks of a dog."

Ahead of them the path curved gently left as the peat hags came in from the right. Where the lime met the peat the sinkholes started.

The sinkholes must have been part of a fault. They didn't commence as simple shafts at the base of funnels but as a long depression with a jagged crevasse in the bottom, masked for much of its length by stinging nettles.

"I don't remember this bit," Pharaoh said.

"You wouldn't have noticed it. The interesting ones are further along, where Rowland — has stopped . . . " His voice died away. Rowland was shouting and waving his arm. They stepped up their pace.

Rowland stopped shouting and turned away, his gun loose in one hand. Harker reached him first and halted, then Pharaoh came up, favouring the bad leg. They stood side by side and no one spoke for a while.

Below them the ground sloped gently to a level sward and a glimpse of rock under the nettles. Parked on the turf was the Honda: red under its dried mud, upright, and possessing the peculiar *waiting* aspect of inanimate objects that have been left only temporarily. They looked around for the owner but with today's visibility they could see a long way across the Scar; if Paul was here he was in a depression.

"How long's it been here?" Rowland asked, but they knew he didn't expect an answer. "Since Friday," he muttered.

"Why did he leave it?" Harker asked.

Pharaoh walked down the slope which

was at such an easy angle that he had no trouble. He felt the engine. "Stone cold," he said. The hole beside the Honda was a riot of ferns below the nettles. He didn't bother to look into it.

"Any sign?" Rowland asked hopefully, although it was obvious that there was none.

"He came back to the path," Pharaoh murmured, returning to them, looking along the continuation of the fault. "And presumably went on."

"Shepherding?" Rowland suggested. "A ewe in trouble perhaps. The boy got lost in the mist . . . " But Pharaoh and Harker were moving away.

The true sinkholes started: shafts below green banks, dark grey vertical flutings festooned with ferns and fragile flowers. They could hear water dripping. At the first hole Harker scrambled down and peered into the depths, stepping from one to the other of the square-topped pillars. Pharaoh moved on. Rowland stood irresolute, watching Harker.

Pharaoh stood on the lip of the next depression and felt the old familiar resignation that is the first reaction of rescuers who have found their quarry after a long search and who know that the interval, for one reason or another, means death. Below him the sides of a black shaft were streaked with orange slime. The vegetation was luxuriant and on the lip the ferns were crushed.

He glanced back. Rowland was watching him, looking expectant. "He's here," Pharaoh called, and they were beside him in a moment.

"We're going to need a rope," he told them, starting the technical process that was as much insulation against shock as the first move in a routine.

They went down carefully; where one had fallen (slipped on wet grass?) others could follow. On the rock they climbed delicately along the lip of the huge cracks, stepping across them with extreme caution. Below them water dripped on something soft: a muffled splat.

At first they were frustrated. With the sun reflected brilliantly off the limestone pavement they could see nothing in depths that appeared bottomless, but whatever the water fell on was close at hand. The ferns were crushed in only one place but although they tried from every angle they could see nothing of what lay below.

"Paul?" Rowland said loudly, without any hope, then shouted, desperately: "*Paul!*"

Pharaoh picked up a small stone and dropped it. The sound came almost immediately, and it had fallen on rock.

"Ten to fifteen feet," Harker suggested. "Listen!"

"What?"

"I heard something," Pharaoh said.

"We all did; the stone — "

"After the stone landed. Something moved down there." He picked up a chunk of rock.

"Careful," protested Harker. "If he's below — "

"The other one didn't hit a body. Now listen — *after* it lands."

The rock fell with a small crash but there was no silence afterwards. Instead there was a scuffle and a whimper.

"It's the bloody *dog*!" Rowland shouted. "All this care and we've found the damn pit bull!"

They retreated and sat on the grass. "What do we do now?" Rowland asked.

"Where's Paul?" Harker looked at Pharaoh.

"Why doesn't the dog bark?" Pharaoh asked, adding, as if to himself: "But it would have barked."

"Oh God!" breathed Harker, and then: "What do we do about the dog?"

"The dog's not important," Rowland protested. "What we have to do now is find Paul; the dog can wait."

They looked at him and then at each other. Harker said: "We think Paul's down there, Rowland. He heard the dog barking, tried to climb down and fell."

The old man stared at him. "Yes," he said after a while. "You could be right; the Honda points to him being close by. Oh, I see what you mean: how do we get past the dog to reach Paul, even to find out if he's down there? That's simple. We shoot it. What are we carrying guns for, eh?"

"Fine." Harker was approving but he stopped there.

Pharaoh put it into words. "How do

269

we see the brute to shoot it?"

"Right." Rowland was pleased to discover a use for his own expertise. "We find a place where the bottom is visible from the top and we drop a sandwich on it. I've got mutton. That'll tempt him out of wherever he's skulking."

By moving about, lying on the lip, shading their eyes, they discovered a position from where they could discern points of light about twelve feet down that must be wet rock on what they hoped was the floor of the crack. While Rowland got into position, ready to fire, with Harker holding him so that he couldn't fall over the edge, Pharaoh dropped a sandwich. They saw the pale flash of it arrested on the gleaming rock. Pharaoh backed away and the others waited, and watched — and waited.

After ten minutes Rowland lowered the barrels of the gun. "It's not hungry," he said.

Pharaoh moved along the tops of the huge cracks. "You've got something in mind?" Harker asked. They were settling down now; this was a technical problem and one unique in their experience. They gave it all their attention. It had the merit of making them forget why they had to distract the dog.

"If these cracks are connected below ground," Pharaoh said, "as they appear to be from this angle, perhaps we could *drive* the dog towards the sandwich."

"You're going to go down?" Rowland was doubtful. "But if it retreats in front of you, you mustn't be too close. I don't feel like shooting if you're down there."

"I thought of dropping rocks: big ones; even the noise should force it to move. It's obviously scared; it's not barking."

"It'll be weak by now," Rowland said.

"It's got water," Harker reminded him, biting off the statement.

When they studied the rock formation they thought they could make out a continuous fault through the maze of subsidiary crevasses. They collected chunks of limestone and positioned them along the lip of the main channel, then Rowland and Harker took their places again at what they hoped was a dead end and where the sandwich still showed on the wet floor, while Pharaoh waited at the other end, some thirty feet away. At a nod from Rowland he pushed the first rock over the edge. It fell with a crash, and it fell a long way.

"That sounded like fifty feet," he shouted. "Don't answer." They had agreed that he should make as much noise as possible; the others would remain silent and immobile. Now they strained their ears.

He moved and dropped the next piece of stone. "Not nearly so deep." He aimed his voice downwards, willing the dog to move. "So at this end there must be a shaft."

Now they all listened, and heard only the larks. Pharaoh moved and dropped the third rock. "It has to shift soon," he called, and listened to the drip of water below. He glanced at the others and held his breath. He didn't think they had moved but there was a tension about them. They would have been stiff before, of course, holding awkward positions. This was different, there was something about Rowland's stance . . .

Noise shattered the moor, resonant in all that stone: the blast of the gun, a squeal, a wild screaming, another blast, silence.

Then they realised that the silence was sweet with birdsong, and when their ears recovered further, they heard the water dripping. Pharaoh licked his lips and climbed carefully back to the others who were peering over the edge. The sandwich had disappeared.

"I fired at his eyes," Rowland said. "I was watching the bread, d'you see, and suddenly it was blacked out. I thought it had gone, he'd taken it, but he must have turned round and his eyes gleamed. Then, when he screamed the fangs showed plainly, so I had two good shots. He's dead, you may be sure of that."

"That's a relief," Pharaoh said. "Thanks."

Harker looked at him sharply. "I'll go down."

"We'll both go; it's not difficult."

"But if the lad fell — " Rowland stopped, embarrassed, remembering that here they were the experts.

"We'll be careful," Harker assured him.

The climb down was not difficult at all, even though they had to straddle, which meant putting weight on one leg. Pharaoh gritted his teeth; the wall there was only about twelve feet high. At the bottom Harker whispered: "I hope he did kill that brute." They had left the guns on top.

"If he hit it twice at that range it's in no condition to attack anyone. And that screaming meant it was hurt badly. Watch it; there could be a hole in the floor. Why have you stopped?" They had been moving one careful step at a time in the bottom of the crack.

"There's something here." Harker bumped into Pharaoh as he bent down. "Wool," he said. "Dead sheep. It's been here ages; it's just bones and fleece."

"Are you all right down there?" Rowland called.

"Fine." Harker squinted at the brilliant sky fringed with black ferns. "Now I can't see," he grumbled. "Here's another sheep. Flies on this one so it's fresh — " There was silence.

"You found him." Pharaoh's voice was without feeling.

"Yes. Clothing, flesh — oh!"

"It's all right," Pharaoh said. "We knew all along why the dog wasn't hungry."

12

HARKER was the obvious person to go for the police; he could travel faster than the others, although speed was of little consequence in the circumstances — it meant only that Pharaoh and Rowland would have a few minutes less to wait. They withdrew to the limestone pavement and sat on the sun-warmed rock. For a while they remained silent and almost immobile, like ancient countrymen. Pharaoh felt no necessity to comfort Rowland and no need of distraction himself. So he forgot his companion and considered idly, almost dreamily, why he was puzzled. When Rowland did speak, it came as a surprise: a human sound in this wilderness of sky and stone, and the dead things in the cracks. "Does anything puzzle you?" he asked.

Pharaoh turned his head slowly, marvelling. "Why was the Honda so far away?" he asked.

"Because he heard the dog barking, so he stopped at the first of the sinkholes and examined each one methodically until he reached the right one. In the cloud it would have been difficult to pinpoint which shaft the dog had fallen down." Pharaoh said nothing. "It's the only explanation," Rowland insisted, with a testiness that indicated, despite appearances, that he was shocked. "That's how you guessed the lad was down there: because the Honda was close by — well, relatively. It's a clear-cut case to my mind — although the boy was mad to climb down and try to rescue the animal with his bare hands."

"He was supposed to be able to handle it, when he had a whip. I suppose that, in the confined space, the dog had the edge on him, particularly if Paul fell as he was climbing down."

After another silence, shorter this time, Rowland said: "I think I can prevail on the police to let me identify him."

"I shouldn't — Oh, that's thoughtful of you."

"We can't have George doing it, d'you see."

"I don't expect so."

"Er — the face?"

"I . . . didn't have the guts . . . the courage for that. There was no question of seeing anything; it was dark down there. I had to feel around. I felt for the pulse in the neck but there was no neck left. The dog must have gone for his throat. Didn't we always say that? That this kind of dog went for the throat? I agree: it's too difficult for the family but then, what about you?"

"It's just a body now; as for the rest, I'm not squeamish. And I had little feeling for the lad when he was alive. I haven't got much time for people who ill-treat animals. All the same we can't have George identifying him."

"Quite."

Having dealt with that they turned to other matters. "How do we get it out?" Rowland asked.

"Clem will bring a rope."

"Of course: you rescue people, first thing you'd think of." After a while he asked curiously: "In that capacity, as a rescuer, do you think these shafts should be fenced?"

"Not at all. Not here. Few people come up to the Scar, according to Clem,and those who do, know the danger. Isn't this the first fatality? And Paul wasn't playing around; he was trying to rescue a dog. The sinkholes are like crevasses on a dry glacier: visible and avoidable. As for children: potentially the shafts are less dangerous than a river. No, they shouldn't be fenced." As an afterthought he added: "And you can be sure that even if you put up chain-link and razor wire, that people determined to explore would get through with wire cutters."

"Good; you've put my mind at rest. The point will be taken up, d'you see, by some cheap tabloid trying to make an issue of it. Where are you going?"

"I need to work out the mechanics: where we're going to put the rope and so on."

He studied the hole moodily. Flowers were jewels against the shadowed walls: cranesbill, herb Robert, buttercups. A door slammed. He looked up in astonishment and saw that a police driver had risked bringing a car along the path. Harker and two uniformed men were approaching.

More cars arrived: the doctor, an ambulance, police reinforcements, a reporter. Harker and Pharaoh viewed the swelling crowd with resignation and, with the kind of black humour that characterised past rescues, observed that television would be a waste of time: the film could never be shown.

Pharaoh was given gloves by the ambulance crew and, with the most agile of the policemen, climbed down and put a rope on the body. The remains were raised to the surface and the rope was lowered again for the dog. Rowland had wanted to leave the pit bull where it was but in the peculiar circumstances the police thought it better that its body should be recovered. After all, a dog had killed a boy (no one who saw what was left of the body was in any doubt about that) and Rowland had deliberately shot a dog. Better, for everyone's sake, to recover all the evidence. To this end a torch was lowered to the officer in the crack and he was told to search for anything that might have fallen out of Paul's clothing, or that he might have taken down with him: a wallet or knife, or a stick with which he'd tried to defend himself and which might provide a clearer picture of the attack. He found nothing.

"Where's Rowland?" Pharaoh asked, having climbed out of the hole. "I don't see him."

"I've no idea," Harker said. "I've been handling the rope."

"He's probably gone down through the quarries. He needs to reach the Rankins before the Press get to them."

"He's going to tell the Rankins?"

"There's no one else, other than the police. He would consider it his responsibility."

A reporter approached: young, fresh-faced, in baggy trousers and Reeboks. He looked sharp but he had no idea that he was talking to two old rescuers, that here was a good story — and neither of them was going to enlighten him. Harker played the elderly retired dullard, Pharaoh was no more than his friend, and their lack of interest in the bizarre circumstances, instead of alerting the Press — two other reporters had approached hopefully — made them appear so ordinary as to be insensitive. They did agree that the sight was nasty, and that vicious dogs should be shot, and it was strange that Paul should have been killed by his own dog. And eaten. "Eaten?" Pharaoh repeated, at last showing a spark of interest. They assured him that the police said parts had been eaten, a great deal, in fact. "Which parts?" Harker asked eagerly, but they found that too repulsive and one who had been fingering his camera lowered it with obvious distaste. Someone asked Harker for his number and he said he was afraid he didn't have a telephone.

When the reporters had left them Pharaoh said with amusement: "I didn't know you had it in you; your tone when you said you weren't on the phone was actually apologetic. The youngster looked at you with contempt. None of them have got any time for us."

"You didn't do badly yourself. It's all right as long as the chickens don't come home to roost."

"We weren't hiding anything."

"A moot point, and you know the Press. Still . . . " he shrugged it off

" . . . I expect we've seen the last of them. Shall we walk down through the quarries? I left your car at home. The police picked me up at the road-end."

The ambulance had gone, and the dog's body had been taken in the boot of a police car. "They've left us to take down that disgusting rope," Pharaoh said.

"It's mine; let me have it."

"No, I'll take it; this shirt's going in the dustbin anyway. The rope will have to be thrown too."

"I'll leave it out in the rain. It's ancient; I don't use it for climbing."

"Just as well." Pharaoh coiled it and settled it gingerly on his shoulder. "Be thankful for small mercies; the cold weather after the storm kept him fresh."

"Yes." They started to walk along grassy channels through the pavement. "How long had he been there?" Harker asked. "I heard him leave around six on Saturday; that's nearly two days ago."

"Why did he stop?"

"You mean stop where he did? I suppose that was the first shaft he came to — "

"I mean why did he stop on the pass? You thought he was going to Ewedale but he must have stopped on top otherwise he couldn't have heard the dog barking. No one would go out to the sinkholes in thick mist unless he had a definite reason."

"Well, that's it! That's why he stopped: he already had the idea that the dog could be down a sinkhole and once he'd turned off the engine he heard it barking. The one time — " Harker stopped suddenly.

"The one time what?"

"I was going to say the one time its barking served a purpose — meaning a beneficial purpose. Of course, it would have been better, at least for Paul, if the dog hadn't barked."

"And he climbed down without a stick."

"But he wouldn't have a stick with him, Jack. If he was going over to Ewedale for an evening's drinking, he wasn't expecting to meet up with the dog."

"No, I suppose not. And when he did he must have thought the brute was so frightened in the bottom of the hole that it wouldn't attack."

"A bit lacking in judgement, wasn't he?"

It was midday by the time they reached the Hall and stopped to find out how Rowland had fared with the Rankins. Pharaoh refused to go inside so Rowland came out and talked to them on the steps.

"Tilly took it well," he told them in surprise. "But the women have gone over to Murkgill to be with her until George gets back. He's away up the dale, still looking for the boy, I'm afraid. For my money it's George who will be the problem when he hears the news. Not that there was much love lost between any of 'em but it's the shock, isn't it? Of course, I didn't tell Tilly what happened."

Harker was amazed. "You had to tell her something!"

"That he was dead, yes, but I said he fell down the sinkhole; going down for the dog, I said."

"She'll guess."

"Well, actually . . . " Rowland looked

guilty. " . . . I told her the dog was already dead — before Paul got there. Shouldn't have done that."

"It's true now."

"Part of it. The point is: it set her off. Not hysterical, not the old screaming Tilly; you know how she loses control: shouting at George and Paul. No, she went quite still, and she stared. I felt like — you know: passing my hand in front of her eyes, and then I wondered if it could be — is it catatonic?"

"It was shock, Rowland."

"I felt very uncomfortable. After a while she said: 'He threw it in the hole.' I told her, no; the dog fell in and Paul climbed down after it. I realised afterwards that he couldn't have known it was there if it was dead, but it was too late. She just looked at me and repeated: '*He* threw it down,' and she gestured towards the cottage. I said: 'Shaw wasn't there, Tilly.' She said: 'He killed it and threw its body down the hole." Rowland smiled wryly. "You see where my good intentions got me, or where they've put young Shaw, except that I hope Tilly will forget. I suppose she was using the dog as

286

a kind of diversion because she couldn't bear to think about Paul. That's why I told Mrs Fawcett and Beth to go over. Tilly shouldn't be on her own when she realises it's her son who's dead, not just the pit bull."

"I suppose Mrs Fawcett can cope with George," Harker said tentatively.

"Of course she can." Rowland was astonished, and Pharaoh had a vision of a ghostly band of Fawcett women bringing restoratives and comfort to centuries of bereaved tenants.

As they walked down to Fox Yards Harker said quietly, as if afraid of being overheard, "We should go across to the Shaws and let them know what Tilly said about the dog. I didn't like that. The Rankins aren't very stable at the best of times."

"We'd better go now," Pharaoh said, surprising his friend who would have expected him to have a bath first, and change his clothes. "I think it's important," he explained, and when they reached the gate he dropped the rope beside the track and they started through the woods, Harker uneasily aware that the path leading to the Shaws' cottage also led to the Rankins'.

As they approached Murkgill the house looked innocent enough but the barn had a sinister air, at least to Pharaoh's eyes. He was unmoved by the pit bull's death but the circumstances that preceded it he found acutely disturbing. He stopped in the yard and stared at the big double doors, at the gap between them, and the ringbolt set in the wall. Harker watched him unhappily.

Shaw was stringing wire between the fenceposts at the back of the cottage. "We've found the dog," Harker said. "And I'm afraid we've found young Paul too."

Shaw glanced from one to the other. "'Afraid'," he repeated. "Something happened to him?"

"He's dead."

"Jesus!" He breathed it softly. "He ran out of road?"

Harker explained. Shaw kept his eyes on him until he came to the part where Pharaoh had moved up beside him in the bottom of the crack and felt for the pulse in the neck to see if there was any sign

288

of life. Shaw's eyes moved to Pharaoh, inquiring.

"The dog went for the throat," Pharaoh said. "There's not much of the head left."

"Anyway," Harker said quickly, "the police came, we got him up, and that's that. The reason we thought you should know, and as soon as possible, is that when Rowland told Tilly, her first reaction concerned the dog. She was shocked of course. She thinks you killed it and threw it down the sinkhole."

Shaw shook his head in bewilderment. "I thought you said the dog was alive when you got there."

"Oh yes, definitely; it screamed its head off between the first and second shots."

"The point is," Pharaoh said, "Rowland tried to spare Tilly the worst, so he said the dog fell in and was killed, and Paul fell climbing down to it. I suppose he implied it was a terrific drop, like falling down a precipice. If Rowland could retract and admit we saw the dog alive it would save you embarrassment but at the expense of letting the Rankins know that Paul was savaged by his own dog — and it was bloody hungry."

"It's not important." Shaw was dismissive. He added hastily: "As it affects me, I mean. Come inside and have a beer; you'll be dry after all the work you've been doing. Sue's shopping in Carlisle with her mother. She'll be delighted to hear about the dog. Relieved might be a more tactful way of putting it." He paused, evidently considering her reaction to Paul's death. "I shall tell her the same version Rowland gave Tilly," he added. "Maybe she'll learn the truth later on but it won't matter so much then."

He was leading the way into the cottage. Pharaoh, glancing at his filthy shirt, shrugged and followed. After all, Susan wouldn't be there.

They sat in the kitchen and drank beer. Shaw seemed at peace with himself, exuding sweat and satisfaction. Harker looked out of the window at the bulk of the barn across the yard. It was very quiet. Pharaoh asked politely: "When do you start your new job?"

Shaw's eyes lit up. "Not for a few weeks. We're having a holiday, Sue and me. We're going to tour the Continent."

"Good." Harker's tone was flat. "But not in the Datsun."

"That heap! It's still stalling. I siphoned off the petrol and refilled the tank too. The thing's only good for the scrapheap. We'll buy a Renault in France." The others made no comment. "Liberia pays well," he added.

"What are you going to do there?" Pharaoh asked. "In Liberia?"

"They say it's training but that's just a formula; everyone uses it. There are nationalist organisations everywhere; training usually means that once you get out there you're on a war footing, putting down insurgents."

"It doesn't bother you?" Harker asked. "Killing for pay."

"You were in the RAF!" Shaw was amazed.

"Apart from the fact that we weren't combat troops — " Harker began hotly, then saw that Shaw was looking at Pharaoh, who said: "Tradition has it that conventional forces fight out of patriotism."

Shaw ignored that. "I do what I'm good

at," he said. He looked round the spartan room. "The money isn't unimportant; Sue wants a bathroom, we need a new car. Wouldn't either of you take a better-paid job to support your wife? Look" — he knew they were unconvinced — "if I didn't do it my employers would find someone else, someone who would most likely make a balls-up of every operation. Western mercenaries are efficient."

"Tools for the job," Harker said.

"What's wrong with that? You've never been in a civil war in a Third World country. If you think the régimes employing mercenaries are oppressive you've got no idea what the situation is like when rebels start a war. And it's not the guys at the top who suffer but the people: peasants, kids, women, old folk. It's scorched earth, intimidation, whole villages set on fire — people roasted inside their huts — just because one guy protested when his kid was raped. That's civil war." The tone was cool but the eyes glittered. "If mercenaries shore up a régime that stops civil war, they can't be all bad."

"You make a convincing case," Pharaoh said.

"Thanks." Shaw looked surprised. His eyes rested on Harker who said heavily: "I can't argue with it."

"Well, at least you're honest. Most people continue to argue and won't listen to the other side. They don't *hear* what we're saying." He grinned. "When you think of all the things you haven't said, come back and discuss them over another beer."

Thus dismissed, they walked back through the woods. "He was convincing," Pharaoh said.

"He's still a paid killer. Which is why Tilly maintains that he killed the pit bull. He didn't, but he's suspect because of his trade."

"The classic scapegoat. When you think about it I suppose a mercenary army is no worse than secret police, or even an open police force."

"Oh, come on, Jack! Police represent law and order, not repression."

"They support the establishment."

"They're impartial."

"That's the theory."

They came to the place where Pharaoh had left the rope, which was attracting flies. "Put it in the beck," Harker said and, seeing the other's expression, "There are dead sheep in all the becks; that extra bit of pollution won't hurt."

★ ★ ★

It was late in the afternoon when George Rankin came to Fox Yards. They were not surprised to see him. There had been no mention of the accident on the one o'clock news; a major earthquake in Iran had crowded out the death of a farm boy in Cumbria. Now, at Fox Yards, standing in the garden, refusing to sit down, refusing a drink, he appeared bewildered. They had, of course, offered their condolences, which seemed to surprise him, as did Harker's inquiry after Tilly's health.

"She's all right," he said grudgingly, and then: "What happened up there?"

"He fell down the shaft," Harker said slowly. "Haven't you seen Mr Fawcett?"

"I heard what everybody's got to say — no, not *everyone* — " His eyes narrowed, the lips thinned and he swallowed. "Now, you tell me."

"He must have been climbing down to the dog . . . " They waited for the question: how did he know the dog was there? It didn't come. "He must have slipped," Harker went on. "And he fell."

"What were — " He stopped as a thought occurred to him. They saw fear replace hostility and it shook them. Belligerence they could understand: the need to blame someone, anyone, for his son's death. But fear was out of context; Paul could get into no more trouble.

"What's on your mind?" Pharaoh asked, then frowned, but the lack of tact didn't seem to bother Rankin. At least, he looked no more frightened than before the question. He licked his lips. "There was no reason — " he started, and stopped again. After a pause he went on savagely: "He never meant no harm, he were going to get rid of the dog; I'd told him to: the dog had to go, I said. His mother wouldn't let it alone; she backed me up. That dog, it were all on account of that dog; he shouldn't never have brought it home. He shoulda buckled the collar tighter. He were only teasing!" He looked from one to the other, pleading with them to make sense of this rambling discourse.

"He was fond of the dog," Harker said cautiously.

"He didn't deserve it; he were only teasing."

"Who was he teasing?" Pharaoh asked.

Rankin turned sideways and hunched his shoulders. He licked his lips and his eyes wandered. He looked very much like the pit bull in a corner, waiting for the whip. It was curious that they should think this because neither of them had seen the dog beaten. Pharaoh frowned in distaste. "Who do you hold responsible?" he asked and then, getting no response: "Who's to blame?"

Harker looked deeply troubled. Rankin said: "I gotta be getting back; she's on her own." He moved away but at the gate he turned and Pharaoh heard Harker draw in his breath. Rankin's face was contorted with rage. "I'm not blaming anyone — yet," he said, "but I got two guns: one for me an' one for 'er." His head jutted at them like a snake striking. "You make sure and see they all knows that. We got weapons, see; we can take care of ourselves."

His footsteps receded. "What the hell!" Harker gasped.

"It's shock. Like Tilly saying Shaw threw the dog down the sinkhole, now George is saying Paul didn't fall, he was pushed. If the dog was dead and couldn't bark there was no way Paul could know it was in the sinkhole. You couldn't see anything in the bottom of those shafts, just a glint of wet rock. George knows that; he probably throws his dead sheep down those holes." He grinned. "Rowland was right; he shouldn't have tried to spare Tilly's feelings. Now, if he retracts, George will think it's because he's trying to protect someone. However, it'll blow over."

"Suppose he goes gunning for this 'someone'?"

"He won't do that; he's more frightened than angry."

"He's both. That's when weak people are dangerous. And he's not frightened; he's terrified."

13

PHAROAH woke suddenly, without any transition between sleep and full alertness. He looked at his watch and was surprised to find that it was only six-thirty. The sun was showing through the tops of the trees across the lane but this was a weaker sun than in past days and the morning carried a different atmosphere. He got out of bed and stood at the window.

The clouds were quite low, at about two thousand feet, he calculated, and they were massed at the head of the dale and moving northeast. There was nothing of June about the day. The wind had backed and the air was cool: a reminder that autumn would come again. Pharaoh thought of winter here: of deep snow and stultifying cold and the dead quiet nights. And he wondered how long it would be before he lost this feeling of delight in the prospect of danger. He dressed and went downstairs to make coffee.

Harker got up half an hour later but they had scarcely time to remark on the change in the weather when Susan arrived, breathless and excited, and having no regard for conventional visiting times. It occurred to Pharaoh that she was aware that Harker was an early riser and was accustomed to coming across at seven in the morning.

"I left Marty asleep," she told them, accepting a mug of coffee. "You'll never guess what he did last night: he locked the door! I didn't know till I got up. We were in Carlisle, Mum and me, and we didn't come back till late. He told me everything and he said I was to keep out of the way of the Rankins because they were hysterical and blaming him. I didn't take any notice then, not till I found the door locked this morning." She laughed and grimaced. "I shouldn't laugh, it's ghastly; Paul, I mean, not the dog, but I'm not *sorry* about Paul. Are you? He was a villain, wasn't he?"

Harker said: "Paul and the pit bull were a lethal combination."

"That's what I said all the time, so I don't think it's wrong to be glad the combination doesn't exist any more. And if Paul was alive he would only get another vicious dog. Well, he can't now," she ended smugly.

"But it's going to take a little while for the Rankins to get over the shock," Harker told her. "Martin's right; you should keep out of their way."

"How did they get hold of this crazy theory that Marty's responsible for what happened? What they're saying is that he pushed Paul, isn't it?"

"Didn't Martin tell you about the dog?"

"Of course. The dog was in the hole too."

"I mean, that it was alive when we found it."

"No, it couldn't have been. What's that got to do with anything?"

"Damn!" Harker turned to Pharaoh. "This has to stop; someone's got to tell the Rankins the truth." He turned back to Susan who was gaping at him. "Look, love, the dog was alive when we got there . . . " He tried to spare her the worst horror but there was no way he could do that once he'd convinced her that the dog was alive after Paul's death. She was aghast.

"The dog killed him?"

"I'm afraid so."

"And then — then it would have — Clem!" It was a whisper.

"Not until after Paul was dead," Pharaoh said firmly, wondering if it were true.

"Oh, my God!" She added: "So Tilly thinks the dog was already dead when Paul fell in, because Rowland told her so. And that would be what she wants to believe — is that right?"

"George doesn't believe it," Pharaoh said. "He guesses that we found the dog alive but thinks Rowland says it was dead from some ulterior motive. He'd never credit Rowland with trying to spare the family's feelings."

"Well, that's all right. All Rowland has to do is tell George he shot the dog himself, and he didn't tell them the truth yesterday because he wanted to give them time to get over the shock, to break it to them gradually."

"Sounds a bit weak," Harker said.

"But it's the truth! I'm going to go

and see Rowland now. He can't do this to Marty. Rowland's landed him right in the soup."

"Hang on, have some breakfast. We haven't eaten yet and we'll go up with you." As she hesitated he said persuasively: "The Fawcetts are old, Sue; we've got to consider everybody."

* * *

They heard Tilly as soon as they came up the steps of the Hall, her voice shrilling from the back quarters. "He's feared, he's gotta carry a gun for his own protection — " Then there was a murmur so soft it was almost inaudible.

Pharaoh pushed the others into the drawing room. "I'll go," he whispered. "I'm neutral; she's not going to be bothered by me."

"I don't know — " Harker looked worried.

"Leave the door ajar; you can hear what's going on."

Susan gave him a grim smile. "I hope you can look after yourself; if you want help, give a shout."

He walked down the passage to the kitchen. Tilly and Phoebe were on their feet, facing each other across the table; Beth Potter was doing the washing-up at the sink. At his entrance Phoebe regarded him with calculation, as if wondering whether his presence would be a help or a hindrance. Tilly was disconcerted by the interruption while Beth, alerted by the silence, turned and considered him thoughtfully. Phoebe asked him to sit down and drew out a chair for herself. "Sit down, Tilly," she said firmly, and Tilly did so. Beth filled the kettle.

"We need to clear the air," Pharaoh said. "Where's Mr Fawcett?"

"With Rankin," Phoebe told him, and then, calmly: "Tilly says Martin Shaw killed Paul and is going to kill them too: George and herself. Mr Fawcett has gone to talk to George while we're listening to what Tilly's got to say."

"I see. And do you all know about the dog?"

"We know everything." Phoebe remained cool. "Tilly finds it difficult to believe."

"Because it's not true!" Tilly shouted. "How could dog be alive? He could never get near t'dog. He had to kill it to get it up to Scar."

"Dog slipped its collar," Beth Potter said, her voice as gruff as a man's.

"You know it did, Mrs Rankin," Pharaoh said quietly. "It was alive when we found it. We heard it yelping. Mr Fawcett had to fire both barrels."

"I don't believe you."

"Why should Mr Fawcett lie?"

"Because — " Tilly flicked a glance at Phoebe.

Beth said with contempt: "He don't have to lie just to get you out. Bad farmers can be evicted without giving no reason."

"That'll do, Beth." Phoebe was sharp, but she repeated part of it gently. "Mr Fawcett doesn't have to lie, Tilly; he's too old to bother."

"Why should Shaw want to harm you?" Pharaoh asked.

Tilly brightened. "Because we knows the truth!"

"And what's that?"

"Why, he murdered our lad, of course!"

Beth sighed audibly and slammed the

304

lid on the tea caddy. Pharaoh asked patiently: "Why did he kill Paul?"

"Because Paul knew he killed dog, that's why."

Phoebe moved as if to cover her face with her hands: a gesture of despair.

"What are you going to do about it?" Pharaoh asked calmly.

Tilly was astonished. "He's got to be arrested and tried for murder. And then he should be hung. If they" — she jerked her head at Phoebe — "if she don't tell police then I'm going to. I've give 'er the chance. She don't believe me, but we can prove it. He's a killer, that Shaw."

"How do you prove it?" Pharaoh asked.

"He threatened us with a knife. He wears it strapped to his leg if he ain't thrown it away. He's trained to kill. George says he killed men in Africa; it's his job. He's one of them mercenaries; there's your proof!"

She stood up but before she could reach the door Pharaoh spoke. "Mrs Rankin." She stopped. "There has to be an inquest," he told her, "and there will be medical evidence that the dog died of gunshot wounds."

"So?"

"That's proof Mr Fawcett shot the animal."

"No, it's not. It's proof dog were shot, not who by or when."

Pharaoh restrained a sigh. "There's further proof," he said quietly. "The dog bit Paul. The doctor will say so at the inquest."

"He's dead, isn't he?" Tilly was beyond reason which, thought Pharaoh, was just as well, considering the extent of the 'bites'. "Of course there'll be marks," she shouted. "Always is, when a child's murdered, in't there? You're all in it together." She blundered out of the kitchen, her footsteps receding along the passage and down the steps.

"You can't reason with that one," Beth said. "You never could. Best thing you can hope for is that they'll leave the dale; if they was to stay, next thing you know, that George Rankin'll be buying some other vicious brute, one of them Rottweilers likely, to protect himself . . ." She faltered as Susan and Harker appeared in the doorway. "She never was what you'd call normal," she ended defiantly.

"She's mad," Susan said. "We heard all of it; we came along the passage and listened from the cupboard under the stairs. Can she do any harm?" She addressed this to Harker.

"I shouldn't think so." But he looked troubled.

"It will sort itself out at the inquest," Pharaoh said. "They'll have to accept the truth then." No one said anything. "She could be blocking it out," he added.

"It's possible," Phoebe agreed. "It may sink in slowly as the shock wears off. Meanwhile we should watch our backs."

They stared at her in astonishment. Harker dropped into a chair as if exhausted. "We came up to persuade Rowland to tell the truth," he told her, "but he was ahead of us, and they don't believe it. There's nothing else we can do; the trouble is, the Rankins are so insensitive that they can't conceive of anyone trying to be kind to them."

"That sort don't know what kindness is," Beth threw out.

Phoebe smiled wanly. "We'll survive.

Mr Fawcett may be able to persuade Rankin not to go about armed but you, my dear" — to Susan — "perhaps you and Martin should go and stay at Grammery until this has blown over."

Susan raised her eyebrows. "I'd go but Marty won't, and I can't leave him."

"It's less than a mile," Harker protested.

"What difference does it make? If George comes gunning for us, he can drive a mile, can't he?"

"He's not after you — "

"I'm Marty's wife — "

"No!" Phoebe raised her voice. "You're not thinking straight, either of you. We're all suffering from delayed shock. It's only a few days that we have to be careful; the Rankins will accept the results of the inquest — "

"That's exactly what I told Rankin." Rowland was standing in the doorway looking tired and unkempt. Everyone was fascinated by the two shotguns he was carrying. "I saw Tilly coming; dodged behind a tree," he said. "Didn't want her to see these." He placed them in a corner. "He can have them back after the inquest."

"How did you persuade him to give them up?" Harker asked.

"I told him to. This is my land and he's my tenant." He stopped there; he'd explained everything. The younger people were speechless.

"Good," Phoebe said. "So you can go home — and anywhere else — without anxiety." She smiled kindly at Susan who blinked and started to get up from the table. "I didn't mean you should go now," Phoebe added gently.

"I have to. I must go and tell Marty that we're safe." She smiled weakly, trying to imply that being unsafe was no more than a figment of people's imagination. "I left him asleep, you see, and the door unlocked. He'll be wondering where on earth I am."

"I expect he locked the door every night since he came home," Rowland said when she'd gone. "He'd be a fool not to with young Paul around. You know" — he sat down and nodded absently as Beth put a mug of tea in front of him — "this situation started before the accident. The Rankins hated Shaw; that's why they think he had a hand in Paul's death."

"We all knew that," Beth said. "There was the money the lad stole from the cottage *and* out of Mrs Winter's car, and Shaw knocking t'lad down; it's been nothing but name-calling and nasty jokes like, and threats, these past two weeks. Why, it goes right back to bullocks in Susan's garden."

"What's that?" Rowland snapped, but Beth turned to the sink, her solid shoulders rigid with defiance.

"It was way back," Harker told him. "Paul put some bullocks in Sue's garden." He couldn't keep himself from smiling. "We didn't tell you; we were trying to spare your feelings."

Phoebe gave him a fond look but Rowland showed a flash of anger. It passed. "No good now," he muttered, shaking his head. "He was a bad lot; when you listen to what *isn't* said, you can see how he retaliated for every action, even every word, that he thought was an insult or a slur."

"He always had to go one better," Harker agreed, but Pharaoh asked: "Were you thinking of something in particular?"

"Not really, not specific." They waited. "He spied on her," he added, embarrassed, as if he'd been guilty of bad manners himself. "I gathered as much from Rankin."

"I'm not surprised," Pharaoh said. "He could enter the barn from one side and watch the cottage through a crack in the doors facing Susan's place."

"What!" Harker glared at him. "Why didn't you tell me this?"

"Hindsight." Pharaoh was equable. "He might have been no more than a Peeping Tom. Watching her, or them, through the crack is worrying only in retrospect."

"Not to say sinister," Rowland put in quickly. "But Rankin is insinuating — no, he's accusing Shaw of something underhand; he says Shaw never went to London to sign on for that job, where was it: Namibia?"

"Liberia," Pharaoh supplied. "Where does Rankin say he was?"

"Actually," Rowland murmured, aware of his wife's eyes on him, "he made it clear that he was only repeating what Paul said: that Shaw didn't go to London, the mileage was wrong."

"That's Martin's business," Phoebe said firmly. "Whether or not he went to London doesn't concern us."

"Of course not." Rowland was indignant. "It was an example of Paul's spying, that's all: checking on the mileage Shaw had done. When I pointed out that Paul must have known what the mileage was before Shaw went away, Rankin said of course he knew; he was trying to get his father to buy the van. He thought Susan would sell it cheaply when it was off the road. Paul discovered the mileage then. Rankin says Shaw's got a woman in Blackpool." He quailed as Phoebe drew in her breath and added quickly: "I don't believe that; I'm just telling you what he said."

"None of this has anything to do with us, nor with the other unpleasant business," Phoebe said with finality and, reverting to the gracious hostess, "You'll stay for lunch, of course."

Harker declined for both of them, citing pressing work on a hen-house. Walking down the drive Pharaoh asked: "D'you put any significance on that:

Shaw not going to London?"

"God, no! Perhaps he didn't, but so what? He could have a number of irons in the fire that he doesn't want Sue to know about — or, more likely, her mother. He's on his best behaviour now."

"He is?"

"Well, he seems to be on better terms with Esme. At least, she no longer holds him responsible for the theft of that two hundred pounds."

★ ★ ★

Over lunch Harker reverted to the subject of the hen-house. He was going to buy some laying pullets when he had made the shed secure against foxes so he proposed to get on with that this afternoon if Pharaoh could amuse himself. Pharaoh said immediately that he would lend a hand with the hen-house. Not at all, Harker said, he should go for a walk; there was only one set of tools and no one should spend the afternoon handing nails.

Half an hour later he was in the woods

beyond the Hall. A bird was singing in a huge oak, thrush or blackbird, he couldn't tell; he would have to ask Harker. Suddenly Pharoah became aware of another sound, increasing in such a fierce crescendo that his immediate reaction was that a low-flying aircraft was about to crash. He halted, waiting for the impact, then he saw it through the tops of the trees: a glitter of sunshine on paint, but it went on and on like a snake in the sky. A train was crossing the viaduct. Trembling, trying to find it amusing, he wondered why more people didn't have heart attacks.

He came to the tall and beautiful arches and admired the masonry: exquisitely shaped blocks of rosy stone. Only one span was used by the path, the rest of the viaduct towered above the woods on the right, and the field called Killing Close to the left. A runnel of water came down from the old quarries — that took another span — but there was a little drainage on the track and in the mud was the imprint of the Honda's tyres. There was no other mark; above the viaduct the terrain was impassable for a Land Rover. Pharaoh would have thought it too steep for a farm bike as well, but as he emerged from the shadow of the span he saw that the eroded track going off to the left, down the dale, might be negotiated by a bold rider.

He stopped at the fork and tried to visualise the map. Weeping Klints was a few miles to the north and when they had been searching for the pit bull two days ago they had gone north from Weeping Klints on a track which must be the continuation of this path. The prints in the mud under the viaduct had been fairly fresh so they could have been made when Paul was searching for the dog. It was odd, thought Pharaoh, that the pit bull should have been seen at Weeping Klints and found some five miles distant, but then it occurred to him that, as there are numerous sightings of suspected criminals in various parts of the country, the same could apply to wanted dogs. Someone had suggested that the person who reported a pit bull among sheep could have seen a fox; he thought it more likely that the animal involved was something like a chocolate Labrador.

Curious, though, that so far no one had found any savaged sheep.

He started the ascent of the escarpment, walking slowly but steadily up the long zig-zags of the sledge road. When he reached the quarries he went into the chasm where he had found the imprint of a boot. That was only a week ago; it seemed like months. The mark had gone now, covered by a profusion of prints made by small cloven hoofs. Nowhere could he see a paw mark.

He found the remains of the cabin where he had smelled bacon, where the small rodent had removed the piece of rind. It smelled of nothing today, and there was no sign that anyone had been there since he'd first come this way.

He climbed past the quarries, having no trouble negotiating the steep slope below the lip of the Scar — ascent was always easier than descent — and came to the tarn which was about a quarter of a mile from the quarries. A sandpiper got up on his approach and fled, shrilling in alarm. He walked round the pool. The only tracks were those made by birds and sheep.

As usual the limestone pavement was alive with birds. Young grouse flew for short distances and then crashed in crevices. He wondered how they would get out again — some of these cracks were a foot deep — but knew it was wiser to leave them to cope rather than retrieve them himself when they would only take off for a few yards and crash-land again. Perhaps he was a substitute for a natural predator; the strongest fledglings would climb out of the cracks, beating their wings, the weakest starve to death in the bottom. What preyed on grouse? Weasels, falcons, foxes? What predators were there on the moor? He was amazed at his own ignorance; for twenty years he'd looked on high places as his own peculiar environment, and yet he didn't know what preyed on grouse.

He came to the sinkholes and sat on the turf above the crucial one, the one where Paul and the dog had died. If this had been a mountain accident — the place where a climber had fallen or a lost walker been found — the family might erect a cairn to hold a plaque: 'In memory of X who fell . . . or died . . . ' What could a plaque say here? 'In memory of Paul Rankin who was eaten by his dog'?

A blowfly buzzed about his head. He got up stiffly and moved along the fault to the depression where the Honda had been parked. It was gone now, presumably taken down by Rankin. He turned and retraced his steps, frowning. Passing the sinkholes he took the path to Black Blote Fell.

The clouds had lifted during the day and visibility was superb. He saw the Lakeland mountains from the summit and appreciated them as background, nothing more. He went down, crossed the lime and stopped on the lip of the Scar to try to identify Fox Yards.

He could see the roofs of the Hall but the green slates of Harker's cottage merged with the foliage. He tried to work out where that roof should be. There was the main road, and a white truck going south, turning left on the Ewedale road. The second turn, the lane that led to Fox Yards and the Hall, was less than half a mile from the junction, and there the truck turned again and would have disappeared in the trees except that, knowing it was there, he could pick it out below the canopy. It stopped in full view. He was, in fact, looking straight down the lane and, over a mile away, he saw a figure cross to what must be Fox Yards' gate and — yes, there was the roof, quite plain when you knew where to look. The white vehicle was Harker's van; he had taken time off to go shopping.

The cottage was empty when he arrived. He took two cans of beer from the refrigerator and went round the back to find Harker in the paddock which he called his orchard. The hen-house stood under a cherry tree. He was screwing a hinge on the lid of the nesting box.

"You should have asked me to do the shopping," Pharaoh said, proffering a can.

"Thanks. You can shop tomorrow if you like. I must finish this."

"But you shopped today!"

"I didn't."

"I saw you."

"Where?"

Pharaoh blinked, stared, looked away. "I made a mistake," he said. "I thought

319

I saw you come home in the van." He regarded his beer but forbore to say that it hadn't been in the refrigerator this morning.

"I went out for beer," Harker explained. "I thought you were protesting about doing the shopping tomorrow. Sorry, we got our wires crossed. Yes, I remembered suddenly that we were low on beer and I knew you'd be gasping for it after a good walk. I nipped in to Kirkby. No time to shop properly. Anyway, the Safeway's in Penrith; that's the place to go for good food. I thought you might like to do that tomorrow at your leisure."

"That's all right. Of course I will. Can I hold that lid for you?"

Harker was a slow and meticulous worker, at least on the hen-house which seemed little different from how it had looked yesterday. But as the man himself said, it was only a matter of eggs and one day more or less didn't make much difference. He seemed to have a fluctuating relationship with this hen-house: casual one moment, panicking the next, because he might not get it fox-proof in time for the pullets and yet, so far as Pharaoh knew, he hadn't even ordered the pullets. He wondered if the hen-house represented something else for Harker, more than just a place to keep a few birds.

★ ★ ★

That afternoon the Rankins went to Kirkby Oswald and presented themselves at the police station with two demands: that the police protect them against Shaw, and that they should be allowed to see the body, in that order. There was no possibility of the latter demand being met but the local inspector thought he could cushion his refusal by attending to the first. He assured them that a police car would be sent to Murkgill 'to sort things out'.

"We'll sort things out when I've seen my lad," Tilly said. "Where is he?"

On being told that the body would be released for burial she pointed out that her question hadn't been answered, and that if her demand to see her son wasn't met she would go to her solicitor and that right now, this minute.

"Weir's a good man — the inspector," Rowland told Pharaoh and Harker. He had called at Fox Yards that evening as he was ostensibly taking the Jack Russell for its walk. Since the pit bull's death the little terrier had its freedom again, so it was being used as an excuse. It looked as if Rowland was in need of masculine company.

"Weir's a responsible feller," he went on. "He could have off-loaded his dilemma, as it were: let them go to a solicitor and when the chap came back to him, briefed him and let *him* explain to the Rankins why they couldn't see their son. Of course they have a legal right, but what man with any vestige of feeling is going to let a mother see a son's remains in that state? Rankin was hopeless; Weir took one look at him and saw he'd had the same thought and was signalling frantically behind Tilly's back. No way would Rankin view the body. He guesses what state it's in but evidently Tilly still won't believe it — " He lifted a hand as Pharaoh went to interrupt. "I know what you're going to say, and he did have the post-mortem report." Pharaoh subsided. "Weir tried everything he could to make Tilly understand although there wasn't all that much he could do: delicate hints, stronger ones. He told me on the phone that this was one case where he couldn't assure the parents that their boy hadn't suffered. The appearances are all to the contrary, backed up, of course, by the post-mortem report. D'you know, he didn't even break a leg, falling down. He was fit enough to put up a fight; there's dog hairs and tissue under his fingernails — those that are left. Perhaps he climbed down partway, then jumped, couldn't get back, dog attacked. Stupid lad! That's by the by; we're talking about Tilly. Finally Weir saw that she had to be told the truth. Someone had to do it; a solicitor or the police. He tried to paraphrase the pathologist's report but it was difficult and he virtually read from it, and then waited for her to ask the obvious questions, like the meaning of trachea and aorta."

"Damage to them?" Pharaoh commented.

"That, of course. You were there, my boy. But they also did a post-mortem on the dog. Not to discover how it died so much — we all know that — but what happened prior to death."

"We know that too," Harker said.

"They need medical evidence, for the inquest. The dog's stomach contained part of the trachea and aorta, along with other bits of organs: lungs, brain tissue and so on, and twenty-seven pieces of human bone."

"It had immensely powerful jaws." Harker looked at Rowland with empty eyes, perhaps visualising what the others would prefer not to contemplate. "Was Tilly convinced?" he asked.

"I suppose so. They left. And they didn't renew the request for police protection then."

"Have they done so since?"

"That I wouldn't know. Weir would only send a patrol car anyway. But if Tilly accepts the results of the post-mortem then she has to accept that the dog, and then the boy, fell into the sinkhole, and that the dog killed the boy. No one killed the dog and put its body down there any more than the boy died by human agency."

"An odd way to put it," Pharaoh said.

"You can't say 'any more than the boy was murdered' because he *was* murdered, but by a dog."

"I'm not sure that — "

Harker interrupted harshly: "Is that the pathologist's findings: that Paul was killed by the dog?"

Rowland stared at him. "What else, Clem? It was an *accident*." He broke off and for a moment they regarded each other blankly. It was Harker who looked away. He got up and went to the kitchen and they heard him filling the kettle. He came back slowly. "The horror of it throws you off balance," he confessed. "Of course it was an accident; we're infected with Tilly's hysteria."

"The papers are going to have a field day with this," Rowland said. "Not a bad thing on the whole — except that someone had to die," he added quickly. "It's ammunition for the supporters of a law to register dogs. I wish they would ban these dangerous brutes; you wouldn't be allowed to keep a leopard on a collar and chain in your backyard and yet this incident is overwhelming proof that dogs can be as vicious as wild beasts."

"As vicious as people," Harker murmured, but Rowland caught it.

"Quite," he snapped. "The owners are equally at fault."

But Pharaoh glanced at his friend's veiled eyes and thought that this had not been what he meant.

14

PHAROAH was astonished at the length of the shopping list. "Do you hate shopping?" Harker asked. "Look, I'll leave the hen-house and come with you — "

"It doesn't need two people. It's just that I thought you lived more simply than this."

"I do usually. There's a lot of booze and party grub. I thought that if we were discreet we might have people in for drinks. It mustn't look as if we're celebrating; that would be crude, but we are free of danger and — "

"And?"

"Of an antisocial element? The threat's gone, Jack! There's a tremendous feeling of relief." Pharaoh was staring at him. "Susan needs taking out of herself," Harker protested. "And her mother isn't getting any social life. She's on holiday, for Heaven's sake! And Juno loves a party."

"Clem! You don't have to justify having people in for drinks."

"I'm not. I wasn't. Yes, I am; I feel guilty about socialising when the boy's not yet buried."

"You think we should pull the curtains, wear black armbands perhaps?"

Harker flushed. "Sue and Shaw are off to the Continent next week, and Esme will be going home — "

"All right, all right! I'm not arguing. I'll buy the stuff."

"You can find nearly everything at Safeway." Harker was suddenly eager. "There's plenty of parking; I'll draw a plan."

Pharaoh was looking at the list. "Safeway sell nails and screws?"

"No, those you get in town . . . "

Pharaoh took his swimming shorts. Since there was no way he could complete the shopping in a morning and get back for a walk he would take his exercise in the town's pool. Harker recommended it. The day had to be organised. Wednesday was early-closing day and what was left of the morning by the time he got there had to be spent buying items in town before the shops closed. Pharaoh had the feeling, as he'd had yesterday, that he was being hustled out of the way. Harker was up to something. Meeting someone? He hoped that it had nothing to do with Susan; surely he wasn't so besotted with the girl that he couldn't wait until Shaw had gone back to Africa. Curious, thought Pharaoh, glancing in his mirror and braking to give a baby rabbit time to find a hole in the hedge: he hadn't known that there were mercenaries in Liberia; Chad, perhaps, Namibia. Maybe Paul had been right when he said Shaw was engaged in something underhand.

Penrith was hot and there were fumes in the narrow streets; for all that, he liked the town and, with Harker's directions and plan, he wasn't subjected to the nightmare of trying to find places to park. Moreover he'd been told exactly where to shop, and although the stores were small and specialised, he could take delight in personal service even when it was slow. However, by the time the shops closed he was tired, and the thought of swimming daunted him. He recovered somewhat by drinking coffee, and then he ploughed up and down the pool until overcome by boredom. He emerged, ate a sandwich in the car park and drove to the supermarket. Finally there was the library but here Harker had erred; on Wednesday afternoons it was closed.

It was four-thirty by the time he returned to Fox Yards, and his leg was aching. The sound of hammering reached him as soon as he switched off the engine but in a few moments Harker came round the side of the cottage to help with the unloading, and to organise space in the refrigerator. A lot of room was taken up by a dressed fowl, swathed in bacon rashers. "It's for tonight," Harker said proudly, switching on the oven.

"You don't get chicken from the supermarket?"

"Never; I always have free-range birds, and eggs. Chicken come from Weepings Klints, and we'll have eggs from there until my pullets start laying. The Klints hens are fed properly. Incidentally, we're having supper early because the others are coming over for the evening."

"You're having a party tonight? You

sprang that on me; I'm worn out."

"It's only drinks. Go and soak that leg in the bath. The water's hot. Then come down and have a Scotch. I'll finish putting this stuff away."

"I'll take the Scotch up with me. Did anything happen today?"

"What sort — ? Oh, you mean concerning the — incident, as Rowland calls it. The Press were around, but they weren't any trouble. They're far more interested in the details of how Paul died than how the body was recovered. Like you used to say in the old days: the circumstances leading up to the accident were far more absorbing than the rescue. You were well out of it today; Shaw too. He just disappeared, is still disappeared for all I know. A reporter came here but I was hard at it in the hen-house and it was easy to play the dumb yokel." He grinned. "I told them about finding the body and paraphrased the post-mortem report. They found me revolting so they won't come back in a hurry."

Susan arrived before they had finished supper and promptly finished off their demi-Camembert. "Fancy cheeses last

331

one day with us," she explained to Pharaoh. "So a day after I've shopped I have to arrive at other people's tables in time for the cheese course."

"I'm sorry, I should have come over and asked if I could bring you anything from town."

"Hell, we've got transport!" It was an odd flash of temper and she regretted it immediately, throwing a glance of contrition, not at Pharaoh but at Harker. "Not back yet?" he asked carelessly, and she shook her head. Pharaoh was absorbed in the colour of his claret. He knew they were exchanging some kind of message.

"Goodness knows where Marty got to," Susan announced in a high artificial voice. "I don't suppose you saw him on the road?"

"No," Pharaoh said, "but I wasn't looking for him."

"He'll be back." Harker was avuncular. "He's a loner; he could have gone to the Lakes, Cross Fell, anywhere." A car drew up outside. "My God!" he gasped. "That's the others. Go and meet them, Jack; keep them in the garden, serve drinks. Sue, help me clear away."

Pharaoh went out to welcome Esme, Juno and Lanty, to seat them in the garden, apologising for the time it was taking to clear the living room, taking their orders. He was putting himself out for them, on his best behaviour: allowing his pleasure to show in the women's appearance, talking man-to-man with Lanty. They had dressed for the occasion in casual clothes, with only a touch of jewelry on the women, and Esme apparently careful not to upstage Juno.

Pharaoh brought the drinks and sat on the log. He was prepared to deputise for the host and make small talk but the women had questions for him. Had he encountered the Press? No. What did the papers have to say? No one took a daily paper at Clouds, except Rowland who had *The Times* delivered with the mail, but no one had had the temerity to call him and ask. The earthquake in Iran was still monopolising the news but Pharaoh said that the *Guardian* had a couple of paragraphs without comment, just facts as they were known; he hadn't seen the tabloids. "They're probably more sensational," he said, "and they could give it even more exposure after the inquest, although they'll be circumspect about the injuries."

"But that's what they're interested in basically," Lanty observed.

"It's the most sensational aspect," his mother murmured.

"I don't think so." Lanty was puzzled. "There's no mystery about that: the dog attacked him. It was obvious to everyone that if the brute slipped its collar a second time it would kill sheep, at least. We were all afraid it would attack people — and then it did: slipped its collar, killed its owner."

"Paul thrashed the animal," Esme said. "Poetic justice, I call it."

Harker emerged from the cottage, responding to their greetings, glancing at their glasses. Susan appeared behind him. Esme looked past her daughter. "Where's Martin?"

"He'll be along." Susan was airy. "Can I get anyone a drink?" This was received in silence.

Esme threw a startled glance at their host who ignored the gaffe and said easily: "The living room is clear now, if you'd like to come inside. It's chilly this evening."

They trooped indoors, Esme going to her daughter's side, murmuring a question. "I don't know!" Susan exclaimed. "He's gone climbing. He'll be back." Esme stared at her.

Juno was saying: "You've had roast chicken. I can smell it. Who did you get it from, Clem?"

"Weeping Klints. It was very tasty. Lanty, beer or Scotch?" He moved around, replenishing glasses, settling people: "Not that chair, Esme; it's got a broken spring. If you insist, here, use this cushion . . ." When everyone was settled there was a brief lull broken by Lanty who said, as if there had been no break in the conversation: "The mystery is how he came to be there. Climbing down to that dog was like shutting yourself in a loose box with a mad bull. I don't believe — "

Susan interrupted, turning on him furiously: "Do we have to talk about that? This is a party, for God's sake! What's it matter whether — "

"Sue!" Harker was incisive, cutting through her protests. She stopped as if a hand had been placed over her mouth, and he seemed to slump a little. "Nothing to get bothered about," he said gently.

The others looked on in bewilderment, except for Esme whose face was alight with interest. She said slowly, feeling her way: "This is the first time we've all been together since it happened, sweetie; we're consumed with curiosity. You've probably discussed it *ad infinitum* but we don't know anything."

"You talk about nothing else." Susan was surly.

"We speculate, naturally, but we have no facts. We haven't seen Jack and Clem since before they found the body."

"So you want to hear all the repulsive details." There was a venomous edge to the girl's tone.

Pharaoh was intrigued by her mood; she appeared to be heading for a public scene. She was, he noticed, drinking whisky, and too quickly. Lanty seemed uneasy, a little frightened by her attitude; Juno was her usual serene self: smiling, attentive. Esme was obviously fascinated but Harker, perhaps because it was his party, was watchful, ready to intervene, even to stop Susan dead, as he had done already. Now Esme, after a pause and evidently thinking that Susan had calmed down, turned to Lanty and said firmly: "You don't believe Paul would have climbed down to the dog. In that case what do you think did happen, because he did go down, didn't he?"

"Not deliberately. I reckon he fell in."

"Oh, that's quite possible," Harker said quickly. "What with all those ferns and the nettles, he could easily have put his foot on what he thought was rock but was just space. He could have slipped; the lime is terribly slippery in the wet. And it was dark."

"It wasn't," Lanty contradicted. "It was daylight and it was dry. You were up on our roof when you heard the Honda go by."

"It was raining by then; we went on working in the wet. And it would have been pretty dim on top with the cloud down."

"And the dog would be barking like mad, confusing him," Esme said thoughtfully.

"I forgot to tell you," Pharaoh began, adding, as everyone turned their attention to him: "I was thinking about the Honda. There are fresh tracks under the viaduct, going towards Weeping Klints. It must be your constant repetition of Weeping Klints that put me in mind of it."

"What are you talking about?" Harker asked pleasantly.

"I think Paul went down the back way to Weeping Klints on the Honda but there's nothing odd about that; someone reported seeing a dog among the widow's sheep. Did she tell you anything, Clem, when you went for the chicken?"

"And eggs," Harker said absently. "I called there yesterday, on my way back from Kirkby. She didn't tell me anything we didn't know already. A man telephoned saying there was a dog among the sheep but there was no way it could have been the pit bull because none of her sheep have been injured, let alone killed."

"Who was the man who called?"

"She doesn't know. Just someone . . . " He trailed off, staring at Pharaoh.

"Yes. Exactly. How did he know who to call?"

"He'd assume those sheep belonged to Weeping Klints," Lanty said. "That would be obvious if they were in a meadow near the house."

Esme ignored him. "The name: that's it! How did he know her number? If he didn't know it already he had to find it in the directory, and for that he had to know her name; he had to know who farmed at Weeping Klints. So it was someone local. OK, we've worked that one out. So what? Another farmer telephoned and didn't give his name. Why is that extraordinary?"

"It wouldn't be," Pharaoh said, "except that the widow thought the caller was a tourist; a townie, she said, who'd thought a ewe on its back was a dead ewe." He leaned back in his chair as they mulled it over. His hip hurt, and the significance of that was that it hadn't hurt before, only the knee and his spine. In a panic he reached for his glass, saw it was empty and caught Harker's eye. His friend rose without haste and started a round of his guests. When he came to Pharaoh he took the empty glass and returned it with a good measure. "You swam too long," he said, and Pharaoh started to calm down. He was right of course, and the glow of alcohol smothered the pain. His face relaxed. He was smiling benignly when Martin Shaw appeared in the doorway and grinned back at him. Conversation stopped and people remembered their manners too late, staring before they broke into tardy greetings. Shaw apologised profusely.

"I had no idea you were having a party, not until I got home and found Sue's note."

"My fault entirely," Harker confessed. "It was short notice, but it's quite informal; those are always the best parties: the sudden impulses. What'll you have?"

"Been on the hill?" Pharaoh asked as Shaw sat down beside him.

"I was on Helvellyn: up Striding Edge, down Swirrel." He saw the other's surprise. "I felt like a fast run," he explained. "Climbing's too slow: I wanted to *move*. I'll have a rum and coke, please, Clem."

"You must have had some fun among all the ramblers on Striding Edge," Pharaoh remarked.

"I climbed round them. It was hairy sometimes; I was expecting one of them to knock me off. People are idiots."

Harker brought Shaw his drink.

"When do you leave?" Pharaoh asked.

Shaw had been intent on Susan who was sitting on the floor talking to Juno. The man turned slowly. "Leave for where?"

"That would be the next question. I asked when."

"Shortly." Shaw didn't take his eyes off Pharaoh. "We're touring; we'll probably end up in the Alps or the Pyrenees."

Harker pulled out a stool. "Did I hear the Pyrenees mentioned?" he asked with interest. They discussed Continental climbing until Lanty joined them. He hadn't climbed abroad and Harker brought him into the conversation by steering it towards British hills. Pharaoh beamed his appreciation of his friend's tact. He realised that Shaw was regarding him with a puzzled air. Shaw, he thought, wouldn't appreciate consideration for a youngster who had never climbed outside Britain. Esme's voice cut across his musings: "This is outrageous: all the men on one side of the room, the women on the other."

Harker disappeared. Esme took his place on the stool. Pharaoh stared at her necklace until she broke off from some exchange with Shaw and said meaningly: "They're Zuni fetishes, Jack; I bought it in New Mexico. People find the little animals fascinating."

"Stylised," he murmured, having difficulty with the sibilants. There was a swirl of movement and when he focused on her again she was beside him and Shaw was gone. "What happened?" came her voice. "How long have you been drinking?"

He hesitated, his mind a blank, except for the question. "You were in Penrith," she reminded him. "You were drinking at lunchtime?"

"Was I?"

"You drove home drunk: along the main road?"

"I never drink and drive. Can't afford to lose my mobility."

"So you started drinking when you came home, and then you had wine with your meal; Jack, lay off the whisky, you're going to make yourself ill."

"My hip hurts. Not now. It did."

"Oh, my dear! I'm such a bitch. I should have guessed something was wrong." He felt a cool hand on his. He heard Harker say something about swimming and a long day, and another voice — Susan's: "Librium?" "Not with alcohol," someone warned, and: "You've had quite enough yourself, sweetie."

★ ★ ★

His mouth was dry, his whole body dehydrated. His hip hurt abominably and there was a terrible emptiness, a profound silence encompassing his world. He was consumed by panic. There was no light and no sound. He waited for thought, not knowing what he was waiting for.

An owl called. Light began to show but only as an absence of pitch darkness, in the form of a rough square. There was a scent of lavender. He felt a chill and realised that he was lying on the floor. Full consciousness returned as panic receded. Now he could discern faint stars through the window. There was a cushion under his head, a blanket covering him, and he was lying on a foam mat. Harker, unable to get him to bed, had made him as comfortable as possible.

He crawled upstairs. Harker's door was open. He listened and heard the sound of breathing. He continued to his own room. He had trouble getting back to sleep again. He was appalled that he should have got drunk in company and wondered what he might have said or done before he collapsed. Then there was the pain in his hip, and that was frightening. He lay and fretted, drifting in and out of sleep until, shortly before the dawn, he was almost there. He heard the approach of the night express, heard the sound increase in volume, change note as it was muffled by the trees, waited for the train to break clear and roar across the viaduct — and knew nothing more. So it was not until the morning that he learned that the express didn't roar across the viaduct on this occasion because it was braking to a halt after hitting Shaw's van on the level crossing.

15

THE driver of the train saw the van but too late. The flashing warning lights were beamed away from the track, towards approaching motorists, and the big pole light that should have illuminated the crossing wasn't functioning. By the time the brakes were applied the train was still hurtling down the dale at sixty miles an hour. Fortunately the van was light and the train was not derailed.

There had been a person in the vehicle, perhaps more than one, it was impossible to tell at this stage. One registration plate had survived intact; it was found, brilliant in the light of the torches, propped like a horticultural label against a clump of yellow loosestrife. Within half an hour a patrol car was at Murkgill.

The Rankins seemed petrified with shock but they managed to direct the police to the cottage on the other side of the barn. The police knocked, then hammered on the door before opening it and shouting; "Anyone home?" Tilly had referred to 'them' at the cottage.

They were met with silence. "D'you think both of them were in the van?" the younger officer asked. "I thought it was just one, from what we could see." He shone his torch round the kitchen.

"Anyone home?" the older man repeated loudly, and they both heard a movement from upstairs. They braced themselves; it could be a dog. "It's the police! Can we have a word?"

There was the sound of bare feet padding over boards. At the top of the stairs, on the edge of their lights they saw the hem of a short nightgown and long legs. "Who's that?" Susan asked shakily.

"Police, ma'am," the older man said. "Would you put something on and come down?"

"Shine the torch on yourself."

He did so, then on his companion. She came slowly down the stairs holding the rail, pushed past them and switched on a light. She returned their careful survey.

"What happened?"

"Are you Mrs Shaw: Susan Shaw?"

"Jesus, yes. What *happened*?"

"Do you own a Datsun van . . . ?" He read the registration number from his notebook. He didn't need to do that but by pretending to consult his notebook he could avoid her eyes.

"It's my husband," she said flatly. "He's had an accident and you've come to tell me." She walked to the window. "The sun isn't up yet."

She knew. She knew why two of them came before sunrise. They watched her warily and, at a nod from the other, the younger man looked around for a kettle.

"Your husband isn't in the house, ma'am?"

"No. Isn't he — with the van?" There was no interest in her tone; she was already in shock, they thought. "Where did it happen?" she asked.

"On the level crossing. It was instantaneous."

"How could it be?"

"It was the night express." He moved close to her but she stood easily, relaxed. Too relaxed? In the background the other man was clumsily filling a kettle, loudly replacing the lid. The noise interested her a little. "The dog's gone," she said dreamily. "If it was barking I'd strangle it. Where are you going?"

"To ask the lady at the farm, Mrs Rankin, to come over. We'll have a nice cup of tea."

She laughed. He put out his hand and she stopped laughing. "Don't *touch* me!" They were immobile, staring at each other. "Don't you dare bring that woman here," she said. "You can take me to my friends."

* * *

Pharaoh came carefully downstairs nursing his hangover and squinted at a note on the kitchen table: "Shaw had fatal accident on level crossing. I've taken Sue to Grammery. Clem."

He rejected the impulse to telephone. Whatever was happening at Grammery, his call would be an intrusion; Harker would contact him as soon as he could. He filled the kettle and, waiting for it to boil, he thought about unmanned level crossings. He was not terribly surprised; he was surprised that it should have happened to Shaw — except, of course, that the Datsun was always stalling.

He sat on the garden seat, drinking coffee, listening to the bees and recovering from the awful night — although not awful compared with Shaw's, he reminded himself — and now Susan had to cope with shock. Esme and Clem would be towers of strength; they wouldn't grieve. Would anyone grieve other than Susan? A strange question, a poignant answer: no. So far as Pharaoh knew, apart from his wife — widow — there was no one to grieve for Shaw.

He was on his second mug of coffee when he heard the sound of an approaching car, but the vehicle that stopped in the lane was a blue Capri, nothing he recognised. Doors slammed and people appeared at the gate, a couple so young that they were girl and boy rather than woman and man. They had fashionable short haircuts, they wore baggy slacks and trainers. He carried a camera, she a shoulder bag, and they looked as if they had just left school.

"We're from the *Herald*," she said, giving Pharaoh a brief smile. "I'm Deborah, he's Bill. Do you live here or are you on holiday?"

"I'm on holiday." He had stood up. "I'm Jack."

"Oh yes." She looked past him and raised her eyebrows.

"My friend is away." Pharaoh emphasised 'friend' and she looked puzzled, trying to work out the significance, if any.

She gave up and asked brightly: "Are we the first?"

"The first this morning. You're early risers; how about a cup of coffee?"

"That would be lovely. We haven't been offered any yet."

"Sit down." It was an order and he waited until they did so; he didn't want them inside the cottage. When he returned with the coffee they were sitting stiffly but he saw that the camera was out of its case. The girl had noticed his limp (it was bad this morning) and she moved along the seat to give him room. The boy got up and sat on the log.

"Who didn't offer you coffee?" Pharaoh

asked pleasantly. "Where have you been?"

"Just the people at Murkgill Farm; they were uncooperative but then they would be: the second visit from the Press in three days, and they're still in mourning." Pharaoh was staring at her. "And there was no one at home at the Shaws' cottage," she went on. "Would you know where the widow is?"

"The widow?"

"Susan Shaw."

"Oh, Susan's not a widow. You've got the wrong lady; it's Esme Dolphin you want." He became mildly censorious. "But we've all talked enough about the accident. It was unfortunate but it's not the first time a dangerous pet has savaged its owner. We were all — "

"There's been another accident," the girl cut in. "And Susan Shaw *is* a widow. The night express hit her husband's van on the level crossing. They've taken the wreck away with the body still inside — "

"They can't get it out," the boy said.

"Shaw?" Pharaoh gasped. "Killed on the crossing? That van's always stalling. . . . Poor Susan. I must go — " Then, furiously: "Why didn't the train stop?"

He subsided. "Of course it couldn't; it's doing sixty when it comes through here. How ghastly for the driver: seeing it on the line, knowing he had to hit it."

"He wouldn't have seen it," she said.

"Heads are going to roll," the boy intoned. "The light had been shot out. If the crossing had been lit it wouldn't have happened."

The girl was doubtful. "There's a curve, and visibility is only half a mile at that point. The driver couldn't have stopped even if he'd seen the van."

"The light had been shot out." The boy was stubborn. "What's the point of having a light there if it's not for the driver of the train? Motorists don't need it; they've got the warning lights flashing when the barrier's coming down. It's vandalism, like putting concrete blocks on the line." He addressed Pharaoh. "Our boss doesn't like vandals."

"No one does." The girl was annoyed, she was supposed to do the talking. "Were you a friend of Shaw's?" she asked Pharaoh.

"I'd only met him a few times."

"You knew that he was a mercenary?"

"Yes." She waited. "I suspect you'll know more than I do," he added.

"What is your opinion of mercenaries?"

"Martin had an interesting theory" — Pharaoh became expansive — "he cited the horrors of insurrection in a Third World country: civil war, scorched earth, famine, and he balanced that against the rule of a more or less benevolent despot backed up by a mercenary army. I couldn't argue with that; I've never been in a Third World country."

"But what do *you* think?"

"Is a soldier who fights for money inferior to one who fights out of patriotism?"

"Kills," the boy put in, "kills for money."

"You've given it a lot of thought," Pharaoh said.

"Isn't it odd that you should have two violent deaths at Clouds in four days?" the girl asked.

"Are you suggesting that there's a connection?" Pharaoh looked interested, but the girl had been looking for argument, not agreement. "Just kicking it around," she said. "I mean: two *horrible* deaths!"

"I'd enjoy hearing your theory of how they might be connected," Pharaoh said.

★ ★ ★

When Harker came home Pharaoh was lying in the grass engaged in deep relaxation. Harker stood at the gate staring. Pharaoh sat up. "How's Susan?" he asked.

"All right. We'll know better when she comes out of shock. The police woke her with the news. Can you believe that?"

"I suppose someone had to. What happened, Clem?"

"You gave the Press an interview." It was thrown out like an accusation.

"That's not what I'd have called it, and I'll believe you any day in preference to the Press."

"But that's how I got my information, such as it is: from reporters and the police. I've been fending off newsmen all morning down at Grammery. Esme was looking after Susan, Lanty and I — well, mostly me, Lanty's on a short

355

fuse this morning — I was coping with reporters. It's the mercenary bit they find intriguing, of course."

"What did they tell you about the accident?"

"Actually there we got more from the police. They wanted to know what Shaw was doing on the road at that time in the morning, what he'd had to drink at the party and so on. I think they have a suspicion there's drugs circulating. They interviewed me for some time, being the host."

"Come on, Clem: what happened to Shaw?"

"Who knows? Obviously the Datsun stalled on the crossing and he must have been trying to start it again when the train hit him. The police want to know if he was drunk. Do you think he was drunk?"

"I wasn't in any condition to notice."

"No, you weren't," Harker agreed absently. "The police are assuming that anyway: he was drunk, possibly had words with Susan, left to go climbing in the Lakes like he did yesterday."

356

"He was going the wrong way for the Lakes."

"What? Oh yes, so he was. That's what the police think all the same. And the Press. What did you tell the *Herald*?"

"I let them do most of the talking." Pharaoh grinned. "I did tell them that the Fawcetts were very old, implying that they were senile. That stopped them going up to the Hall. I'm sorry I couldn't think of a way to stop them coming to Grammery without alerting their suspicions."

"What suspicions?"

"I mean, if they thought I was trying to dissuade them they could have wondered why. It was to protect you all, particularly Susan, but they were in a mood to see sinister pointers everywhere."

Harker's eyes narrowed. "Because Shaw was out so early?"

"That, but also the light being shot out: the one above the level crossing."

"That's not sinister. People — young boys — are always shooting out streetlights. They think of it as target practice."

"You mean Paul, of course."

"Why 'of course'?"

"You couldn't mean Lanty?"

"Lanty's too old for vandalism; he shoots animals, not light bulbs."

Pharaoh studied his friend's face. He said slowly: "They were also interested in the fact that there had been two violent deaths here in four days. When I took the girl up on it initially she pretended to be surprised, but it is odd, Clem."

"The police are satisfied," Harker said, as if by rote, then he caught the other's drift. "Are you hinting that *Paul's* wasn't an accident? No, that's Tilly's crazy theory. Why are you looking at me like that? You're not serious! The dog killed Paul."

Pharaoh said slowly: "I was thinking that if there was a connection between the two deaths then it's possible that neither of them was an accident."

Harker sat down on the garden seat. "God, I'm tired." He rubbed his eyes. "You're suggesting that they were — ? No, I don't believe it."

"Why not?" Pharaoh got up from the grass and sat on the log. He stretched his legs like an old cat, one at a time, carefully. "I'm tired too," he said.

Harker sighed and, as if he had

expelled evil with his breath, his face cleared and he said cheerfully: "You punished the whisky bottle last night. How's the leg?"

"Better. I'll have to watch that: using alcohol as an analgesic. Too easy for it to become an excuse. Thanks for covering me up. Did I make a fool of myself?"

"Not at all. You passed out where you were sitting. I explained to people that you'd overdone it: swimming. Everyone was very sympathetic. You couldn't have been too bad; you didn't make a sound when you came upstairs. What time was that?"

"I've no idea. Long before dawn. My God!"

"What?"

"I couldn't get to sleep. I heard the express come through."

"Oh. Nasty."

"What do *you* think he was doing on the road at that time in the morning? Didn't Susan say anything — in confidence?" Pharaoh shook his head to clear it. "I must still be drunk. What I mean is, do you think she knows and isn't talking?"

"She has no idea, and it's something we'll never know now. Everyone's asking the same question. Susan didn't even know Martin wasn't in bed until the police woke her up after the accident. They brought her over here, you know. She was badly shocked. I did what I could and when it was light I took her down to Grammery."

"I didn't hear a sound."

"We didn't want to wake you. We were very quiet."

There was a pause. Pharaoh looked thoughtful; Harker watched him anxiously. Pharaoh said: "There are a number of questions: loose ends, odd occurrences about Paul's death."

"Oh, Paul." He was dismissive. "Such as?"

"Of course there are, Clem! There's the dog for a start. Why did Paul climb down when he knew the dog was so vicious?"

"It doesn't matter. He did go down so there's no argument." Harker gave a thin smile. "And in case you're suggesting someone killed him and put the body down, there was tissue and dog hairs under his nails, remember? He was alive when the dog attacked him."

"Suppose he was pushed into the hole?"

They were silent again, Pharaoh quite still, Harker fidgeting and frowning. At length Harker asked: "How did — how could Paul be persuaded to go to the top of the sinkhole?"

Pharaoh was ready for that one. "He heard the dog barking." After a moment he amended it. "Someone else heard it bark and that person told Paul." After another pause he added: "The chap who — put the dog down?"

"Oh, was that pushed too? How do you push a pit bull? How do you get it up to the Scar in the first place? And why kill Paul? Come off it, Jack."

"The Honda was used." Pharaoh was following another line. "But the weirdest thing is that telephone call to Weeping Klints. It had to be a local man — well, a man with local knowledge — and presumably a man, although women with deep voices, or who can drop their voices, can be mistaken for men. Accent. Did the widow say what accent the caller had?"

"Like a tourist, she said. Not a local. To the farmers round here 'tourist' means merely that a person hasn't got a north-country accent."

"So you asked her. You didn't tell me that before." Harker said nothing. Pharaoh studied his face, then looked away.

"I had the feeling," Harker said carefully, "that it might be better to let sleeping dogs lie, particularly when they are friendly dogs."

"Did you have suspicions?"

"Of course."

"Lanty." It wasn't a question. "But it couldn't have been Lanty," Pharaoh went on. "He was cutting up a tree when you were on the roof."

"What roof?"

"Grammery, of course. That was when you heard the Honda go by on Saturday afternoon. Susan was helping Lanty." Pharaoh's eyes glazed.

Harker smiled. "Susan's a lovely girl but she hasn't the brain for the logistics involved, and all in order to put a dog down a shaft for the purpose of luring Paul to the edge and pushing him in. Apart from the fact that no one could approach the dog — and Paul would be highly suspicious of anyone approaching himself, let alone Susan — Lanty and Susan were in the kitchen when I came down from Grammery's roof. And the Honda had gone by not long before, a matter of minutes."

Again Pharaoh didn't appear to be listening. "I wonder what Shaw was up to," he mused.

"You mean when he was supposed to go to London and didn't?"

"Paul told his father the mileage on the Datsun was wrong."

"Shaw had a lot of irons in the fire."

"You know that now for a fact?"

"It's more than a guess. You thought he was living in the old quarries before he arrived down here."

"Not necessarily living; but someone had spent the night there or, at least, cooked a meal, and he did approach us from that direction the first time we met him up on the Scar; he wasn't coming from Ewedale where he said he'd spent the night."

"If Shaw did bivouac in the quarries it could only have been to spy on Sue, and that suggests he suspected she was having an affair with Lanty or me — "

"More likely someone from further afield. He'd have seen the Range Rover outside his cottage and would want to find out who the owner was."

"I hadn't thought of that. How did he know which was his house? This was his first visit to Clouds. Last time he came back to the UK Sue met him in London. I suppose if he'd been keeping watch for some time, with binoculars . . . or he could have come down at night . . . " Harker grimaced. "It sounds unpleasant, Jack, to say the least. And if he spied on his own wife, who else did he spy on? I mean elsewhere? A man like that makes enemies."

"Who could have followed him here. I came to that conclusion when I read your note this morning and I was wondering how many people would grieve for him."

"The police are treating it as an accident; Paul's death too. Paul was killed by a dog, Shaw by a train. In fact, Shaw's could have been suicide, except that he didn't seem to be a suicidal type, whatever that is. But he did know that van was stalling like mad."

"Everyone did. Shaw thought Paul put something in the petrol."

"That's one person then who couldn't have had anything to do with Shaw's death. Paul's been dead for four days. Unless you're suggesting that by putting sugar in the petrol Paul did manage to kill Shaw even though the lad was dead himself. What's funny?"

"Not funny: ironical. I wonder if it *was* Paul who shot out the bulb in the light above the crossing."

16

"**H**OW thoughtful of you, Jack." Phoebe peered inside the carrier bag. "Clem keeps us in salad vegetables through the summer. Did you have a good party?"

"Most enjoyable. I missed you and Mr Fawcett."

"We're too old for parties." She unpacked the bag, removing the lettuces with a puzzled air. Pharaoh realised that he should have cut off the roots; now she would guess that Harker hadn't sent the produce, that he had brought it on his own initiative. "I was on my way to the Scar," he said, and decided to come clean, to declare his interest. "Has Mr Fawcett learned anything that might explain matters?"

"I don't know how much you know."

"It's puzzling that Shaw should have been on the road so early. Clem reckons we'll never know the answer to that one."

"We don't need to." Rowland had entered the kitchen by the back door, the Jack Russell at his heels. He nodded to Pharaoh. "Tilly's better," he said, with a kind of triumph. "No doubt about it; that woman was terrified of Shaw. Makes you think, don't it?"

"And George?" Pharaoh asked.

"Didn't see him. He's up on the Scar. I called on Tilly to see if she needs any help with the inquest on Monday, but it doesn't hold any terrors for her. A bit surprising, that; the Coroner's bound to come down heavily on Rankin for allowing the lad to keep a pit bull."

"He can't," Phoebe said. "They lost their son."

"True, true, but he'll have something to say about the keeping of dangerous dogs, can't avoid it; he has his duty. And now the level crossing. It's been one thing after another since you arrived, Pharaoh. I assure you, it's not like this all the time."

Beth Potter shouldered her way in from the passage, burdened with a carpet sweeper and dusters. "Just as well," she put in. "Wouldn't be many of us left if it happened often."

Rowland gave a bark of laughter. Phoebe, unmoved, twisted the tops off beetroots as if her sole concern was the preparation of food.

"Did the police let you in on any secrets, sir?" Pharaoh asked.

"There are secrets? No one told me. They're going to have to do something about the crossing, of course. Case of bolting the stable door, eh? Although all the time that crossing's been in existence, there's never been a fatal accident, not even a cow. Funny thing, that."

"Cows don't get drunk," Beth said.

"Was he drunk, Pharaoh?" Rowland was sharp. "What was he drinking?"

"Rum and coke, when I saw him."

"What on earth's that: coke? *Coke?*"

"Coca Cola. It's an American soft drink."

"Oh that. What's it taste like?"

"Like cough mixture. Very sweet."

"Revolting. It must kill the rum."

Pharaoh left the Hall and took the familiar track to the Scar. The ruts of the Honda still showed in the mud below the viaduct, now overlaid by the tread of

368

a gumboot. As he climbed the zig-zags to the quarries he thought yet again of the other footprint, in the bottom of the chasm. As he'd told Harker, there were questions to be answered. He didn't know why they should be answered; only that a question was half a concept; it was unfinished, it demanded an answer, and Pharaoh had a tidy mind.

As he approached the quarries he saw that sheep were drifting in front of him, moving up to the Scar. He thought of dogs immediately but these sheep showed no panic, they moved like an orderly gathering, stopping occasionally to look back. The object of interest was a black animal stationed on top of a spoil heap like a sentinel. Pharaoh halted when it dropped down from the spoil heap, fluid as a fox. Moving like that it could only be a dog and, because the sheep were undisturbed, it must be a collie. Pharaoh moved again, upwards towards the quarries.

The afternoon was warm and still and the birds were quiet, or perhaps there were few birds on the escarpment but he hadn't noticed their absence until today. His footsteps scrunched loudly in the abandoned workings, water dripped down the walls and in the place where he had found the mark of a climber's boot there was now the print of a gumboot, fresh and clean, moisture still seeping into it. He felt the cold edge of excitement, of danger. He moved loosely, forgetting his game leg, noting every stone and shadow, alert for movement.

Something growled, menacing as the growl of a lion. He stooped and came up with a rock in each hand. A few yards away was the entrance to a level, like a cave. He could see nothing within but he sensed a presence. "Ah, Rankin," he announced cheerily. "We wondered where you'd got to. Is there a sheep inside?"

"Dead." Rankin stepped into the sunshine, two collies slinking behind him. "Dogs went in, found a ewe; her died lambin'."

Pharaoh looked politely interested but he was sweating with relief; Rankin wasn't carrying a gun. He dropped the rocks.

"Harker with you?" the man asked, his eyes ranging the spoil heaps.

Prudence dictated a lie. "No, Mr Fawcett was. Not now; he turned back. He said it was you. He called on Mrs Rankin earlier."

"Did he now? So did the police and the Press. Everyone's calling on us; we're popular all of a sudden."

Pharaoh walked to the edge of a turfy platform. Rankin moved after him and they looked out over the woods of Clouds. A goods train was crossing the viaduct. Pharaoh suppressed a smile. He had remembered that Rankin couldn't be armed; Rowland had taken his shotguns. "He'll give you the guns back now," he said.

Rankin turned towards him. "You reckon so?"

"Shaw's dead."

"So we're all on same side."

"We weren't before?"

"*He* were on t'other side." Rankin had a sly gleam in his eye. "We all know that, don't we, Mr Pharaoh?"

"You're saying Shaw was against all of us? How do you make that out?"

Rankin grinned. "He stole from his wife's mother, he likely stole from his own wife, if she had anything worth stealing. As for the men . . ." He paused and looked away. " . . . 'Course, you hadn't been here long enough for him to have anything against you" — the tone was ingratiating — "but Lanty Dolphin . . . Why d'you think Lanty were never seen without a gun? Lanty knew before us."

"Knew what?"

"That Shaw carried a knife. Susan woulda told him, told him to be careful."

"You're saying that Shaw was jealous of his wife's friends?"

Rankin shrugged and his eyes wandered. Pharaoh said easily: "So you knew all along that Shaw was up here in the quarries. He wasn't as clever as he thought, was he?"

"He were tidy." Rankin sounded as if he approved the tidiness. "He left marks of his boots but they coulda been made by any hiker passing through. All the same they was his boots, same as tracks round his house. And he couldn't hide his traces from the dogs; they sniffed out

372

where he'd been. They told me he were up here."

"How long do you reckon he was here? We thought several days."

"Two, p'raps. Dog barked a lot; the other dog: pit bull. That would be why he had to kill it." Pharaoh opened his mouth to protest but Rankin overbore him: "I know what you're going to say, but Shaw put dog down hole, so he were responsible for its death, same as for lad's."

"How the hell did he 'put' the pit bull down the sinkhole?"

"I don't know. You work that out; you're the one with the education, but it don't matter. Dog's dead." His face was stony. "Like my son," he added.

Pharaoh looked around, found a rock and sat down. Rankin was not averse to continuing the conversation; he sat on a bank, his stick between his knees, while the collies watched from the shade of boulders, their tongues lolling in the heat.

"Who was he spying on?" Pharaoh asked.

Rankin opened his mouth, there was

373

a fractional pause, then: "His wife, o'course."

"And?"

"That fellow'd think his wife were going with everyone, anyone, even me."

"Did Paul tell you where Shaw went when he pretended to go to London?"

"He didn't know, but it were a hundred and seventy-five miles, the round trip."

"Did you or Paul have any ideas about that? What places are there within ninety miles?"

"T'lad said Blackpool. It's not my problem. Fellow's dead. Whoever — " Rankin caught his breath then went on in a rush: "Whoever he went to see is better off without him; he were a killer — Shaw." He was sanctimonious. Pharaoh nodded his agreement and stood up. He was about to say: "You've got nothing to worry about anyway," but he refrained; the Rankins had the inquest on Paul to get through, then the funeral. Nothing to worry about perhaps, but devastating, far worse than worry. And yet Rankin seemed untroubled by grief, untroubled by anything. Yesterday, two days ago, he had gone armed against a killer who he swore was after him and Tilly. Now the killer was dead and he guessed Rankin had been about to say: "Whoever killed him done us a good turn," or something similar, which meant either that Rankin had had no hand in Shaw's death, or that the man was a superlative actor.

Pharaoh left him and continued to the plateau. As he threaded his way through the bone-white lime, he pondered this passion of a man who spied on his wife for several days because he suspected she was living with another man. But Shaw had never shown any sign of being passionate; on the contrary, he was a cold fish, ruled by his head — except just that once when he had knocked Paul down and reached for his knife because a trailer was obstructing the lane. That was when he drove off in Esme's Range Rover. Pharaoh stopped short. Shaw had gone out to telephone after he received a letter from — where? Someone had deciphered the postmark: Esme or Susan. Susan had thought at the time that it was from a woman. What was that postmark: Glasgow, Blackpool, Lancaster? It wasn't far away; could it have been 87½ miles: half of the 175 that Paul had calculated from the Datsun's mileometer?

He came to the sinkholes and found his way to the top of the maze where Paul had died. He studied the plants there. Many were crushed but some had bloomed afresh and vividly; the dropped petals were dull but in one place so brilliant that they could have been made of nylon. They *were* nylon. He teased a silky pink fibre from the rock, and then remembered that Harker's old rope was pink and green: dirty on the outside but still bright where it was frayed. This was where Harker had stood when they recovered Paul's body, securing himself to a limestone bollard. The lip of the crevasse was five feet from the bollard. He peered over the edge and saw another pink fibre caught on a bulge where the rope had rubbed, and one or two pale strands, like hair. Paul's hair was dark, and the dog had been a rufous shade. To his knowledge no one had descended or climbed out at this point. He lay down and, at full stretch, he could reach the hairs.

It wasn't hair but thread of some kind. He studied it, bemused, knowing it to be familiar but unable to put a name to it. He had his wallet with him so he put the threads in the fold of his driving licence, then walked along the line of sinkholes to the one where they had found the Honda. Standing on the lip of the depression he considered the terrain for a while then retraced his steps along the fault, turned and came back.

★ ★ ★

"There was no need," he told Harker an hour later. "I'd already worked out the significance of that particular spot; it was the only place where the Honda couldn't be seen until you were right on the lip of the funnel, and yet it still looked quite a natural spot for a farm bike to be parked because it was a shallow depression, one you could ride down into."

"Meaning?"

"Meaning that, being out of sight, the Honda wouldn't be found until the dog had mutilated the body sufficiently."

"What on earth! Sufficiently for what?"

"To destroy something: a bruise or a laceration." He paused. Harker said nothing. They were sitting on the ragged lawn behind Grammery where he had run Harker to earth when he came down from the Scar. Now, as they talked, Lanty approached and with a fine disregard for their privacy settled himself beside them. Pharaoh considered him thoughtfully and came to a decision. Taking out his wallet, he extracted the pale threads and passed them to Harker who accepted them gingerly as if they were animate.

"What's that?" Pharaoh asked. Lanty hitched closer to see.

"Animal hair?" Harker suggested, holding a thread against his jeans. "It's not wiry enough to be from a horse's tail."

"It's from a rope," Lanty said, "or binder twine."

"Binder twine's mostly brightly coloured," mused Harker. "Rope? Well, it's not nylon or perlon, that's for sure; it's too stiff. Hemp? A hemp rope?"

"Sisal!" Pharaoh exclaimed. "Who uses sisal?"

"Probably every farm's got old hemp or sisal ropes hanging around. They were used for tying loads on wagons. What's the significance of this, Jack?"

"A sisal rope was used to lower the pit bull into the sinkhole, and then Paul."

Lanty gaped.

"Impossible," Harker said flatly, but after a while he went on: "They would have to be unconscious: both the boy and the dog."

"The dog, yes," Pharaoh agreed, "but it could have been tranquillised. As for Paul, he was conscious when the dog attacked him because he scratched it. Was he unconscious when he was being lowered?" He considered his own question but Lanty was puzzling over the technicalities involved.

"What about knots?" he asked. "The guy on top couldn't go down to untie a knot; the dog would've attacked him."

"He could go down if it was still tranquillised. He'd undo the knot, climb back, retrieve the rope. As for Paul, he wore a belt. The rope could have been run through that and the boy lowered on a double rope — no knot required;

all that had to be done when he was on the floor of the crevasse was to pull the rope through the belt."

"Come *on*!" Harker jeered. "You're going to lower a conscious person like that? Paul would have struggled like mad. So he'd have to be lowered unconscious, and we know he wasn't because he tried to fight off the dog."

Pharaoh nodded. "But at some point — " He was suddenly alert. "Look at it this way: he'd knocked Paul out, with a blow or a drug, it's immaterial; he had to in order to get him there in the first place, but he kept him at the top of the sinkhole until he showed signs of coming round, when he'd lower the lad to the bottom and pull the rope up."

"The dog would attack immediately," Harker said.

"Not if stones were being thrown at it to keep it at the other end of the system. That way Paul would have time to recover in the bottom of the crevasse. Once he was fit and shouting for help the man on top would walk away, leaving a clear field for the dog."

"That's obscene," Lanty said.

"It answers a lot of questions."

"Why?" Harker asked. "I can see him dumping the dog like rubbish but why kill Paul — or was he rubbish as well to Shaw?"

"Shaw?" repeated Lanty. "Shaw did this?"

"Who else?" Pharaoh was running out of steam. "You met him. I'd say he was capable of it, but motive's another matter. He didn't do this on impulse; it was very carefully worked out. Could he have been so angry with Paul that it festered, or did he plan it as a kind of exercise, something amusing to do?"

"You don't know it was Shaw," Lanty pointed out. "It could have been anyone."

Harker turned to him. "Who else had it in for Paul?"

"Everyone!" Lanty was astonished. "He was trouble long before he brought that dog home. Afterwards he was lethal. Sue was terrified of the pit bull."

No one responded to this and they were so preoccupied with their own thoughts that they were startled when Esme asked: "Is this a private party or can anyone join in?" She stood behind them, neat and clean and smelling of talc but looking tired. "She's asleep," she said in answer to the unspoken question. "I had to come out for a breath of fresh air."

"What's she been doing all this time?" Lanty asked roughly.

"What would you expect?" Esme was tart, then she softened, forgiving him on account of his youth. "She talked, she dozed a little, drank some wine. In fact, that's probably what made her sleep in the end." They remained silent. She went on with a hint of defiance: "And if you're wondering how much she really knows about last night, what she didn't tell the police, the answer's nothing. She'd had a lot to drink and she didn't even know that Martin hadn't come to bed." She paused. "Or that if he did, when he got up again. She's as bewildered as any of us. You look very intense, Jack; what is it?"

"You remember Martin pinching your Range Rover, driving away to telephone?"

382

"Ye-es." She drew it out, her eyes fixed on his.

"He had a letter that morning. What was the postmark?"

"Newcastle."

Pharaoh turned to Harker. "How far is that from here?"

"Around — let me think — Bowes . . . Bishop Auckland: around eighty miles. Why?"

"He was in touch with someone: someone in Newcastle. There was the letter, then he needed a telephone; he wouldn't phone from Fox Yards, the call was private. And it couldn't wait; he had to take a car without permission. Then he went away, ostensibly to London but he covered less than two hundred miles. Newcastle fits."

"And he wouldn't take Susan," Esme put in. "She's maintained all along that he had another woman."

"It's immaterial now," Harker said.

"Divide and rule." Lanty looked smug.

"What's that?" Esme was nonplussed.

"Two villains." Lanty was pleased at the attention. "One murdered the other and then gets himself killed by a train.

Not divide and rule so much, but one cancelled the other out." He beamed at them.

"Are you telling me Martin murdered Paul?" She was horrified. "I don't believe it."

"Everything points that way," Pharaoh said quietly.

17

AT the inquest on Paul Rankin the verdict was death by misadventure, with the Coroner adding a rider on the methods employed in restraining dangerous dogs, and of keeping them in the first place. A Coroner's court in sheep country looked askance at a pit bull that twice slipped its collar. There was no suggestion, even from the Rankins, that the collar had been deliberately unfastened.

The Rankins seemed resigned to events; the results of the post mortem had finally convinced Tilly of the facts of her son's death, and nothing was left but censure. "The Rankins," Harker remarked to Pharaoh as they drove home after the inquest, "are scapegoats; it's a case of give a dog a bad name. Those dead sheep, for instance, George didn't put them there; if he couldn't sell carcasses to the knacker, he'd push 'em down a sinkhole. One of his neighbours unloaded those beasts in

Tranna Mire, knowing George would get the blame."

It was four days since Shaw had died, and the second inquest was scheduled for Wednesday, in two days' time. Rowland had told them that there would be no surprises; the verdict would be accidental death, with the Coroner expected to emphasise that it was the responsibility of the public to recognise the danger of unguarded level crossings. In other words, Shaw's death was his own fault. As this information was disseminated through the community at Clouds it was met with a thick silence; people accepted the theory of Shaw's culpability without comment, in order to spare Susan's feelings.

There was a visitor at Grammery Bank who contributed to the polarising of attitudes. When the reporter from the local paper wrote her story, concentrating on the glamour of the mercenary but saying nothing unusual, she had named her informants. Two days later Alice Ward arrived: a lean person in her sixties, wearing a crumpled Dior suit and driving a Lotus Elan. She was a freelance journalist and she looked capable of turning Clouds inside out in twenty-four hours. Instead she wandered about, seemingly without any particular target, meeting people by chance. She prevailed on Juno to rent her a room at Grammery; she drank moderately, ate like a bird and *lurked*, according to Susan who escaped to Fox Yards to get away from women, she told them meaningly. The men noted with relief that she seemed to be recovering from her initial shock.

Apparently Juno and Esme were fascinated by Alice Ward, although Susan thought that her mother was probably impressed by the Dior suit. Harker, after he met the woman, said that she was all right but that he found women like her creepy. Pharaoh thought that his friend had lost his sense of proportion, was perhaps, like Susan, overawed by all those dominant women down at Grammery.

The weather wasn't conducive to rational judgements. Another heat wave had descended on Cumbria and the dale sweltered. The level of the river dropped, grass turned brown on the Scar and the rock was hot to the touch. Like animals people were active only in the early morning and evening, and even the meadows seemed devoid of life.

After supper on the day of the inquest Harker went to the Hall to install an extra socket in the Fawcetts' bedroom, having prevailed on them to use an electric blanket next winter. Pharaoh strolled through the woods, grateful for the comparative cool of evening, and started up the escarpment. Someone called his name; Susan was coming fast up the zig-zags behind him.

"You're too quick for me," she gasped, arriving and flinging herself on the turf. "I've been calling you from the bottom; you must have been panting too hard to hear me." She was wearing a white tank top and denim cut-offs. She carried nothing.

"You're not dressed for the hill." He was disapproving.

"Neither are you."

"I know what I'm doing."

"Do you?"

He stiffened. She lay on her back, her eyes closed. "Tell me what happened to your family," she demanded. "I joined the club. I want to know how survivors cope."

When he didn't respond immediately she started to fidget. Seeing this he said quietly: "The marriage wasn't working out — but I don't think the depth of a person's feelings has much to do with grief. There's still guilt. At the time I didn't analyse my reactions."

"But it wasn't only your wife." Pharaoh looked at the haze that hid the mountains. Susan was frightened; she had gone too far.

"Yes." He sighed. "I loved my daughter."

"I'm terribly sorry." She sat up and touched his hand. "I shouldn't have compared us. My feelings for Martin were nothing like that."

"Well, as deep, but different."

"It was one-sided." She looked out over the valley. "He never loved me."

"He must have done. He married you."

"God knows why. Lust perhaps, wanting

a home base — or just because it was what everyone else did. The Army forces you to conform. But he changed."

"When he became a mercenary?"

"That's right; in the SAS he was just a soldier but the first time he came back from Africa he hadn't altered so much as *intensified*. He was harder, although that's the wrong word too. He was cool, but I don't just mean laid-back, he didn't seem to have any feeling left, not even about the men he'd killed. He'd say things like 'someone had to do it' or that he was efficient. That was gross: efficient at killing! And he didn't care about me any more. He even — Oh, it's so boring to talk about money. I won't."

"Was he violent?"

"You know something? He didn't care enough to hit me. He wasn't bothered by me nagging about money; hell, he wasn't bothered about Lanty!" He said nothing. She went on the defensive. "Marty was gone for months at a time — imagine: in the summer" — she gestured angrily, indicating the lush valley, the heat, two young people thrown together — "how could he expect — "

"He couldn't expect it. No one could."

"*He* said that." Her eyes were wide, pleading for enlightenment. Evidently she hadn't received it from Harker. "He didn't care about me going to another man. Of course he *said* it had to stop but then d'you know what he did? He went to Clem and asked him to take care of me! I mean, it was sort of selling me, wasn't it? Passing me from hand to hand."

"Did he have another woman?"

Her face changed. The eyelids drooped, the lips were compressed. "It had to be that. He got a letter from Newcastle, made a phone call; he probably went over there. I don't know. I don't care. I thought she might arrive when she heard about his death but there are no strange women around."

"Except Alice Ward."

She gave a noncommittal grunt. "It was the house he wanted."

"The cottage at Murkgill?"

"Yes. Amazing, isn't it? He loved the place. If I'd left he'd have kept it on. Of course, I wouldn't have left; I loved the guy. He was trying to make it up to me — at the end." She winced. "I thought everything would come right when we were on holiday; we've never had a proper holiday and it would have been fun touring the Continent and not having to bother about money — " She stopped suddenly. "Forget I said that."

"I was there already." He was reassuring. "Have you told your mother the truth about the money?" He held his breath for the answer.

She grimaced. "Not yet. I don't know how to. Clem says he'll put it in the hedge in a plastic bag and smear it with gravy and the Jack Russell can find it. That way Mum will think that Paul stole it."

"Clem didn't tell me he was going to do that."

"He'd feel guilty about putting the blame on Paul. So am I actually. What do you think?"

"I don't think it matters now."

"Yes, everyone's dead, and the verdict's official. And just because he dropped the dog down the sinkhole doesn't mean he had anything to do with Paul's death. And so what? No one's going to say anything. It's not as if I had any part in it: accessory or whatever it's called; you don't have to protect me. I'm rather surprised that Clem told you, in fact." She realised that she sounded pained. "No offence," she added quickly.

"None taken." He was casual. "I'd guessed anyway. And Clem and I go back a long way. You get to know who you can trust in our job, our old job. As for the accessory angle: an accessory has to know he or she is helping. You didn't know."

"Not really." Her gaze wandered and came to rest on the trees about Clouds. "I suppose you think the same way as Clem," she mused. "And that must be the explanation. I mean, Marty: doing his own washing? Never!"

"It depends." A comment for all seasons.

"What, jeans and boots: scrubbing the boots?"

"He had to give some explanation."

"I told you — I mean, I told Clem: I

never asked for an explanation. I wasn't going to ask Marty why he washed his own jeans."

"I wonder if it could have been blood." He said it as if it were a recurring problem, already discussed in depth.

"Not blood. Mud. Remember that night: it was hectic; there was water and mud everywhere." Her face softened but she frowned immediately. He thought her eyes were wet. "I wonder if he did it for me: killing that bloody dog."

"He didn't kill it. We were there when Rowland shot it."

"Oh, I know *that*, but Marty put it down the sinkhole; we all know that; well, the three of us do."

★ ★ ★

"Susan's been talking to me," Pharaoh said.

"I know. She came to the Hall and I said you'd gone up to the Scar."

"You sent her after me? Why?" Pharaoh couldn't see the other's expression; the sun had set and Harker hadn't turned on a light in his living room. "You expected her to confide in me. So why didn't you tell me yourself?"

"I had the idea that we might keep it as something between ourselves: me and Susan."

"What made you change your mind?"

"Because you've changed, Jack. You've become curious — and it's not idle curiosity either. You were crowding me. I felt you wouldn't rest until you'd discovered the truth — and I didn't want you talking to other people."

Pharaoh twisted in his chair and switched on a lamp. Harker was obviously uneasy, turning away from the light. Pharaoh said neutrally: "And you reckoned I'd be more sympathetic if I learned it from her rather than you?"

"She hasn't done anything criminal, Jack."

"No?"

"Of course not." He was indignant. "She suspected Shaw had been out that night — "

"She knew he'd been out."

"All right, she knew. It didn't have to be anything to do with the dog. After all, everyone thought it couldn't be approached, except by Paul, and he had to carry a whip."

"We've discussed that. It had to be tranquillised."

"We only worked that out with hindsight. Susan didn't, and at the time she was confused. Esme was badgering her to leave the cottage, Shaw was trying to persuade her to stay and at the same time she knew he was keeping something from her. To Susan, because she's like that, the secret had to do with a woman. It would never have crossed her mind that he'd gone out that night to get rid of the dog."

"All I suggested was that she might not be completely innocent, that she convinced herself it had something to do with a woman rather than the dog because the alternative was terrifying, once the dog was connected with Paul's death. Of course, she's made the connection now, or you made it between the two of you. What I'd like to know is what motive you arrived at. Why did Paul have to be killed?"

"We never considered it; we didn't

discuss anything. You seem to think we sat down and had a rational discussion like two detectives working it out. It wasn't like that at all. For one thing, we were pushed for time: I didn't know when you'd be back from Penrith — "

"You sent me to Penrith so you could get together with Susan! So that's why you gave me so much to do. I thought at the time that you were getting me out of the way." Harker looked uncomfortable. Pharaoh studied him closely. "It was something more than that. You couldn't have been thinking that Susan had a hand in Paul's death?" Harker shifted uneasily. "No, of course not," murmured Pharaoh.

"I had to drag it out of her," Harker said quickly. "It was disjointed: lots of extraneous information. I had to piece together the pertinent bits, the deciding factor being that Shaw had washed his jeans and scrubbed his boots. The inference was that he'd got them filthy the night before but all she knew was that he'd been out in the storm after she'd gone down to Grammery. Where could he have got the tranquilliser for the dog, Jack?"

Pharaoh was silent. "Would mercenaries carry tranquillisers?" Harker wondered. "To subdue village dogs, for instance?"

"Most unlikely. They'd use poison. They'd kill village dogs, not tranquillise them."

"What about sleeping pills?"

"I've no idea how they'd work on a dog, nor what dosage to use, so I doubt if Shaw would have known. He'd have used a drug that's specifically for animals. He'd get something from a vet." He thought about that for a moment. "And if he couldn't get it legally, if the vet demanded to see the dog, suspected he was up to mischief, then he'd get it illegally, by breaking into a vet's dispensary."

"He threw the dog some meat with the drug inside? How did he get the animal up to the moor?"

"Carried it, of course, like shepherds carry a sheep, round their shoulders."

"It must have weighed a ton!"

"Seventy pounds?" Pharaoh hazarded. "I've carried children weighing more than that over rough ground, so have you. Shaw was a powerful fellow, he could have done it. He'd be more likely to do that than risk using his van; he never knew when it would stall on him, and there was no other vehicle available — My God, the Honda!"

"The Rankins would have heard him start it."

"No, I changed direction: I'm thinking of Paul. That was how Shaw got the boy up to the sinkhole; you heard him pass, remember, just before you came down off Grammery's roof that evening. You heard the Honda go by and we thought Paul had gone over to Ewedale. His parents had driven down the dale and he was on his own at Murkgill. That was when he made the tracks under the viaduct, looking for the dog on the back way to Weeping Klints. When he came back, Shaw would be waiting. Sue was at Grammery cutting up the fallen tree with Lanty; there'd be no one at Murkgill except Paul and Shaw. He must have knocked Paul out and ridden the Honda to the sinkholes carrying Paul on the back."

"In broad daylight?"

"It was gloomy before the storm and I doubt if there was much traffic on the road. He might have worn the boy's anorak, he could have wrapped fertiliser sacks round Paul. But Shaw wasn't a prudent man, Clem."

"No. He was lucky all the same, not to be seen. So that's how it was done: set up as an accident. Dog barks, Paul hears it, parks the Honda, climbs down to rescue it, dog attacks. Only the last bit is how it was — and Shaw walked away. Or do you think" — came the cool voice — "he stayed and listened?"

"Forget it, Clem — "

"He came over here and asked me to take care of Susan next time he was away."

"She told me. Did you think that showed a total lack of imagination or was it how he got his kicks? Apparently he wasn't bothered about her affair with Lanty either."

"It wasn't an affair; it was a one-off, and she was consumed by guilt. She tells me everything; I've always been a kind of Dutch uncle to her." His eyes were shadowed but the pain was there in his voice.

"You're rid of him now," Pharaoh said absently. "What I can't understand is why he didn't walk out and leave her. She says he was attached to the cottage. Why? The place is a slum."

"It's a safe house. Not in the usual sense, but it's a sanctuary for him, is how she puts it. Why do I talk in the present tense? The fellow's dead. He never had any feelings for anyone, he rolled over them like a juggernaut. I can't believe he's got — that he had a woman in Newcastle, unless she served some ulterior purpose — like Susan did. That's why he wanted to keep her, you know; because she looked after the cottage. If she wasn't in it while he was away Rowland might let it to someone else. It was so important to him that to keep Susan there, to keep her feeling secure, he'd encourage her to have a relationship with me. I'm a steadying influence, you see; that's what he meant by looking after her. It amazes me that he should have stolen from Esme; he could have got on the wrong side of Susan there" — his voice dropped — "except that she adored him."

"He wanted the money so he took it, and it was easy to throw the blame on Paul. A man like Shaw will always take what he wants, although — "

Pharaoh stopped and Harker leaned forward. "Although what?"

"There's always Nemesis." Pharaoh shook his head and went off at a tangent. "If he didn't care for Susan, what was he doing in the old quarries? Rankin swears it was him; he says the tracks in the quarries were the same as those round the cottage. If it was Shaw, why?"

"I don't think it was him." Harker sounded as if he'd given the matter a lot of thought. "The chap in the quarries could have been watching for Shaw; he could have had a connection with Newcastle. Perhaps there is a woman in Newcastle after all and her husband was here waiting for Shaw to come home."

"Someone certainly knew his address because of the letter, someone who was important enough that Shaw had to telephone, had to take Esme's Range Rover, steal — Clem! Where did Susan find that money: the two hundred pounds he took out of Esme's wallet?"

"She told you that too? Under a loose floorboard in their bedroom."

"Of course! He needed the money to go to Newcastle. Was it all there?"

"Less than half. Over a hundred was missing."

"I'd give a lot to know the identity of the person who wrote that letter."

"Why, Jack?"

Pharaoh caught the serious note, the demand for satisfaction. "Doesn't it nag at you?" he asked, surprised. "We know everything else, we worked it out and it fits beautifully, like a jigsaw puzzle, but we can't quite finish it, there are pieces missing, but the pieces exist, we could find them."

"A husband," Harker said flatly. "Or — even better — another mercenary catching up with him, avenging some wrong done him by Shaw out in Africa. He'll be clever, like Shaw, no, more clever . . . " He trailed off. Pharaoh was nodding agreement.

"Oh yes, he has to be superior to Shaw. A benefactor, you might say. I'm not concerned with him at this moment; I want to know what's behind this Newcastle connection."

18

PHARAOH had met Alice Ward once, when Juno asked him and Harker to dine at Grammery Bank. The woman had fascinated him. There was a moment when their eyes met across the table that he was aware of something like recognition, and which initially he found incomprehensible. She had watchful amber eyes. He was reminded of wildlife films and a lioness in tall grass on the fringe of a herd of wildebeest, looking for one with a limp. So he wasn't greatly surprised, on the morning after the inquest on Paul, when he turned up at Grammery with a contrived excuse, that she should be in the kitchen with Juno. They had gravitated together. They exchanged polite smiles but it was Juno he addressed as he started the ball rolling: "I thought I'd go up Black Blote Fell before it gets too hot. Do you think Susan would like a walk?"

"How sweet of you, Jack, but we're

going shopping in Kendal when she wakes up." As Juno hesitated, evidently thinking that shopping wasn't a suitable occupation for a man, Alice said calmly that she would accompany him. It was as easy as that and only Juno was surprised.

They drove up to the pass in the Lotus. She was wearing sandals but, when she opened the boot, under the clutter of plastic bags and trainers and an old raincoat was a rucksack and a coiled rope. She retrieved a climbing boot and hunted for its mate. He caught the unmistakable clink of carabiners and he moved away, disorientated. As they started along the green track he said with a touch of resentment: "I didn't know you climbed."

"Why should you? I was never a tiger."

"Nor was I."

"Top climbers don't become rescuers. They're too selfish."

She didn't say that other people had filled her in on his background nor did she ask if he still climbed; she took it for granted that he'd know she had done her homework.

"What angle are you going to take

with this story?" he asked. "Actually, I don't see that there is a story. Is it Paul you're interested in: dangerous dogs and irresponsible owners, or are you investigating mercenaries?"

They were walking slowly and the turf was smooth, the conversation seemed almost casual. "This is field-work," she told him. "I like to approach a place with a clear mind, with no preconceived theories. The angle evolves — although sometimes there isn't a story at all. In that case I cut my losses and go away." She looked around. "We must be approaching the sinkholes. This must be where it all began, as far as you're concerned, right?"

"Around here, yes." He thought back to the morning he had first come this way with Harker, with the lapwings flapping about them, and the figure of a man silhouetted on the edge of the escarpment. His eyes sharpened. "As far as I'm concerned? You were involved before that? How?"

"I think we both have a lot of gaps to fill in. How about you starting? You met Shaw — "

"This sounds like a trade."

"You could call it that." She was amused. She reminded him a little of Shaw, with his predator eyes and boyish charm, but when she smiled her eyes held feeling. They were seductive, yet as soon as he formulated the thought he knew that there were other forms of seduction besides sexual. "There have to be questions you'd like answered," she prompted.

"What makes you think that?"

"You're like me. You have to know; it's what makes you tick. Now tell me how it started."

He didn't think he was that curious; all the same, if she was going to make a stab at answering some of his questions, he'd oblige, although the early events were public knowledge: Shaw's tale of hitching north, of having spent the night before his arrival at Clouds sleeping out on the high ground between Ewedale and the Scar. He pointed across the lime. "That's where we saw him first, and just below the edge are the old quarries where I found the boot mark. Did you know — did Harker tell you about the print?"

408

She nodded and didn't seem surprised when he said that Rankin was certain the print had been made by Shaw because he'd seen the same tracks round the cottage at Murkgill. Almost certainly she'd met the Rankins. She guessed the thought. "Rankin talked to me before Tilly shut him up," she said. "Rankin's stupid; Tilly's careful. Her tantrums are contrived, they're a form of power. Now tell me about Paul. I take it this is a sinkhole."

They were at the depression where the Honda had been parked. He told her how they'd found it, and then the dog and the body. As he talked they moved along the fault to the crucial shaft. He laid the facts before her as they had appeared at the time of the discovery, and then he listed the steps that led to the Coroner's verdict of misadventure. "Now," she said, sitting down on the lip of the depression, "tell me what really happened."

"You can get a copy of the Coroner's report."

"I mean, tell me how Shaw worked it."

He said carefully: "If I were to tell you

what we dreamed up as an alternative theory of how Paul died, and you printed it, wouldn't you be subject to a libel action? Can you libel the dead?"

"Oh, I wouldn't print a theory, but I see your point, so I'll tell you what could have happened. Let's say Shaw drugged the dog and put it in the sinkhole. Then he made a hoax call to a farm down the valley, saying the dog was among their sheep. The purpose of that was to draw attention away from the Scar and split the Rankin family. As they panicked he would expect to get Paul on his own at some point. That phone call was made from Harker's place." Pharaoh gaped. "You were at Grammery Bank," she reminded him, "and Harker doesn't lock his door. Some time before six o'clock his mother and father were away and Paul was alone at Murkgill. Shaw knocked him out, probably tied and gagged him, put him on the Honda and came up here. He lowered Paul on a rope — taken from a barn? Don't stare at me, that particular piece of information came from Lanty Dolphin. Am I right so far?"

"It could have happened that way." So Susan hadn't told her that Shaw had washed his jeans and scrubbed his boots after the stormy night — more important, that she had told Harker. Aloud he said: "It's all circumstantial, of course. And what makes you so sure Paul didn't have an accident — or that if there was foul play, Shaw had to be responsible? You said you came here with an open mind, so this implies you formed the theory since you arrived that Paul was murdered by Shaw, but people here think it was an accident."

"The Rankins don't, and other people may accept the inquest verdict and still hold their own opinions. Shall we walk on? And they talk — my, how they talk, contradicting each other — but I believe the Rankins come near the truth."

"They believe what they want to believe. George could have been mistaken about those footprints, in which case, if it was a stranger in the quarries, the fellow could have come down to Clouds when Shaw was away, or at night. The dog barked; someone had to be about."

"Not necessarily. Susan said the dog

often barked just because it was bored."

She started to draw ahead and he lengthened his stride to keep up but he couldn't close the gap and he wouldn't ask her to slow down. Disgruntled he resumed his comfortable amble and the gap between them stayed just too wide for conversation.

The path fined down and started to rise. She dropped back a little but they were still in Indian file. He wondered if she was considering how much information she should trade, and how much he could risk disclosing. He was wishing he hadn't suggested this walk. She knew too much; she wasn't what she appeared.

When they came to the summit of Black Blote Fell he was sweating like a horse but there was only a light sheen on her face. He had to fight to retain any advantage over this woman, and advantage he needed, for by now he was thinking of her as an antagonist.

When they reached the cairn they sat on stones a few feet apart and contemplated a line of mountains fine as cobweb beyond the Vale of Eden.

"Have you climbed on Scafell?" he asked.

"Yes. I prefer Gimmer. It's lighter; I'm too old for Scafell. Who killed Shaw?"

"What," he corrected, sidetracked by a vision of Gimmer in the sun. "What, not who; it was a train killed Shaw."

Her expression was inscrutable. Resigned? Contemptuous? "You met the man," she said. "If he stalled on a level crossing and the barriers came down, was he the type to sit there and wait for the train to hit him? He was a devious guy with fast reflexes; he would have guessed that van had been tampered with at the same time that he was jumping out of it. You can't believe he was alive when the train hit."

"You're saying someone put his body in the van and placed the van on the line. And shot out the light," he added, remembering the broken lamp.

"No. A stone was thrown at the light. A shot is too noisy."

"You know this — or you're guessing?" She was silent. "You're not guessing. It was the stranger in the quarry," he ventured. "Would that be another mercenary, someone out of his past, a revenge killing? Are you going to tell me you know who it was holed up in the quarries, watching his cottage?"

"It was Shaw."

"Well, that's what we — I — thought all along, but how do you know?"

"I know a great deal about Shaw."

"In that case" — he was tart — "you must know what he was doing watching his own cottage."

"That's simple; he was watching to see if the coast was clear to come down."

"We were right about that too?" He couldn't hide his astonishment. "You're not saying he was watching to see if Susan had a lover! He didn't care for her that much. You're saying he was making sure that no one was waiting for *him*. Who?" Very delicately she licked her lips. "You?" he breathed. He felt suddenly vulnerable: lame, alone in a remote place with a person who seemed fully in command of the situation — but when she spoke she was quite composed.

"You're getting ahead of yourself. I'm an investigative journalist." But she said it deliberately as if trying to imprint a fact on a difficult pupil. "I'm part of a team. Shaw was afraid of anyone who got close, like the Press."

"I see." He was staring at her. "And Esme's Range Rover — "

"No. He'd have had binoculars so he'd recognise his mother-in-law. But he had to make sure there were no other visitors — in the other houses, the woods, anywhere. He was in a good position for that."

"Why was he so wary of the Press? Why didn't he just tell you to go to hell? He was into something else, wasn't he? You're not interested in mercenaries; there's an ulterior motive here."

"He wasn't a mercenary, not any longer. He had been but he was drummed out of his mercenary unit for the same reason he was discharged from the SAS, only worse: brutality. It was fighting in the Army — ostensibly — but there was a fatal stabbing. The authorities couldn't make a charge stick, or didn't want to — for the good name of the regiment and all that — but he had to be given the push. He wasn't a mercenary for long either; he was too fond of killing. He was also an ingenious torturer. Torture is extraordinarily effective."

It was a while before he could comment, and then all he said was, "You've done your homework."

"It's my job."

"What is your job? Was it Shaw?"

She resumed at a tangent. "The IRA have problems with accents." She smiled without amusement. "Nowadays, with a bombing campaign in progress, everyone: the police, the public, is suspicious of Irish accents, even of a working-class Englishman in a place where he shouldn't be, but who's going to question a self-assured mid-Atlantic accent in a club say, or an Army mess, a nuclear power plant, you name it? Shaw could fade into the background anywhere: as a yuppie or a junior officer, even a detective. He was under contract to the IRA, he was a contract killer."

There was a thin scream and a swift skimmed past the cairn, chasing flies. Another followed, and another; suddenly the summit was alive with birds. Pharaoh stared through this aerial show without seeing it. "Newcastle!" he exclaimed.

"Who sent the letter from Newcastle?"

"Ah, that would have been his contact." For the first time she seemed ill at ease. "He's a teacher, an elderly bachelor, a maverick. I thought I'd won his confidence but something must have aroused his suspicions. My cover was a different kind of reporter: social problems, the child abuse scandal in the Northeast, you know? My hotel room was burgled. They found nothing. I should have had fake documents; finding absolutely nothing, no background material, must have alerted them. An innocent reporter would have had notes, letters, tapes. My man must have written to Shaw telling him to telephone and as a result Shaw took off for Newcastle. He did go there, he was seen to meet the contact. Maybe he wasn't meant to go, but Shaw wrote his own rules. I don't think he would have lasted long with the IRA either. Whatever he went to Newcastle for: to discuss a change in schedule or to pick up something, while he was there he obtained the tranquilliser for the dog. It had to be killed because Susan had given him an ultimatum: either it went or she did. The dog was an acute embarrassment but it wasn't until Shaw came back to Clouds that Paul became the major threat." She gave a snort of laughter. "That boy had to be crazy except, of course, he didn't know what he was up against: entering the cottage, stealing from Susan's purse. If he could do that, what might he discover about Shaw? He could be stopped, nothing easier for Shaw, but he couldn't get rid of the lad as he would in Africa; he had to stage an accident. The pit bull was made for the occasion."

"Did they find traces of a drug in its stomach?"

"No. If they looked, too many days had elapsed for anything to show. But how else could he have got it up to the Scar alive? And a vet's surgery in Newcastle was broken into the night Shaw was there. No prints, the chap wore gloves. A number of drugs were taken but among them was acetyl promazine. It's a tranquilliser for dogs."

"He adapted to circumstances," Pharaoh said thoughtfully. "If you're right, originally he could have meant just to drop the dog down a sinkhole and leave it; we'd have thought it fell in when it was trying to reach a dead sheep. But he came back from Newcastle with talk about a highly remunerative contract that he said he signed in London. That had to be so that he could keep Susan sweet, but she broadcast it and when it reached Paul, who had read the mileometer and knew he hadn't been to London, if that boy taunted him with the mileometer reading, Shaw would have flipped."

"Not to show it." She smiled thinly. "But he'd be watching for his opportunity."

"He got it with the storm, and took the dog. What a devious fellow he was! He devised the perfect murder."

"Not quite. You suspected. We did — or I did, after I'd listened to people here, but I knew considerably more than you to start with."

"You still do. You implied we should exchange information but there are big gaps in yours."

"Such as?"

"Why did Paul have to be killed? Shaw could have faded away. He was footloose enough, God knows."

"He could have cut his losses and established another safe house but that takes time and here he was working to a tight schedule. His operation, his part in it, was going down very shortly, within a matter of days. And Paul might even be teasing him with threats of the police, because I don't think Paul stole that two hundred pounds." She glanced at him, paused, but he didn't rise to the lure. "Shaw must have been on a very short fuse," she went on. "He was about to leave for Germany, and he needed Susan. No way could he find another bolt-hole just for a few days. What reason could he give her? The simple alternative was to kill Paul; in fact, being Shaw, he would have preferred it that way."

"How was Susan involved? She said they were going on a touring holiday."

"They would have gone to Germany. Susan was perfect cover." She saw his shock. "Oh, she had no idea what was going down, she hasn't now — "

"*What* was going down?"

"It was to be a bomb: in an officers' mess, at a party. Maybe it's still on and they've found a substitute for Shaw, but that's not my concern. I needed to find out who killed him."

He made no comment. She didn't seem to expect it. Staring at the blue hills he felt drained. At length he said: "If you've come to the conclusion that Shaw was murdered, the police must have their suspicions." When she didn't answer, he turned and looked at her. "Won't they?"

"I expect so." She was equable.

"So? What will happen at the inquest? Rowland Fawcett told us there wouldn't be any surprises."

"There won't be. The verdict will be accidental death, the same as the verdict on Paul."

A cover-up, he thought as she continued: "But we all want that, don't we? No one is going to talk" — she held his eye — "least of all yourself."

★ ★ ★

"What on earth was she getting at?" Harker asked. "What *is* she?"

Pharaoh leaned back in his chair, easing the bad leg. "As for what she is, I suppose she could have trained as a journalist but that has to be cover for some kind of anti-terrorist organisation, something that we don't even know exists. She knows too much, far too much. Sinister, when you think it through. I felt it up there: a sense of intimidation, not coming from her so much as the people behind her."

"But she told you so much — I mean, a police cover-up! I can't believe it. What about the police themselves?"

"They'll have their orders; no one's going to open an investigation with the possibility of uncovering a can of worms. I get the feeling that Shaw isn't the only terrorist who's met with a fatal accident, so-called. The difference this time is that it wasn't authorised, not by Alice Ward's mob anyway; that's what got them puzzled and why she was sent here to find out what happened." Pharaoh paused. "She reckons it was one of Susan's lovers — "

"But Susan — "

"That's what Alice thinks. It wasn't Lanty, he's too thick, and of the two of us she appears to favour me, although it could be you." He smiled. "And we're not going to say a word about an illegal anti-terrorist squad and a police cover-up because Alice can spill the beans on us. One of us, or both."

Harker stood up and went to the kitchen. Pharaoh sat still, hearing the refrigerator door open, and close. The shadow of a bird flicked through the sunlight.

Harker returned and placed a can of beer beside his friend's glass. He stood looking out of the window at his garden basking in the afternoon sun.

"There's no proof, Jack."

"I should hope not," Pharaoh murmured. "What about the autopsy?"

"He was alive when the train hit him, and even if there's enough of the stomach contents left to analyse, who's going to trouble when a man was hit by a train? Besides, you say the police won't investigate."

"What would they find in the stomach if they did analyse the contents?"

Harker sat down heavily. "It was Phenergan. It's a liquid given to children, another tranquilliser. It was in his rum and coke."

"Really. I hope you got rid of the bottle."

"What do you think?"

"And you slipped this stuff into Susan's drink and mine as well?"

"Oh no, that wasn't necessary; you were both lapping up the Scotch that night. It was just whisky that knocked you out."

"Do you realise that the train could have been derailed?"

Harker closed his eyes for a moment. "That horrifies me, even the thought of it in retrospect. The possibility of derailment almost put me off, but I convinced myself that the van was light enough to be thrown clear by the impact. It was a gamble though, there was no way I could be certain; I could only hope that if I was doing the right thing then the train wouldn't be derailed. I had a bad time there, Jack."

Pharaoh was awed. "How long had you known that Shaw was responsible for Paul's death?"

"Known, as opposed to suspected?" Harker looked embarrassed. "I was ahead of you much of the time, but then Sue was confiding in me. When she told me he washed his clothes after the night the dog went missing, that was the clincher. Once I knew he was responsible for the dog's disappearance then the connection with Paul's death was obvious. You know, I never had any feeling for Paul until the end; it was the method Shaw used that convinced me I had to do something to stop him."

"The ultimate pit bull."

"Worse, he had brains. But you're right: he was a finely tuned animal, a credit to his handlers." Harker was bitter. "He was trained to take people out, to waste them."

"And you were trained to save lives."

"That's irrelevant. Shaw was mad and he was put down like a rabid dog. The reason I set it up as an accident was that I certainly wasn't going to risk life imprisonment for him. Nothing altruistic about that."

"No sweat." Pharaoh was cool. "It was an accident. What proof can there be that it wasn't one of our own hit men, a contract killer on the right side?"

"That's immoral." Harker was shocked.

"How can you say that?"

"What I'm saying is, if there are official hit men in this country it's as immoral as employing a public hangman: getting someone else to do the dirty work."

"So you take the dirty work on yourself."

Harker shrugged. "I had nothing to lose."

Pharaoh thought about the train and its passengers. Looked at one way putting the van on the line had been the most irresponsible act imaginable; yet from a different perspective, Harker could be seen to have assumed full responsibility for behaviour where there could be no atonement if the plan had gone bad. Suicide would have been the soft option. "I don't understand you," he said.

"You know what they say about curious cats. Let's take our drinks outside and enjoy the garden. Tomorrow we'll go to the Lakes and climb in the sun." Harker smiled, thinking curiosity could cure a cat too. Pharaoh was interested in people again.